TURQUOISE MENAGERIE SYNDROME

Adventures from Law Enforcement

Steven D. Thomas

Foreword

Steven Thomas has hit it out of the park, presenting his passion for law enforcement emergency management in his new book *Turquoise Menagerie Syndrome*. As the Sheriff of Orange County, Florida, it was my responsibility for the safety and security of over one million residents and millions of visitors to Central Florida and its many attractions. To help accomplish that task, we created the Orange County Sheriff's Office Homeland Security Section. Steven Thomas was an intricate part of that section as a member of the Critical Infrastructure Protection Unit and the Critical Incident Management Team.

Over several months, Sergeant Thomas helped develop the first-ever interactive Critical Incident Command training course in the United States. Our desire was to create a training environment wherein command and supervisory personnel could practice incident management with the realism necessary to enforce the need to manage major incidents from the first critical hour. This intense hands-on training brought together law enforcement, fire rescue personnel, public education officials, school principals, and other government entities to practice and implement the principles of the Incident Command System while increasing their level of efficiency and effectiveness in responding to an actual incident, whether it be a national disaster or a terrorist attack. Once the daunting task of constructing the training props and developing the curriculum was completed, the design team, along with Steven, undertook the task of "Training the Trainers." This was the only training of its kind in the United States at that time and was accepted as a best practice by the U.S. Department of Education. Sergeant Steven Thomas and the Command School Design Team were commended for their dedication to helping others develop the skills necessary to assist them in protecting and serving their community.

Turquoise Menagerie Syndrome is the story of three high school friends who decide to enter the mysterious world of law enforcement and emergency response. Through their travels, they each encounter a variety of characters and events that will change each of their lives. *Turquoise Menagerie Syndrome* is both well-written and entertaining. Steven Thomas is able to thread the main theme of command and control throughout the book while simultaneously interspersing it with illuminating and amusing "cop stories." Steven Thomas has not only "talked the talk" but also "walked the walk." The credibility of both the author and the characters is especially important in this great read.

Over the succeeding short stories, you will be introduced to what turns out to be an ever-changing and growing, sundry cast of fascinating supporting characters, each of whom is described in detail with the added bonus of assigning them colorful, lighthearted, yet entirely appropriate nicknames. Thomas provides the right amount of backstory for each character without diminishing the flow of the story.

Over the past fifty years, law enforcement and emergency responders have evolved and improved their equipment and tactics. The *Turquoise Menagerie Syndrome* will show how law enforcement has failed to change accordingly to keep up with the times and world of mass casualty incidents that would have been unheard of fifty years ago. Each agency that provides "traditional" emergency response services needs to change its current response to a culture of "Control and Command" to effectively manage these mass casualty incidents and accomplish the mission it chose and swore to undertake.

I hope you enjoy *Turquoise Menagerie Syndrome* as much as I did!

Kevin Beary

Kevin Beary
Sheriff (Retired)
Orange County, Florida

TURQUOISE MENAGERIE SYNDROME

Adventures from Law Enforcement

A Novel

by

Steven D. Thomas

To

My beloved wife Michell,

"My Reason for Everything"

and

For all the Jack Webb Cops

and

All the Joseph Wambaugh Cops

and

All the Cops in Between

For you must teach others those things you and many others have heard me speak about. Teach these great truths to trustworthy men who will, in turn, pass them on to others.

2 Timothy 2:2 (TLB)

Contents

Introduction

Turquoise is a greenish-blue color that best describes the wave of various first responders as they arrive at a natural or man-made disaster scene. This response can be unpredictable, reckless, and emotional, where responding assets haphazardly and uncontrolled self-deploy and respond without direction, or instructions, going to where 'they think' is best. Or there can be a professional response where every first responder is controlled by a command and given a specific assignment. Specifically, law enforcement will respond and accomplish their duties and responsibilities. In many cultures, turquoise brings luck, peace, and protection. Time will tell. Mass response of uncontrolled or unmanaged assets is the first symptom of the Turquoise Menagerie Syndrome.

Once the assets start arriving at the location, without Command and Control, they will deploy themselves hither and yawn many times, appearing confused or worse, clogging ingress and egress of the scene. This action forces others who were specifically requested or needed to park and walk a great distance to get to their assigned mission location. At this point in the law enforcement response, we appear to be a strange and diverse collection of people, uniforms, and rolling stock such as command post vehicles or specialty units on display. As if we were kept in captivity, ready for exhibition to show how good we are. Without Command and Control, this law enforcement menagerie will stay stagnant, and the community will start questioning why we are not doing our jobs. Law enforcement must stop the shooting and the dying. The menagerie is the second symptom of the Turquoise Menagerie Syndrome.

First-responding professionals are made up of a characteristic combination of opinions, emotions, behaviors, experience, and training. The turquoise menagerie often occurs simultaneously or right after the other, causing an inadequate and inefficient response to these critical incidents. The lacking quality or element in the Turquoise Menagerie Syndrome is Command and Control. A committee cannot manage critical incidents. Trained professionals must handle them. All law enforcement executives must ensure all their employees are trained in the response process and responsibilities of 'Incident Command.'

Otherwise, these law enforcement leaders will experience the Turquoise Menagerie Syndrome firsthand. Who knows, someday, a Chief of Police may be terminated for failure to act. Responding personnel to the critical incident may be called out in a public meeting by a ten-year-old little girl who lost her sister in the event. She may declare, "All of you officers who responded, take off your badge because you don't deserve to wear it!"

"to protect and to serve"

As a child of divorce in the 1960s, Tom Stevens would spend the summers with his father and stepmother in Chicago and return to live the remainder of the year with his mother and stepfather in Los Angeles. Tom's Father and wife were staunch Democrats, and his mother and husband were diehard Republicans. In the summer of 1968, Tom and the rest of the country watched as the Chicago Police Department tried to deal with the demonstrators at the Democratic National Convention. Tom's Father's office building was near the Union Stockyards, and they watched the news channels, not knowing if there would be a building standing in the morning. For years we've seen that footage played time and again as the poster child of how law enforcement should not respond to civil disorder.

When Tom returned home late that summer, he remembered a Los Angeles Police Department black-and-white pull-up and park right in front of his house in Pacoima.

Two officers exited the car, and as they were putting on their hats and placing their nightsticks in the rings on their Sam Browne belts, one said to Tom, "Hello, son."

Both men gracefully walked over to Tom's neighbor's house. The officers were there to investigate a report of a lion in the neighbor's front yard.

Tom's sister Sharon, seven years younger than him, came running into Tom's room around 1:00 A.M. this morning, almost screaming, "There's a lion next door! There's a lion next door!"

Tom replied, "You're crazy. Go back to sleep! It was just a dream."

Sharon persisted, "I'm telling you, Tom, come see!"

Tom got up from his bed and went next door to Sharon's bedroom window that faced the neighbor's front yard. Tom peered out the window through the delicate curtains, and sure enough, there was a carefree lion cub in the neighbor's front yard.

A man was playing with the nine-month-old cub that weighed about forty pounds.

Tom ran to his mother's bedroom and excitedly told her, "There's a lion in the neighbor's front yard!"

Tom told his mother about Sharon coming into his room and what she had told him. Tom told his mother that he got up to confirm her claim, and he saw for himself. Tom's mother went into Sharon's room to look for herself.

Tom's stepfather worked as a bartender at a dinner house and cocktail lounge in Van Nuys and would be coming home soon. Tom's mother was worried about what would happen when his stepdad got home. Her thought was, where there is a cub, there is a mamma lion! Tom's mother thought, would her husband be attacked by a lion? Tom's mother called the Los Angeles Police Department to investigate what was going on next door because she was worried. As is standard practice in the LAPD, the call was received, prioritized, and placed in the hopper pending assignment.

Tom remembered how awe-struck he was when he saw that car park right in front of his house, both officers getting out of that car, and how professional they looked. Tom's Mom told him always to respect the police and do whatever they told him because they were there to protect him. Tom believed her because, after all, it said 'to protect and to serve' on the side of their car.

The officers came back to Tom's house and told his mother that the neighbor was a manager at Lion Country Safari in Orange County, and he had brought home a baby lion to show his children.

Everything was all right. The lion cub would be returned to Lion Country Safari later that day. Tom's stepdad, who made it home without incident, once told Tom that he had wanted to join the Los Angeles Police Department, but he was only five foot seven inches tall, and unfortunately, he was not tall enough to meet their standards.

The Laguna Fire

It was hot and dry this Saturday morning in San Diego County! The Santa Ana winds started early and were already blowing close to thirty-five miles per hour in a south-westerly direction. Most Californians were familiar with the Santa Ana winds and the destruction they left behind. Some flustered residents have described these winds as the west's version of a hurricane. Many have joked about having to vacuum bars of soap in their family bathrooms to help clean up the fine sand deposits left by the winds.

Gary and Dina Stevens liked living in east San Diego County. They had called Pine Valley home for the past twelve years. The Stevens worked in downtown San Diego, and neither considered it a burden driving to and from Pine Valley daily. After all, everyone in southern California commuted. Gary was a project manager with a pharmaceutical company, and Dina worked as an Executive Assistant with a new technology group recently transplanted from the Midwest.

Gary and Dina often hiked the hills near their home and trails at Kitchen Creek in the San Diego County foothills with their grandson, Tommy Stevens. Tommy was a good-natured kid living in the San Fernando Valley. Tommy visited his grandparents whenever he had the opportunity. Tommy liked to watch *Dragnet* and *Emergency* on Saturday nights, but he was hooked on his favorite police television show, *Adam 12*. Tommy would recap each episode to his grandparents' ad-nauseam. He told his grandparents he would be a policeman just like his hero *Pete Malloy*!

On a given day, the Stevens awoke early to drive to Kitchen Creek to beat the effects of the growing Santa Ana. When they returned to their car, both Gary and Dina were exhausted from the heat and the force of the winds. As they pulled out and headed home to Pine Valley, the local San Diego rock station was playing the Temptations' *Ball of Confusion*. One might say a 'Da capo' regarding what all Californians would witness and experience during the following two weeks!

Tommy Stevens had no idea how the following two weeks and their results would impact his life and family.

As Gary and Dina Stevens turned their car northbound on Kitchen Creek Road towards Sheepshead Mountain Road, minutes from Pine Valley, a massive gust of the Devil Santa Ana wind blew over a weakened and aging oak tree. The tree fell into power lines igniting what would eventually become the second-largest fire in California's recorded history. Gary and Dina Stevens lost everything in that fire!

As it would become known, the Laguna Fire was named after the Laguna Mountain Range in eastern San Diego County. During the next thirteen days, seven-hundred-seventy-three wildfires would break out during the Laguna Fire. These combined fires included the Wright, Clampitt, Bailey, Agua Dulce, Rankin Ranch, Red Mountain, Verdemont, and Speedy Bogart Fires.

Mutual Aide was requested throughout the state as the California Division of Forestry and San Diego County Fire Department valiantly and desperately attempted to gain control of these fires. Eventually, over twenty thousand firefighters responded to assist. In addition, hundreds of law enforcement officers responded for crowd control and eventual evacuations. Public Works personnel and equipment from several cities, counties, and the state responded for traffic control and other duties as assigned. Additionally, numerous civilian emergency support groups such as the Red Cross, Salvation Army, and many churches and civic-minded groups responded to help with food, clothing, and other donations.

California has a rich history of responding to natural and artificial disasters, including fires, floods, mudslides, and earthquakes. However, the Laguna Fire of 1970 brought issues that had been disturbing and plaguing the fire service for a long time. Upon arriving at the scene of an incident or possibly while en route, a first responder's number one job is to establish command and control. Time and resources are wasted or delayed until these two tasks are completed.

Command of the Laguna Fire and a command post location were not communicated to all responding units. Incident objectives such as life safety, incident stabilization, property preservation, or environmental protection were not explicitly determined or shared. Responding fire departments thought they would do as they always do, "Put the wet stuff on the red stuff!" Law enforcement thought, "The fire department will call us when they need us." Finally, Public Works thought, "Ok, we're here; now what?"

The major obstacle faced was communication with all agencies responding to the Laguna Fire. Not just that their radio frequencies did not synchronize or work together, but the professional language used to describe tactics and equipment in this fire suppression effort was inconsistent. In addition, many of the responding fire departments did not speak the same vocabulary.

To illustrate, law enforcement did not train regularly with the fire service. There was no common language that the fire service, law enforcement, public works, and medical responders used or could use universally to communicate effectively.

Furthermore, resource management and asset tracking were hit-and-miss at best, and the planning process, if considered at all, was accomplished at each fire scene precisely. Information and intelligence were not gathered or shared. Consequently, documentation was inconsistent and only agency-specific. When it was over, the Laguna Fire burned from Harbison Canyon to El Cajon, burning over one-half million acres of land. Seven-hundred-twenty-two homes were destroyed, and sixteen civilians were killed. Several persons who died may have been illegal aliens, as their bodies were never identified. Gary and Dina Stevens, along with numerous other families, lost their home and its contents in the Laguna Fire.

The Laguna Fire's total cost was two-hundred-thirty-four-million dollars.

After reviewing the 1970 fire season in California, the federal government set aside over nine hundred thousand dollars to research fire command and control systems improvements[1]. In 1971, Firefighting Resources of Southern California Organized for Potential Emergencies. (FIRESCOPE) was created to develop a Multi-Agency Coordination System[2]. After five (5) years of dedicated work, in 1976, FIRESCOPE released the Incident Command System (ICS). This system would be adopted by the Federal Emergency Management Agency (FEMA), which used the Incident Command System (ICS) in the development of the National Incident Management System (NIMS).

---

[1] https://www.emsics.com/history-of-ics/
[2] https://en.wikipedia.org/wiki/Laguna_Fire

The Grand State of Jefferson

1972 was an exciting year in politics in America! In May, Governor George C. Wallace of Alabama was shot by Arthur Herman Bremer at a Laurel, Maryland, political rally. In June, the first United States Libertarian Party National Convention was held in Denver, Colorado. Additionally, in June, five men were arrested for burglarizing the offices of the Democratic National Committee at the Watergate Hotel Complex in Washington, D.C. The scandal would continue for two additional years.

Locally, after eight decades of planning, debating, arguing, and compromising, a new frontier was forged in the west. Amendments were filed by both Oregon and California legislators. Both state assemblies approved the motions. The results were sent to the voters in each of the two states, where they received overwhelming support. Finally, it was approved by the United States Congress according to Article 4 Section 3 of the United States Constitution; the Grand State of Jefferson was formed.

This 'Greater Jefferson,' so-called as it was more significant than the original proposal of 1941, consisted of southern Oregon and northern California counties. Located in Lakeland County, the new state capital is Santiago Springs. Governor-elect Oliver Scott has vowed that through planned development and working with conservation, Jefferson will be in the top ten convention destinations in the country. Scott stated that his plans include casino gaming integrated with the convention industry and family theme park vacation destinations.

Many people in California, including Tom Stevens's parents, were waiting for Jefferson to add a star to the American flag in anticipation of an improved lifestyle. Most people had high hopes for the new state and the country's future. Finally, in November, President Nixon was reelected in one of the most significant landslides in American political history!

Welcome to Hudson Falls

Tom Stevens had spent the last three years attending the Northridge Military Academy in the San Fernando Valley in Southern California. His stepfather and mother, Daniel and Barbara Thomas, were deeply troubled by the increase in gang activity and the drugs that seemed to run rampant in their Pacoima neighborhood. The Thomas' would do whatever it took to get their son Tom out of that environment.

Daniel and Barbara started researching and looking for a new community to call home. As a result, they stumbled across a town called Hudson Falls in Greenwood County, Jefferson. Hudson Falls was not far from Reno, Nevada, and the Thomas' had spent their honeymoon in Reno fifteen (15) years earlier.

Hudson Falls was a retirement community of approximately 23,000 people. The main street through Hudson Falls is State Highway 76, California Boulevard, in the city limits. It is said that California Boulevard is fourth in the nation with the number of banks, including the amount of money contained in each of those banks, only behind Wall Street in New York, Michigan Avenue in Chicago, and Florida Avenue in Hemet, California. Therefore, Hudson Falls sounded like the perfect place. After all, the star of the television show *Winning the West* owned a vast ranch in Hudson Falls, and no other down-to-earth American could be more trusted than Lance Bigelow! Tom's parents thought they might have found a little slice of heaven!

As the research continued, the Thomas family subscribed to the *Hudson Falls Herold*, the local newspaper, to check out all that was happening in the community. Tom's parents' favorite section of the newspaper was *Police Blotter*. Every day, this section would report on all the criminal activity in the City of El Camino, right next door and north of Hudson Falls, and the unincorporated area of Greenwood County. To illustrate, the Hudson Falls Police would report to the *Hudson Falls Herold*:

Wednesday, July 7, 7:15 a.m. Petty Theft Garden Hose 700 block of East Juniper Avenue.
Thursday, July 8, 8:15 p.m. Verbal Disturbance: 200 block of North Hawthorn Street.

Thursday, July 8, 10:00 p.m. Barking Dog: 100 block of South Aspen Avenue.

Daily, similar reports were made by the El Camino Police Department and the Greenwood County Sheriff's Office in the *Hudson Falls Herold Police Blotter*.

After reading several weeks of the *Hudson Falls Herold* and the *Police Blotter*, Tom and his family packed up. They moved from the San Fernando Valley in California to Hudson Falls, Jefferson, continuing the search for the American dream!

"I'm Doing This for the Rest of My Life"

Tom Stevens was doing well as a sophomore at Hudson Falls High School. Specifically, he was several credits ahead of most of his classmates. Like most young men, Tom was anxious to start driving and gain independence. The only delay was the Driver Safety Course and Driver Training behind the wheel of a vehicle provided by Sears Roebuck and Company. This car was maintained by and kept at the high school. Driver Safety was part of the Civics Course taught in the classroom. Mr. Nick Komitas had taught Civics for years, and he would determine who the Driver Training students behind the wheel would be based on their class participation.

An extra credit portion of the Civics class was for the student to ride along with the Greenwood County Sheriff's Department for a week and document their experiences, observations, opinions, and relevance to civics. The Hudson Falls Lions Club sponsored this program. Additionally, the student would be required to provide an oral presentation to the rest of the civics class. Most people can relate to the fear of public speaking.

Tom was not about to let that opportunity slip through his fingers, so he was one of the first to sign up. Tom was selected rather quickly by Mr. Komitas to ride with the sheriff's office. Tom never expected that assignment to change his life the way it did.

Tom arrived at the Hudson Falls Sheriff's Office at evening shift change; four black-and-white patrol cars were backed into marked stalls at the rear of the building adjacent to the public parking. South of the marked vehicles were three detective units. In the 1970s, you could make a Dodge or Plymouth unmarked cop car a mile away.

The front door of the sheriff's office was in the far southwest corner of the Greenwood County Government Complex. As you entered this public entrance, there was a small waiting area with four chairs, tile flooring, and a reception area staffed with a sheriff's dispatcher matron. The dispatcher, dressed in uniform, was sitting behind a glass window with a small round hole for speaking and non-bullet-resistant protection. She sat at a desk with a Motorola tabletop radio console, base station, and a stand microphone.

Behind a closed closet door next to her was an ASR 33 Teletype terminal. The Teletype was quite noisy during the operation, loud enough for Tom to speak up when he told the dispatcher he was there for the Lions Club ride-along program. Tom was said to have a seat, and the sergeant would be up in a minute.

On the waiting room wall was a black and white photo of Sam Baldwin, the Sheriff of Greenwood County. This photo was prominently displayed. Sheriff Baldwin had a grey flat-top haircut and wore a grey suit, white shirt, and thin black tie. This photo looked like his employee identification photo taken when he started with the department in 1950.

When the sergeant opened the office door, he said, "I'm Sergeant Hall. You must be Tom Stevens!"

Tom said, "Yes, sir, I am."

"Follow me and keep quiet. We are going into the briefing. After the briefing, I will introduce you to everybody."

"Sounds good."

Sergeant Jack Hall was a slight but impressive man who demonstrated absolute command presence. He had five gold stars embroidered on his long-sleeved uniform shirt above the left cuff. He looked like a cross between Paul Newman and Mr. Rodgers. However, his personality screamed 'no-nonsense.' Tom would later learn that Jack Hall's troops would follow him anywhere into battle.

The Hudson Falls station briefing room was in the back of the building. Sitting around a rectangular wooden table were four deputies. Sergeant Hall stood at the table's end as if he were a conductor about to start the symphony. He removed a pair of readers from his left front shirt pocket and began to read and comment on each of the calls handled by Hudson Falls Station during the past twenty-four hours. After reviewing all the teletype information and stolen vehicle information from the county and surrounding agencies, Sergeant Hall started with the introductions of his squad.

Before the introductions, Sergeant Hall reached into a black basketweave pouch on his gun belt opposite the ammo dump pouch containing .38 caliber issued rounds. Inside the second pouch was a pack of Camel regular cigarettes. One cigarette was removed and placed into his thin-lipped mouth in one easy motion. The sergeant reached into his left front uniform pants pocket and pulled out a Zippo lighter that was a gift from his wife. He lit his cigarette. The other deputies around the briefing table followed suit in this daily ritual.

Tom soon realized that everybody in law enforcement went by a nickname. Sam 'Thumper' Robinson did not get his nickname from the rabbit in the Disney movie.

Jacob 'Heifer-hauler' Murphy was a truck driver on his off-duty times and hauled, you guessed it, cattle across southern California.

Ethan 'Frank' Mitchell, who always had perfect hair, was nicknamed 'Frankenstein' due to his size.

Joe 'The Sicilian' Toarmina was on a regular day off.

And finally, there was Roberta 'Bobbie Boobs' Lee, who……. well, we know how she got her nickname.

Sergeant Hall told Tom, "The dispatcher you met upfront is Stella 'Green Springs' Bartley." She got her nickname after a famous peach wine she was intimately familiar with at shift parties. Stella's go-to 'Ghetto wine.'

Hall then said, "Stevens, you're with Robinson tonight."

Before leaving the briefing room, Tom saw a large metal storage cabinet. Curiosity got the best of him, so he asked Sergeant Hall, "What is kept in this locked cabinet?"

Hall replied, "I'll show you." He unlocked the door and opened the cabinet to reveal several items of U.S. military surplus.

"Here we have our CS and CN gas and gas gun."

There were also four Winchester .30-30 rifles and ten ammunition boxes for these rifles.

Sergeant Hall said, "These rifles are in case we need heavy arms in a hurry. SWAT would require a two-hour response time from Greenwood!"

Once they got outside, 'Thumper' said, "We lucked out tonight. They are letting us take out the new patrol car!"

Tom said, "Very nice. Which one is it?"

"The new 1973 Plymouth Satellite with the new lights and siren called the Federal Signal Twinsonic Code 3 lightbar."

'Thumper' proudly said, "Wait till you see this thing lit up!"

Tom noticed that the other three patrol cars only had a red spotlight and amber and red light mounted on the rear deck on the driver's side. The vehicle they were driving tonight was the latest in law enforcement technology!

Tom rode with all Sergeant Hall's squad members during that week-long ride-along program. Tom fondly remembered the suicide by hanging 'Thumper' investigated in Moonglade on his first night. After no communication for a week, a distraught mother found her twenty-five-year-old son in a shed at the back of his property.

The young man left a note saying he couldn't take it anymore. Tom also remembered the bar fight at the Brush Popper Inn, where 'The Sicilian' was the only unit available. He talked all the parties down without further injury or anyone going to jail. 'The Sicilian' also took the time to explain how to talk to people and how a good cop rarely has to fight.

Likewise, the compassion and professionalism 'Bobbie Boobs' showed while investigating a violent rape of an ex-girlfriend by the suspect. The victim received counseling and additional assistance due to the deputy's efforts, and the suspect was arrested the next day by detectives.

Tom would remember the commercial burglary in progress call in Evergreen. 'Frank' Mitchell, with the help of his squad, was able to place the meth heads under arrest as they were backing out of the building. Tom also recalled the shots fired call on the Adahy Indian Reservation and the attempted murder charges between two families in an ongoing tribal war.

Finally, Tom remembered the last night of this experience when 'Thumper' arrested two migrant farmworkers for possession of heroin at home in Grove Valley. When they returned to the Hudson Falls Station from the county jail in Greenwood, 'Thumper' asked Tom, "Well, what did you think of this experience?"

Tom asked, "You get paid to do this?" He then proudly declared, "I'm doing this for the rest of my life!!"

Your Honor

When Tom Stevens' parents moved from California to Jefferson, they decided it was time to change their lives and geography. Tom's Dad, Daniel Thomas, gave up bartending and went to school to become a licensed real estate agent. Daniel completed the agent training but also completed the training as a real estate broker. Tom's Mother, Barbara Thomas, also attended classes and became a licensed real estate salesperson. Barbara specialized in residential properties, and Daniel specialized in commercial and ranch properties. Eventually, the Thomas' opened their real estate office downtown, Hudson Falls.

Daniel had just closed on a one-hundred-acre ranch property south of Hudson Falls near Emerald Valley and was in the mood to celebrate. Barbara was tied up showing residential property, so Daniel decided to call his son Tom to see if he wanted to get a bite to eat. Tom was always ready for a good meal! The father and son met at Alphy's coffee shop at California Blvd. and Aspen Street. The Alpha Beta Supermarket chain owned Alphy's coffee shop, and the two were never far apart. In Hudson Falls, the supermarket was on the southwest corner, and the restaurant was on the northwest corner. Alphy's décor was classic 1970s with dark wood with orange, gold, and red interiors.

Tom arrived at the restaurant and found Daniel seated at a booth in the center of the main dining room. Daniel knew that Tom always had the same thing at Alphy's, so he had already placed the order. Tom had no problem with this because his dad was right. After a few minutes, Tom noticed a couple of booths over. A single man was staring at them consistently. The man was a professional-looking individual, approximately forty years of age, wearing a gray flannel suit with a white dress shirt with French cuffs. In addition, he was wearing gold cuff links with green stones and a black tie. The man seemed deliberate yet approachable. This gentleman was a cross between Cary Grant and Efrem Zimbalist Junior. Tom and Daniel were served their lunch and were almost finished when the well-dressed man approached their table.

"Pardon me for interrupting but aren't you Daniel Thomas?" Tom's dad shifting into real estate broker mode, smiled, stood up, and as he shook the man's hand, confidently said, "Why yes, I am! The man said, "I'm Richie Cappalli......from Tiny Naylors!" Tom's dad

13

was speechless. Tom stood up and introduced himself to Richie. Tom offered Richie a seat, and Richie joined Tom and his dad. Daniel finally said, "Richie, I can't believe it! The last time I saw you was when you graduated high school and were going off to college."

Tiny Naylor's was a chain of drive-in restaurants started in 1949 in Southern California. Their most prominent location and the busiest drive-in west of the Rockies was the Tiny Naylors restaurant at Sunset Boulevard and La Brea Avenue in Hollywood. Tom and Daniel finished their meal, and the three men enjoyed coffee. Tom learned for the first time that his dad was the manager of this restaurant from the mid-1950s to the early 1960s and that Richie Cappalli worked for Daniel as a busboy and then cook.

Richie shared his whole story with both Tom and Daniel. Richie's father was an L.A.P.D. Motor Officer. One night when he was coming home from the San Fernando Valley at about 2:30 A.M., he was run over and killed on the Golden State Freeway by a drunk driver. Young Richie took the death of his father very hard and started to become more than his now single mother could control. Richie's mother and husband had been regular customers of Tiny Naylors, and Daniel knew the married couple.

After explaining her situation to Daniel, she asked him if her son could go to work at the restaurant to keep him on the straight and narrow and give him a new path. Daniel agreed and started Richie as a busboy. Richie was a sophomore attending Hollywood High School. Richie told Tom that his dad was the greatest thing that ever happened to him. Daniel was tough but fair and taught Richie his strong work ethic. Richie worked at Tiny Naylors for three years, and after one year as a busboy, Richie was promoted to line cook.

When Richie graduated from Hollywood High School, he went to U.C.L.A., where he studied political science. Next, he went to Loyola Marymount University Law School, where he graduated with a Juris Doctorate. Richie confirmed that all of this was possible because of Daniel's impact on him as a young man. Richie concluded that once he passed the bar, he moved to Jefferson, where he opened his law firm in Hudson Falls. Richie practiced law for eight years when he ran and was elected a Municipal Court Judge in Hudson Falls.

Richie Cappalli has been a Municipal Court Judge for ten years and had just finished a cup of coffee with his high school mentor and son.

Greenwood County Fire Department

Tom Stevens completed his driver training course, and on his sixteenth birthday, he purchased his first car. Tom had been saving all of his money earned over the past two years working around the neighborhood, washing cars, mowing lawns, and working as a busboy at a local dinner house. As promised by his parents, they matched the money he had raised towards purchasing the vehicle. As a result, Tom purchased an emerald green 1969 Dodge Coronet R/T hardtop coupe with a Magnum 440 V-8 engine. Tom purchased the car from a recent widow. The vehicle belonged to her husband, who bought it to "desperately cling to his youth," according to his wife.

When Tom drove the vehicle home, all neighbors came over to admire Tom's new pride and joy! One of the neighbors was Russ Martin. Russ was a Division Chief with the Jefferson Division of Forestry who took a shine toward Tom when Tom started mowing his lawn for extra cash. Tom and Russ had talked for hours on end about careers in emergency response, and Russ had told Tom that once he was ready, he would help him. Today, Tom told Russ he was ready.

The Greenwood County Fire Department is a volunteer fire department minimally staffed with Jefferson Division of Forestry members. Round Lake Fire Station 26 was east of Hudson Falls towards Evergreen, not far from Tom's residence. Chief Martin called Station Captain Paul Warner to ask for his assistance in helping Tom join the volunteer fire department. Chief Martin and Captain Warner had been friends for many years, and they both agreed to give Tom a chance.

Round Lake Station 26 was located in a remodeled farmhouse with a newly constructed engine house for the new fire truck. The new Engine 26 was a 1970 American LaFrance Pioneer Pumper Truck. This engine replaced a 1955 International Harvester R-176 Fire Truck, now the backup pumper truck at Station 26. In addition, the volunteers recently purchased a 1969 Dodge utility truck from Greenwood Power and Light and are converting the vehicle into a rescue squad for Station 26.

It was a cool, crisp, and clean mountain air Saturday morning as Tom swiftly walked up the driveway to Station 26. The bay doors of the fire station were rolled up, and both engines were facing the street, ready to respond. The radio in the sallyport was blaring to be heard throughout the compound. Ironically, the Cornelius Brothers and Sister Rose sang *Too Late to Turn Back Now*."

Tom saw some movement towards the back of the station, and upon further inspection, he found Captain Warner restocking one of the cabinets on the side of Engine 26. The Captain wore his daily fire uniform consisting of green pants and a short-sleeved tan shirt. The Jefferson Division of Forestry patch was on one sleeve, and the Greenwood County Fire Department patch was on the other.

Tom introduced himself, "Good Morning! My name is Tom Stevens. Chief Martin suggested I come down and speak with you. I'm interested in joining the volunteer fire department."

Paul Warner replied, "Yes, Chief Martin did call me about you. Welcome, and come on in. Do you drink coffee?"

Tom enthusiastically said, "I sure do!"

The two went inside the station, where they talked for over an hour. Captain Warner invited Tom back to the next Volunteer Training Meeting to meet the crew.

Tom attended two additional Volunteer Training Meetings. On the third meeting, the members voted Tom in as a probationary firefighter for the Round Lake Station 26 Firehouse of the Greenwood County Fire Department. One of the greatest moments in Tom's life so far was when the volunteers issued him his firefighting equipment, including a Plectron R19 single-channel emergency alerting radio receiver used to activate emergency response personnel. Tom also received a brand-new yellow Cairns composite fire helmet with '26' in white reflective tape on the sides. He also received his multi-purpose gear, pants, a bunker coat, and a new pair of Fire-Dex structural firefighting rubber boots.

When Tom went home that night, he tried on all of his new equipment again and stood in front of a full-length mirror to see how he looked. As he was staring at the image in the mirror, Tom questioned if he would have been able to save his grandparent's home with all their memories from that San Diego fire many years ago. He vowed that he would always do the best job in that situation!

Tom worked as a volunteer firefighter for just over a year, and during that time, he was exposed to various calls for service and training opportunities. Working at Station 26 allowed him to work and interact with the deputies from the Hudson Falls Sheriff's Office he met and rode with during the week-long civics class event. Tom learned about the two agencies' close relationship and how each needs to get along and work together to accomplish the mission's objective.

Deputies often would come into Station 26 and have coffee or bring their reports into the station to finish them up. Just as Tom was approaching the completion of his probationary period at the Greenwood County Fire Department, he realized that when he went through that week-long ride-a-long program with the sheriff's office, the law enforcement bug bit him hard. All he wanted to do was work in law enforcement and become a deputy sheriff. That opportunity was just around the bend.

The Boys

Tom Stevens's best friend throughout high school was Jim Scott. The two met in Mr. Komitas's Civics class, where they discovered a shared love for law enforcement. This resulted from the week-long ride-a-long program both of them completed with the sheriff's office. A friendship was forged, and the two became inseparable. Jim was tow-headed with brilliant crystal blue eyes. He was charming when he had to be but didn't like people. Jim was on both the varsity football team and the varsity wrestling team. He wrestled in the heavyweight division at five foot ten inches tall and two hundred thirty pounds with very little fat.

In contrast, Jim also sang in the Hudson Falls High School Choir and Acapella Choir yet never attended church or participated in a church choir. Jim's parents were in their early sixties when Jim entered high school. He was a 'change of life baby. To illustrate, Jim's older brother was fifteen years older than him, and his sister was twelve years older than Jim. Jim once told Tom he always hated his parents for being a change of life baby raised alone by elderly parents.

Jim's father, a quiet man, was a retired concrete truck operator and his mother was a retired middle school teacher from El Camino. When Tom first met Mrs. Scott, he thought how sweet she was. Jim lived in his deceased grandmother's house during the school year. The house was towards the back of his father's farm. This small wood farmhouse was over one hundred years old but was refurbished by the Scotts for Jim's use. Both Jim and Tom believed the Scotts were glad to have him out of the way in the back of the property. Jim worked for the Lake Hudson Municipal Water District as a groundskeeper at the Lake Hudson campground, thirty miles away, near the national forest during the summer. The Scotts kept a travel trailer in the campgrounds year-round so that Jim could live close to his work.

Jim drove a brown-and-white 1967 Ford F250 pick-up truck with gun racks on the rear window that his dad gave him. Then, in the spring of his high school sophomore year, Jim bought a used Harley Davidson 1200cc Electra Glide motorcycle from the Greenwood Police Department public auction. This decision came after Jim saw the movie

Electra Glide in Blue, starring Robert Blake. Jim knew then that being a law enforcement motor officer would be his destiny.

Tom still officially lived in his parent's home in Hudson Falls but spent most of his time with Jim at the farmhouse during the school year.

Tom would be staying at his parent's house for only one additional summer. On the first Saturday afternoon in February after his birthday, Tom received a call from Jim, who was very excited about what he had learned.

Jim told Tom that he read an article in the Greenwood Examiner newspaper that the Greenwood Police Department was looking to expand its department with young people interested in a career in law enforcement. Therefore, the department was conducting an introductory meeting for the Explorers at the Greenwood Police Department next Wednesday at 7:00 P.M. Jim told Tom they would be at that meeting.

The City of Greenwood is a forty-five-minute drive northeast of Hudson Falls, with a population of approximately three hundred thousand. The three-hundred-member police department is located downtown. When Jim and Tom arrived, they found a three-story red brick building with three flagpoles, one for the American flag, one for the State of Jefferson flag, and one for the City of Greenwood flag. Over one-hundred police cars, marked and unmarked were parked in the lots to the rear of this building. To the right of the entrance was a law enforcement memorial. It contained a list of all the officers who gave their lives in the line of duty since the city was incorporated in 1901. Twenty-three officers had died, with the last one being killed just three months ago in a domestic violence investigation.

It was a fantastic Wednesday evening when Jim and Tom arrived at about 6:45 P.M. They were greeted by a couple of younger Explorers dressed in their 'Class A' uniforms. The two asked how they could assist and when Tom replied, the two Explorers explained the meeting was on the second floor in the community conference room and pointed to the elevators in the first-floor lobby. Tom and Jim made their way to the elevator, and once the doors opened on the second floor, they saw a group of about twenty people talking amongst themselves outside the closed doors of the community room. Within two minutes, these doors were propped open by two officers also dressed in 'Class A' uniforms. 'Class A' uniforms consist of long-sleeved shirts and ties. Both officers were warm and welcoming to the crowd, who later learned that these two officers also served as Advisors to the Greenwood Police Department Explorer Program.

They listened to a presentation on the Boy Scouts of America and the Explorer Program's history, how the Police Department trains and develops the Explorers, and the program's benefits. After about a twenty-minutes, one of the Advisors introduced the Captain of the Explorers for his testimonial.

Explorer Captain Robert Henry was a young man of 18 years of age who stood six-foot-two inches tall and weighed approximately one hundred and eighty-five pounds with dark hair and eyes. He had an athletic build and wore his 'Class A' uniform from the top of his round navy-blue hat to the bottom of his high gloss oxford shoes like a model on a Paris runway. His appearance was impeccable.

Tom and Jim would have sworn they heard a couple of girls in the crowd swoon as he approached the podium where he began to speak. Robert Henry was as charming as he was good-looking. He was the perfect representative for the explorers, or even the police department, for that matter.

After the presentation and a short question-and-answer period, Robert Henry came over to Tom and Jim and introduced himself to the boys from Hudson Falls. The three young men took a shinning at each other, and Robert invited Tom and Jim to join him for dinner at Coco's, an upscale coffee house in Greenwood across from the Greenwood Entertainment Plaza.

Tom and Jim followed Robert to the restaurant. Robert drove a new yellow 1972 Ford Ranchero GT with a 351 Cleveland engine. With Goodyear racing tires, Robert had Cragar Mag wheels all the way around, and the back end raised slightly. The truck had dual exhaust with Cherry Bomb Glasspack Mufflers. Tom and Jim agreed; Robert's truck was as pretty as he was.

Once the three arrived at the restaurant and parked their cars, the new friends headed toward the entrance. As they approached, Robert told

Tom and Jim that Wednesday nights were Explorer Meeting nights for the Greenwood Police Department and the Greenwood County Sheriff's Department. Robert added that his girlfriend Zoe Acker, an explorer with Greenwood County Sheriff's Department, would be joining them tonight for dinner.

As the three young men waited for Robert's girlfriend to arrive, Tom and Jim discovered that Robert had worked for Vaughn's Market in Greenwood for four years. He started as a box boy and now works as a checker. His parents have been married for twenty years, and they lived in the same house, in the Greenwood Country Club, for sixteen years. Robert's father is an aerospace executive with Lockheed Martin, and his mother is a homemaker and socialite. Robert's father is a twin. His brother is a Captain with the Greenwood County Sheriff's Department and Station Commander of the Pine Ridge Sheriff's Office. Robert joined the Greenwood Police Department Explorers because he wanted to make it independently. Everybody knew that if he joined the sheriff's office, like the mob, he would be a made man because of his uncle.

When Zoe Acker and her friend Maria Perez entered the restaurant, they made quite an impression on Tom and Jim. The two young ladies looked like a pair of cheerleaders in deputy sheriff's uniforms. Zoe was a blond-haired, blue-eyed beach bunny about five foot four and weighed a buck twenty. Maria was a Mexican beauty with shiny raven-colored hair and deep brown eyes who stood five-foot-seven inches tall with a sleek build. Whenever Tom saw her, he thought of the Marty Robbins song *El Paso*.

For this Wednesday night and the following three Wednesdays, Robert, Zoe, and Maria made it a point to recruit Tom Stevens and Jim Scott for each of their respective agencies.

Zoe and Robert had been together for two years, yet they seemed to drift apart. Zoe had started to hang out with an older and smaller version of Robert by the name of Richard Campbell, who was a member of the Greenwood County Sheriff's Department program. To make it worse, Campbell was known as a 'snake in the grass' who got away with murder because he was the brother-in-law of the sheriff's department explorer advisors.

Within six months, Zoe ended her relationship with Robert. But unfortunately, Zoe was the love of Robert's life. Tom later told his wife how Zoe treated Robert and ended their relationship. This break-up permanently impacted Robert and how he treated women for the remainder of his life.

Tom and Jim attended two Greenwood Police Department Explorer Meetings and two Greenwood County Sheriff's Department Meetings. At the end of the second meeting with the county, Tom and Jim decided to join the Greenwood County Sheriff's Department Explorers.

Tom Stevens, Jim Scott, and Robert Henry would remain friends for the rest of their lives!

The Advisor

The Advisor of the Greenwood County Sheriff's Department Explorer Post was a deputy by the name of Alexander Lee. Alexander worked as a patrol deputy in a contract city for the sheriff's office out of Greenwood Station. When the opportunity was presented, he took on the Explorer Program four years earlier as an additional responsibility. Alexander said he liked working with kids. Alex was married, and his wife Olivia was an emergency room nurse at the Greenwood General Hospital. Olivia had a heavy Russian accent and sounded like she had just gotten off the boat from Moscow. Alex and Olivia had been married for just over two years.

Tom Stevens and Jim Scott had attended several meetings in Greenwood. They were unhappy with the exposure to the sheriff's office and volunteer opportunities out of Greenwood Station. After all, there were thirty explorer post members, and each had to be allowed the chance to participate. Alexander was also committed as an officer in the Naval Reserve and spent many weekends on military leave.

Tom had always admired Alexander Lee because Alexander had lost close to one hundred pounds two years ago, as other deputies had told Tom. Alexander often seemed standoffish with Tom and Jim, but the two assumed that he wanted to spend time with the younger members of the post or did not like that Tom and Jim were from Hudson Falls. Regardless, Tom and Jim met with Alexander and requested permission to work and volunteer out of the Hudson Falls Station.

Alexander agreed with Tom and Jim's plan and told them to make sure all of the time worked at that station was documented for the annual report to the administration. Alexander requested a supervisor from the Hudson Falls Station call him to confirm the Station Commander's approval.

The Pitch

As Tom Stevens came to a stop sliding in the dirt in front of Jim Scott's house, he interrupted Eric Clapton as he was singing, *I Shot the Sheriff* by turning down the radio in his car and yelling, "Come on Jim, we are going to be late!"

Jim could be heard from inside the house, "I'm coming. I'll be right there!"

Tom and Jim were heading to the El Camino Junior College, where they had signed up for a few police science courses.

It was Monday night, so they were headed to Sergeant Jack Hall's class. Sergeant Hall taught at El Camino Junior College for about ten years to pick up some extra money for his wife's planned European vacation. Sergeant Hall taught the Introduction to Law Enforcement class on Monday night, and both Tom and Jim signed up for the course as soon as they could while still in high school. Sergeant Hall knew the two students from their ride-along experiences and active class participation. The part-time professor learned that the two had joined the Sheriff's Department Explorers in Greenwood. So tonight, during the break, Tom and Jim had planned to ask the good sergeant if they could work and volunteer for him in the Hudson Falls Station.

Professor Hall was a no-nonsense man and conducted himself accordingly as a sheriff's sergeant and a college professor. He was more professional than friendly, but the two cohorts knew he liked them despite his outward appearance. During the break, Sergeant Hall listened to the pitch and asked a couple of questions. Sergeant Hall had already made up his mind about using these two. He concluded this meeting and told the two to get the approval of Station Commander Liam Allen.

Greenwood County Sheriff Department Captains had quite a reputation during the 1970s and 80s as empire builders, with Captain Liam Allen of the Hudson Falls Sheriff's Station no exception. Most of the deputies under his command disliked him. The others just tolerated him. Captain Allen is of Korean heritage and was adopted by a white couple when he was three. Captain Allen was also the most egotistical person many have ever met. He had a four-foot oil painting commissioned wearing his formal dress uniform, including a General Dwight D. Eisenhower jacket. The oil painting hung over the mantel in his living room.

The exciting part of this story is that he had this done when he was promoted to sergeant and had the uniform in the painting updated with every promotion since then. Captain Allen's wife looked like and reminded most of Miss Prissy in the Warner Brothers cartoons featuring Foghorn Leghorn. The Allens had no children between them.

Captain Allen also taught at El Camino Junior College. He led a Criminal Law course on Wednesday nights from 7:00 P.M. to 10:00 P.M., but unlike Sergeant Hall, his ulterior motive was to impress young ladies with his power and position. Tom and Jim had also signed up for Captain Allen's Criminal Law course.

During the first break of the evening, they could speak with Captain Allen alone. Tom and Jim told the captain about joining the explorer program in Greenwood. He had heard about his department's program in Greenwood but was not thoroughly knowledgeable about how the program functioned.

The two schemers took a deep breath and asked the captain to work and volunteer in his station. Captain Allen thought a moment and then thought he could do something none of the outlaying substation captains had done by having these Explorers work for him! Nevertheless, he agreed to Tom and Jim's request. This was solidified when Tom, not yet knowing about politics in law enforcement, mentioned that someone from Hudson Falls needed to call Deputy Lee in Greenwood to confirm Hudson Falls' approval of the assignment.

Captain Allen thought no patrol deputy in Greenwood would tell him how to run his station. The captain ended the meeting with, "You both can start on Monday. Report to Sergeant Hall at 1600 hours for additional information and training." Tom and Jim's law enforcement careers took off within a moment.

It Was a Different Time

Sheriff Sam Baldwin had been with the sheriff's office since 1952. He started as a supervisor in the forensics section. At the time, it was known as the Identification Bureau of the Greenwood County Sheriff's Department. Sam had a degree in biology from the University of Maryland.

Sam started his career as a lab technician with the Federal Bureau of Investigation in Los Angeles in 1948. Baldwin was currently in his third term as Sheriff of Greenwood County, and the citizens loved him! During community meetings, he would often tell the citizens that the sheriff's department was a response agency only, not a patrol agency.

The early 1970s was long before negligence and liability were the driving words behind day-to-day law enforcement supervision and management. Response times to calls for service were often over an hour. Professional and aggressive law enforcement was the priority, not the public perception of the Greenwood County Sheriff's Department or Sam Baldwin's political career.

The General Orders of the Greenwood County Sheriff's Department consisted of approximately thirty pages printed out and handed to each employee in a sage green paper binder like the ones used by college students submitting end-of-semester term papers.

Modern law enforcement supervisors and managers would cringe or shudder in disbelief at how the law enforcement mission was accomplished during this time. However, the average tenure of a station commander, Captain, with the Greenwood County Sheriff's Department was fifteen years, and each one of the Captains ran their station as if it was their empire. The only thing similar between each of the Greenwood County Sheriff's Stations was the uniform the deputies wore and the stars on the doors of the black-and-whites assigned to each station.

There was no central communications center, nor was there anything called 911. Each sheriff's station thought they were the best and the toughest, and rarely would they consider asking for help from each other, yet when they did, assistance was provided without hesitation.

There were no computers, no cell phones, and no body cameras. Most cops were male and Viet Nam war veterans. Many cops only had a high school education yet considered themselves professionals, along with lawyers and doctors. Cops stuck together and supported each other. They wanted nothing to do with the administration because everyone knew that sergeants ran the show. Most thought the profession a calling, and most could not imagine doing anything else.

Paying Your Dues

Tom Stevens and Jim Scott anxiously arrived promptly at the Hudson Falls Sheriff's Station at 3:45 P.M. for their history-making first shift for the acclaimed Sergeant Jack Hall. Sergeant Hall had already briefed his troops about the new additions and told them that if they were interested, they would be teaching the Explorers how to do the job of a Deputy Sheriff. However, the impatient sergeant also added that the squad would not be seeing them around for a little while as the two went through an orientation program and some basic training to introduce them to the sometimes focused and mediocre realities of police work. Most of Sergeant Hall's troops seemed interested and comfortable with this new program.

When they arrived, both eager friends wore their Explorer uniforms, like that of a Deputy Sheriff. The shirt was the same except for the patches on the sleeves and a cloth badge that read 'Explorer Greenwood County' instead of the metal badge, which read 'Deputy Sheriff Greenwood County.' The uniform pants were the same except for the tan stripe on the side, which the explorer pants did not have. Explorers wore the black basketweave 'Sam Browne' belt minus the gun, holster, and ammo dump pouch. Keepers, handcuff case or two, and radio case was the same. When the Watch Commander, Sergeant Hall, took the two comrades back to the small and crowded briefing room, 'Thumper' chimed in about how the two smelled like a uniform store. In those days, cops bought their uniforms and equipment, as did the explorers.

Sergeant Hall comfortably and systematically read the call log from the past twenty-four hours and APR (All Points Radio) board for wanted persons, cars, and patrol information from throughout the county. When completed, the relaxed sergeant lit up his first Camel unfiltered cigarette of the shift. Several deputies followed suit. As is custom for new 'boots' after their cigarette, 'Thumper' and 'Frank' both told the new Explorers to carry their briefcases and pursuit bags out to the units. Both newbies came to attention and simultaneously shouted, "Yes, Sir!"

Once outside, both 'Frank' and 'Thumper' took the time to show Tom and Jim the proper way to check the patrol car for equipment and how to document any shortfalls found before the shift. The Explorers were also shown where the station's supplies were kept and how to restock the patrol cars. This task would later become one of their daily routines. As the evening shift patrol units were now clearing the parking lot, Tom and Jim excitedly reported back to Sergeant Hall, who was now in his overstuffed and cluttered office.

"Napoleon," as many deputies at the Hudson Falls Sheriff's office called the pertinacious Sergeant Hall, told the two colleagues, "The essential thing a cop has is their professional reputation." He had described it many times in their class at El Camino College.

"The second most important thing is to pay your dues!"

If the impatient and cynical sergeant heard it once from a young person, he heard it a thousand times, "Yes, I want to be a cop, but I want to be a detective like the ones on television!"

No one ever starts as a detective! Instead, everyone begins on patrol and earns their way to the detective bureau. Tom and Jim were no exception, and Sergeant Hall told both of the 'specialized and important jobs' he had in mind for each of them so that he might see their caliber.

Transitioning, the tense Sergeant Hall issued Tom and Jim their key to the station, a shotgun key, and a county '102' key, which opened every county padlock used at county facilities or county gates.

Sergeant Hall thoughtfully told both Tom and Jim that they were not allowed to work the same shift and they would both have to work at least two shifts (sixteen hours) a month, like that as reserve deputies are required. The seemingly demanding sergeant told Tom and Jim to provide him with their schedule by the end of the week. This simple gesture made both Tom and Jim feel like team members.

Tom was disappointed to learn that his first assignment was to update the Fictitious Business Name File in the Sergeants' Office. He was handed a two-foot dusty stack of yellowed classified ads from the two local newspapers, and his mundane job was to cut out the fictitious business name statement listed in the paper and staple the notice onto a three-by-five card. Tom would turn the card over and write the name of the business allowing it to be filed in a three-by-five card file cabinet in the shared Sergeants' Office.

There were approximately five hundred fictitious business names posted in these newspapers, although the number in Tom's mind seemed tenfold. This project took Tom about two agonizing weeks to finish while working for 'Napoleon' on the evening shift. During this time working for Sergeant Hall, Tom noticed that after reading most reports submitted by the deputies, Hall would type up correction notices for each report and return these reports to the deputies for corrections. Tom always thought that his professional life's goal would be to work for Sergeant Hall and submit reports error-free with no returns.

Sergeant Hall knew that Jim Scott worked at the scenic Lake Hudson Campground and was an avid hunter with his father, so he was given the job of cleaning all the shotguns and 30-30 rifles in the Hudson Falls Sheriff's Station. He was tasked with cleaning and restocking all the filthy and neglected print kits to ensure each had enough cards, powder, and tape. Jim completed this tedious and time-consuming task in a fortnight while working the day shift with Sergeant William 'Big Bill' Johnson.

The next task 'Napoleon' wanted Tom to master was the jail. Four different experienced deputies were assigned to train Tom on how to receive a prisoner from another agency. How, safely, to search prisoners. How to book these prisoners, obtain their fingerprints, and correctly take their mug shots. Tom was also instructed on the detailed process of entering each of these prisoners into the jail population 'stats.' These records were maintained at the central county jail. Additionally, Tom was shown how to properly place a prisoner into a cell after completing the booking process.

Finally, he was instructed to remove the prisoner from the cell, search them, obtain all the appropriate paperwork, including the booking sheet and property bag, place them into a pre-searched patrol car, and then transport the prisoner to the central county jail, Greenwood. The training concluded with safely delivering a prisoner to the central booking desk in the county jail from the substation. Jim would also complete this same intensive and demanding training.

After four months, Tom was assigned by Sergeant Hall as the evening shift jailer freeing up patrol deputies to get back out in the field. Tom would receive prisoners from outside agencies, book them, and place them in holding cells before transporting them to county jail. He would later transport up to three prisoners without assistance to the county jail for processing.

Jim's next assignment in the training program was the evidence locker. He was trained to remove evidence from the patrol lockers where the deputies place the evidence obtained during their investigations and to log it into the system. Educated in the evidentiary chain of possession, Jim transported evidence to Greenwood headquarters for storage and additional processing as needed. Finally, Jim helped prepare and inventory evidence to be destroyed or sent to a public auction. Tom also completed this same detailed and time-consuming training.

This initial training for the new Explorers took about six grueling months. Tom and Jim ended up volunteering anywhere from forty to sixty hours a week at the sheriff's office, and they spent the time of their lives doing it. As Sergeant Hall described, professional reputations were developed. Restriction on the office environment was eased as time went by.

Tom and Jim were now riding with the deputies more and more. Most of the deputies treated the two like Reserve Deputy Sheriffs. When Tom and Jim would ride, they kept the patrol log and wrote the reports for the deputies. Many of the deputies told Tom they should have him write their reports all the time since Sergeant Hall rarely kicked back any of Tom's reports for correction. If they only knew, Tom would have been more than happy to do that!

My Goat

One thing you never do in law enforcement is share your feelings, fears, or emotions with your colleagues. You never provide them with the material and the information they need to push your button, and you never tell them where you keep your goat! This basic concept was especially true for Sergeant Jack Hall's crew. Tom Stevens and Jim Scott would learn this fact of life the hard way!

The Boy Scouts of America is a fine organization that does a fantastic job of educating and developing the future leaders of our country. The Explorer program also allowed young people to glimpse into and experience the ins and outs of a specific career to help map out their future career paths.

The problem was that after six months of volunteering fifty to sixty hours a week at the sheriff's office, Tom and Jim felt comfortable as if they were a part of the Greenwood County Sheriff's Department. To illustrate, if the devil himself had shown up at the Hudson Falls Sheriff's Department, both Tom and Jim would have sold their souls to be Deputy Sheriffs for that department. For some reason, Tom disliked being tied to the Boy Scouts, and he would periodically mention that feeling to the deputies with whom he and Jim worked.

One afternoon towards the end of Sergeant Hall's briefing, the sergeant mentioned that a large Boy Scout group was attending a significant event at Lake Hudson. As a result, the scouts and campgrounds requested extra patrol from the deputies. 'Frank,' feeling very jovial this afternoon, took a verbal poke at Tom and said, "Your people have come to town." Tom replied, "They are not my people!"

'Thumper,' not wanting to let this golden opportunity pass, said, "You're right, these are Boy Scouts. You look more like a Cub Scout!"

Then, Jim entered the briefing room to finish his dayshift paperwork.

'Thumper,' on a roll, said, "Look at you two. We have a Chubby Cubby and a Stout Scout amongst us!"

At that very moment, Tom and Jim earned and were christened with their new nicknames. These nicknames held especially true once the squad saw the grimaced look on Tom's and Jim's faces when they heard it for the first time.

Coffee Mugs

In police stations and sheriff's offices in America in the 1970s and 1980s, a pot of coffee was on for employees or guests. Hudson Falls Sheriff's Office was no exception. The Kitchenette break area was near the detective's offices next to the evidence lockers. This area consisted of a sink, refrigerator, and counter, which held the large coffee urn for the day shift crew and the regular pot of Mr. Coffee for the evening and midnight crew. Suspended above the sink were racks of coffee cups uniform in appearance. The Greenwood County Sheriff's Office Star was on one side of each cup with the deputy's last name under the star. The deputy's nickname was on the opposite side of the cup if they had one. Otherwise, the cup was blank.

Early during the training program, Tom and Jim were instructed by Sergeant Hall that it was their responsibility to ensure the coffee pot had coffee twenty-four hours a day. Jim took care of it for the day shift, and Tom did the same for the evening and midnight shifts. Both Explorers also ensured the area was kept clean and the cups were replaced in the rack once cleaned.

About a week after Tom and Jim had been christened with their new nicknames, Sergeant Hall ensured that both day and evening shifts were in the briefing room for a brief presentation during this shift change. Once everyone had gathered, Sergeant Jack Hall presented Jim with a new coffee mug identical to the ones currently on the rack in the kitchenette. The mug had the Greenwood County Sheriff's Office Star on one side with 'Scott' underneath. On the opposite side of the cup was a caricature of a red fire hydrant with the words 'Stout Scout' above the fire hydrant. Many of the deputies teased Jim that he was built like a fireplug.

After the presentation to Jim, Sergeant Hall presented Tom with the same cup, only on the opposite side from the star, and his last name was a caricature of a Boy Scout in his green uniform saluting the Boy Scout three-fingered salute. Above the Boy Scout read 'Chubby Cubby.'

Over forty years later, Tom still has this coffee mug on display in his office at home with the Boy Scout side showing!

The Detectives

This was the second career for Detective Harmon C. Harmon. When he was eighteen, Harmon joined the Navy and retired as a Master Chief at thirty-eight. He returned home to Greenwood County, where he joined the sheriff's department as a patrol deputy. Seven years later, Harmon took the Detectives test and was subsequently promoted to Detective and assigned to the Hudson Falls Substation. Twenty years have passed since he started working in the Detective Bureau, and he has seen generations of 'assholes' come and go through his and other Detectives' doors.

As Harmon washed his hands in the men's room sink, he looked down at his age-spotted and freckled arms and saw the remnants of two navy tattoos, a ship, and an anchor. Both tattoos had faded and now looked like two green-black blobs on his forearms. As he glanced in the mirror when leaving and saw his thinning white hair, he thought it was time to retire. At sixty-six years of age, Harmon was ready for that trip to Europe about which his wife, Edith, had always talked. Five years ago, Harmon had a cancer scare and lost part of his lung. The cancer was from years of smoking in the Navy and as a patrol deputy. Additionally, his change of life daughter, Bonnie, had just graduated from Hudson Falls High School with Tom Stevens and Jim Scott. Bonnie was engaged to a lovely young man who worked as a manager at the Firestone Service Center in Hudson Falls.

The Grand Master of the Hudson Falls Detectives was John 'Johnny' Miller. Johnny Miller had been a widower for five years. He had been with the sheriff's department for thirty-six years. A thoughtful man of German descent, Johnny had been a detective for thirty of his thirty-six years. He was five foot ten inches tall with a frumpy build. His index and middle fingers on his right hand were yellow from the four packs of Pall Mall regular cigarettes he inhaled daily. Detective Miller had just finished sending his second son through medical school. His eldest son is a surgeon in Denver and his second son is now an emergency room doctor in Boston.

Detective Miller, a master at interview and interrogation, could also review a police report and determine who the suspect might be, based on the method of operation. Miller would then check his files and make a phone call to the suspect. Amazingly, the suspect would come to the sheriff's office to meet with the detective and confess to the crime. Detective Miller would often make a case and clear the investigation with an arrest without ever leaving his office. Considered to be one of the best interviewers in the sheriff's office, Detective Miller taught Detective Harmon how to work cases based on the method of operation review. Also, using other investigative skills, the two cleared much paper and made many arrests over the years. Most of the time, Johnny Miller worked as a loner, and he had no intention of retiring soon.

Charles 'Charlie' Wilson was a hard-charging hard-drinking detective cross between a used car salesman and a college professor. He was loud, in your face, and always ready for action. Charlie Wilson celebrated his twentieth year in the Detective Bureau with a weekend getaway to Las Vegas, where he dropped a grand on the craps table. Charlie had a photographic memory that helped him with the significant economic crimes he worked on as a specialty. Charlie was divorced from his third wife, but according to him, he was 'banging' a gorgeous state trooper from Duncan on the side.

After only three years on patrol in Greenwood, Charlie started his time as a detective. He was recruited for the Organized Crime Squad because of his youthful appearance and accounting degree from UCLA. He worked on an Internal Revenue Service Task Force for five years dealing with east coast transplants and high-rollers in Mountain Bluff. Charlie's skills with numbers brought him to the Economic Crimes Unit out of headquarters and then to Hudson Falls, where he and Detective Harmon have been working as a team for the last couple of years.

The new kid on the Hudson Falls Sheriff's Office Detective Bureau block was Benjamin 'Benny' Wright, with fifteen years of experience as an investigator. 'Benny' Wright was a large man who stood six feet five inches tall and weighed approximately two hundred ten pounds with little body fat. 'Benny' was also a pleasant man who did not take advantage of his position or the people he worked with. Benny's head was cocked to the right slightly due to an on-duty injury he sustained while working patrol as a rookie in Pine Ridge. 'Benny' was chasing an armed robbery suspect on the interstate when a semi suddenly pulled out in front of him, causing the patrol car to flip several times before resting in a dirt field next to the interstate. 'Benny' sustained a broken neck, and it took the jaws of life to free him from the patrol vehicle. In addition, he had a broken back, and he thought he would never walk again. After nearly a year in physical therapy and several surgeries, Detective Wright was cleared for full-duty status. 'Benny' was married with two daughters, ages twelve and fifteen.

'Benny' met 'Charlie' Wilson three months before 'Benny' was promoted to Detective. 'Benny' was working patrol out of the Greenwood County Sheriff's Office Mountain Bluff office when he received a request to back the Economic Crimes Squad at a Mob-owned-and-run brothel. The victim reported to the Vice Unit that one of the girls gave him a dose of the clap. She threw him out when he requested the madam to pay his medical bills. The victim then drove to the sheriff's office to report the crime and assist in the investigation. The victim not only filed criminal charges for himself, but his wife filed for civil damages as well. His wife lacked consortium due to her husband's inability to obtain and maintain an erection during his recovery.

Due to the media circus, the sheriff's office also decided to bring in Economic Crimes to work the organized crime angle with the mob and the Internal Revenue Service. So 'Benny' Wright transported 'Charlie's' prisoners. That was the beginning of a true friendship!

The Hudson Falls Sheriff's Office detectives have eighty-five years of investigative experience. This situation holds at most of the sheriff's office substations. The problem with the system is that Detective is a tested rank. When a person tests and is promoted, many stay in that position for the remainder of their career. The problem lies in that most patrol sergeants have no investigative experience. This is a substandard situation Tom Stevens would witness many times in his career.

My Best Day, My Worst Day

As in most households, the Sunday evening meal was time for the family to catch up from the past week. It was no exception in the Thomas household. On the first Sunday of December, Barbara made her specialty fried chicken with mashed potatoes and white chicken gravy. Nothing but pure health. Boy, was it good? Sharon, Tom's sister, and his stepfather Daniel were all in the family room when Tom's mother called them into the dining room for dinner. Although Tom's mother was raised Southern Baptist, and Daniel was raised Catholic, the family never said grace or gave a blessing before a meal.

The mood was light and friendly, the food being passed around along with compliments to the chef. Sharon started the conversation about what she had done in school this past week. When she got into the weeds about boys and what each girlfriend thought about them, Barbara would cut her off and redirect the conversation to Tom. Tom then worked full-time and donated approximately twenty to thirty hours weekly to the Greenwood County Sheriff's Office. Daniel had been needling Tom for several weeks about donating too much time to the sheriff's department. On this night, Daniel started again; only he was pushing very hard on the issue.

Tom could not understand why Daniel was so upset about donating time to law enforcement.

Tom told Daniel, "Dad, I am doing what you always told me to do. I am developing my professional reputation. I am showing them what good work I can do. I am showing them that I want to be there and work for that organization!"

Daniel replied, "They are just taking advantage of you!"

Tom knew that his stepfather always wanted to be an L.A.P.D. Officer, but he was only five foot seven inches tall. The minimum height for an L.A.P.D. officer, at the time, was five foot eight inches. Tom believed his father was jealous and just being ridiculous, and he told him so!

Tom then told his family that this whole conversation was almost laughable because he was receiving the standard 'You are hanging out with the wrong crowd!' speech reserved for the sons involved with gangs or drug users in 'B-movies' from the forty's and fifty's.

Tom said that for his mom's benefit because she was such a fan of all the old Hollywood movies.

Daniel then spoke the line that all fathers say to their children at some point in their lives, "As long as you live under my roof and eat my food, you will follow my rules!"

Tom lost control of his outside voice and said, "You're crazy."

Daniel stood up, unknown if to strike Tom or to position himself in a more superior position. Still, as he did so, Tom also stood up, not clenching his fists or in a fashion that he was about to attack but displaying command presence. Tom had learned about command presence and its importance. All the deputies he had ridden with and worked for taught this – the lifeline of all good cops. The lesson stuck.

While this was happening, Sharon yelled Tom's name.

Tom's mother cried, "Both of you, stop it!"

Several moments passed that seemed like hours, and when Daniel realized that Tom was not going to back down, Daniel turned away and said, "I am done with this!"

Tom turned to his mother and said, "I'm sorry, Mom!"

With that, Tom left his parent's house and had his Sunday dinner at Jack in the Box in Hudson Falls. Like many sons who have gone through a similar situation, Tom thought today was his best day when he realized he could take his dad! And it was his worst day when he realized he could take his dad!

After two weeks of avoiding the family, Tom's mother called him at the sheriff's office and told him the family had bought a new home in southeast Hudson Falls. They would be moving to this new house within the month, but Tom would not be joining them. Instead, Tom's mother had rented him a furnished bachelor's apartment near downtown. Tom moved into his new digs and realized that he was on his own and a grown man when he ran out of toilet paper, and there was no one around to call to bring him some.

When Tom was hired full-time by a law enforcement agency, his stepfather never congratulated him.

Baby Cakes

Tony Sullivan was a lateral transfer from the Pomona Police Department in Southern California. Tony had been a road manager for Dick Clark Productions before becoming an officer, and he shared plenty of stories about the folks he worked with, known and unknown in the entertainment industry. At the time, Pomona had a reputation as being a rough town in Los Angeles County. So, Tom Stevens was naturally drawn and intrigued by Greenwood County's new deputy.

Tony was married and had a young daughter. His family was happy they left Southern California and relocated to Hudson Falls. Tom, who welcomed Tony on his first day, started to develop a friendship immediately, and once Tony completed his training program, Tom was the first to ride with him.

Tony was surprised when Tom got in the car with him. Tom immediately offered to work the radio for him, keep and complete the patrol log, and write any reports they may take that night. Tony, assigned to the evening shift with Sergeant Jack Hall, did not realize that Tom had been doing this for the last eight months. Tony was surprised and grateful at the same time. Tony told Tom that he would teach him everything he knew about being a cop, both good and bad. Tom never knew what spawned it or where it came from, but halfway through their first shift together, Tony started calling Tom 'Baby Cakes.' It was not to embarrass him or to push his button. It was just a nickname that Tony came up with for his new protégé.

Two nights later, after the briefing, when Tom got into the patrol car, Tony asked 'Baby Cakes' if he had ever been in a fight wearing that uniform.

When Tom replied, "Never,"

Tony said, "Well, that will change today."

Tony said, "We need to see what you are made of!"

Tom asked, "What are we going to do?"

Tony said, "We will get you into a fight with your first arrest!"

39

The young Explorer was excited in anticipation. The two drove towards the east end of the El Camino Valley towards Evergreen, which is farmland and where the immigration camps are located.

Tony told Tom, "When we see our target, we will get out of the unit, make contact, and I will get him to swing on you. When he does, your job is to take him into custody as swiftly and quickly as possible."

Tony confirmed, "You have your cuffs on you, right?"

Tom said, "I sure do!"

Tony said, "Great, we will be in business!"

As Tony and Tom were driving towards Evergreen, Tom thought about how 'Thumper' and 'Frank' had choked out people in the Hudson Falls jail or on the street when they made arrests. These two seasoned deputies had instructed Tom on the finer points of the carotid sleeper hold as it was formally called, and the two told him many times, "You got it!" when he would apply the hold to them in training. Tonight was going to be Tom's first application in a real-world scenario.

Tony Sullivan pulled off the main drag in Evergreen onto a dirt road alongside one of the many plum tree groves, where he saw three men around a small fire.

Tony told Tom, "We are going over there to contact these three suspicious persons around this suspicious fire to investigate. During our investigation, we will determine that they are in the country illegally and place them under arrest. The subjects resisted during the arrest process, and appropriate force was used to effect the arrest. Got it?"

Tom replied, "Got it!"

Tony concluded, "Watch the bad guy's hands. You will know when he is about to fight. When that happens, take him down and place him in custody. Now, call it in!"

Tom Stevens grabbed the mic from the center console of the patrol unit and dispatched, "Hudson Falls 540 out with three and a suspicious fire in the plum tree grove in the 26500 block of Fairview Ave."

The Hudson Falls dispatch acknowledged the call, and Tony and Tom started walking toward the three men. As Tony and Tom approached, two of the three men got up and started running toward the center of the plum tree grove.

Tony told Tom, "Let them go; we will deal with this one."

When Tony approached the now lone man, he asked him in Spanish, unbeknownst to Tom, "What is your name?"

The man replied, "Pedro Perez Rodriguez."

Tony, who learned Spanish after working the streets of Pomona for a couple of years, continued,

"Where were you born?"

Pedro replied, "Ensenada, Mexico."

Tony's final question was, "Do you have papers or a green card?" and when Pedro replied, "No,"

Tony told him he was under arrest for being an illegal alien. Then Tony asked Tom in English, "Are you watching his hands?"

Without waiting for an answer from Tom, Tony told Pedro in Spanish, "If you can kick this kid's ass, you are free to go!"

Pedro cocked his head as he looked at Tony in disbelief when he suddenly clenched his fists and took a swing at Tom Stevens. Using Pedro's forward motion, Tom eagerly spun him around and applied a carotid sleeper hold of which 'Thumper' and 'Frank' would be proud. Next, Tom quickly and smoothly reached into his handcuff case, removed the cuffs, and applied them in one swift motion while the suspect was still limp.

Tony proclaimed as Tom was helping Pedro back to his feet, "You done good, 'Baby Cakes!'"

When they returned to the patrol car, Tom placed Pedro in the back seat and notified dispatch, "Hudson Falls 540, we have one in custody for Title 8 Section 1325 and 1326 USC. Notify Border Patrol to respond to the Hudson Falls station to pick up the prisoner."

Pedro was only charged with being an illegal alien and not the assault on a peace officer charge. Tom completed all the paperwork and booking as if Tony Sullivan had made the arrest. However, this was all Tom, who was on cloud nine for the remainder of the evening. Tom told Tony that he could not wait to call his best friend and fellow Explorer, Jim Scott, to tell him about his first arrest.

Tony Sullivan ended the shift with one of his daily words of wisdom to 'Baby Cakes.'

"Always wave at kids on school buses!"

In the Wee Hours

Tom Stevens had applied at several law enforcement agencies for civilian positions. However, he still had two years to go until he was twenty-one. In the meantime, Tom took a job as the midnight clerk at the 7-Eleven store in east Hudson Falls. The store was located at the northwest corner of California Blvd. and Cottonwood Avenue and backed up to a residential area known as Sullivan Ranch, between Hudson Falls and Evergreen. One of the benefits the owner of the store, Alfred Flores, enjoyed was Tom working Wednesday through Sunday from 11:00 P.M. to 7:00 A.M. every cop in the El Camino Valley knew Tom worked at this store, and it became the midnight cops hung out. To be sure, with the owner's blessing, Tom always cared for the cops with drinks and snacks.

It was a cold winter night in Hudson Falls. Tom was working this first night back and knew it would be a long shift. After the usual midnight rush, customers in the store had slowed to a trickle. The evening shift of Greenwood County Sheriff deputies had been in to finish their reports and have the last orange Slurpee of the shift. The midnight crew of G.C.S.O. deputies had made their initial stop around 12:30 A.M. Each deputy left to run out to their beats to check their commercial areas for prowlers or any suspicious activity. Hudson Falls Police were not far behind the county and stayed for about an hour until the Jefferson Highway Patrol swung by for a quick coffee before the bar rush. California Boulevard was the main road to Lake Hudson. The 7-Eleven sold various items, including camping gear and equipment, and had just received new fly rods and other fishing equipment. Tom, an avid angler, could hardly wait to try these new fly-fishing rods out.

It was about 2:30 A.M. when Ethan 'Frank' Mitchell and Jacob 'Heifer Hauler' Murphy were at the 7-Eleven, sucking down a cup of coffee and a handful of mixed nuts from a display case when the silence of their radios was broken.

"1 David 20 Hudson Falls."

'Frank' grabbed the radio, "Hudson Falls 1 David 20 Go Ahead."

Dispatch continued, "1 David 20 Assist Jefferson Highway Patrol with an unknown injury traffic collision on California Blvd near the Cranston Ranger Station. Reporting party advises that the vehicle flipped and rolled off the roadway. The reporting party will flag you down."

'Frank' Mitchell replied, "1 David 20 en route from California Blvd. and Cottonwood Ave."

'Heifer Hauler' Murphy said, "Hudson Falls 1 David 10 will back from the same location."

With that, both deputies took off with lights and sirens eastbound on California Blvd. towards Evergreen. The Cranston Ranger Station was approximately ten miles east of Cottonwood Ave.

The store was finally empty, and Tom walked over to the new fishing equipment sales display, where he removed one of the new fly-fishing rods. He ensured the rod was ready to test when he walked outside in the parking lot towards the north edge of California Blvd. No traffic was out, and Tom enjoyed his casting across the five lanes of California Blvd. and onto the sidewalk across the street. Tom was outside the store for several minutes, improving his distance with each cast, when he turned around and noticed a customer walking southbound on Cottonwood Ave from the residential area.

The customer wore a black motorcycle helmet, a black tee shirt, and a black leather jacket. He was also wearing blue Levi's and a pair of black motorcycle-style boots with a dull finish. This individual appeared to be about five foot seven inches tall and weighed approximately one hundred and thirty pounds. Tom turned around and started walking back inside the store, not thinking anything about this suspicious person.

As Tom and the subject got closer to the store, Tom told the customer, "I'll be right with you."

The subject replied, "OK."

Tom beat the person to the door in seconds, and when Tom entered the store and started to walk towards the employee's entrance to the front counter, the suspect pulled a blue steel revolver from his waistband and pointed it at Tom's head.

The suspect sounded like a young white male and told Tom, "Give me the money!"

Tom, surprisingly not scared, replied, "No problem." As he did so, he noticed through the clear visor of the suspect's helmet his piercing pale blue eyes and a small mole near the corner of the suspect's right eye.

Tom placed all the money in a plastic bag from the store and handed it to the suspect, who extended his left hand to grab the plastic bag. Tom also noticed that the suspect had 'Mi Vida Loca' tattooed on the web of his left hand, and the suspect was a white male. The suspect told Tom to lie on the ground and count to one hundred before moving.

Tom again said, "No problem."

The suspect exited the store and fled on foot in an unknown direction.

Once Tom confirmed that the suspect was gone, he initiated armed robbery procedures for the store, including locking the front doors and calling the Hudson Falls Sheriff's Office. Two Hudson Falls Police units were en route to the 7-Eleven for something to eat and drink when the call came out. When the broadcast was made, most cops in the El Camino Valley could not believe it.

Unlike most victims of armed robbery, Stevens gave a complete and detailed description of the suspect and the weapon used. Within minutes all available law enforcement units in El Camino Valley were in the area looking for the suspect and eventually checking on their buddy, the one that got robbed.

Several minutes after the radio broadcast, Jacob 'Heifer Hauler' Murphy checked out with a subject matching the description northeast of the store in a residential area in Sullivan Ranch that backed up to agricultural land. When searched for officer safety, the suspect was found to have a four-inch blue-steel Smith and Wesson Model 10 .38 caliber handgun in his possession and a white plastic 7-Eleven bag with a couple of hundred dollars in paper money. 'Frank' Mitchell backed Jacob on his stop, and Sergeant Elliott Donato, the Greenwood County midnight shift sergeant, came to the 7-Eleven to pick up Tom for an in-field lineup.

When Sergeant Donato arrived at the 7-Eleven store, six patrol cars checked to ensure Tom was all right. Before Tom left with Sgt Donato, the six law enforcement officers told Tom not to worry about the store. They would watch it for him! Tom had already called the owner and told him what had happened. Tom replied to the cops, "Yeah, that scares me!" The owner was currently en route to the store with a thirty-minute response time.

When Tom and Sergeant Donato arrived where the deputies had the suspect detained, Tom told the sergeant that he needed to see the suspect up close. Typically, in-field lineups were conducted at a distance for the benefit of the victim or witnesses.

When Tom approached, the suspect surprisingly spurted out, "So, we meet again!"

When Tom came up, he looked the suspect in the eye and saw the same small mole near the corner of his right eye. The color of his eyes was just as he remembered. Tom asked to see his left hand. 'Mi Vida Loca' was tattooed on the web of his left hand.

Tom stated, "That's him!" The suspect, who had a criminal history of commercial armed robbery, was arrested and transported to the Hudson Falls Sheriff's office, where he was booked for the crime.

By the time the owner of the store, Alfred Flores, arrived on the scene and he and Tom went over everything that happened, it was approaching 6:00 A.M. Mr. Flores was thrilled that Tom was safe.

Moreover, nobody was hurt. He was even happier when the deputies told him the suspect was arrested and the money was recovered. Mr. Flores gave Tom the rest of the morning off with pay.

At about 8:30 A.M., Tom arrived at the Hudson Falls Sheriff's Station for a scheduled shift. Tom, who was now in uniform, saw that the suspect was still in custody, and Detective Johnny Miller was moments away from interviewing the suspect. When Tom Stevens entered the jail to check on the prisoners as he always did as part of his assigned duties, the suspect came up to the bars and said, "Oh Fuck, you're a cop?" Tom said nothing to the man. Moments later, Tom escorted the prisoner to the interview room where Detective Miller was waiting. Once Mirandized, the suspect admitted to that and four additional robberies in the El Camino Valley and surrounding areas.

"Back the Boobs"

Sergeant Jack Hall took the first three hours off his shift to see his daughter's Hudson Falls softball team play against their arch-rivals at El Camino. Tony Sullivan had taken a comp day off, and Sergeant Hall left Sam 'Thumper' Robinson in charge while he took the three hours off. 'Thumper' was a tough-as-nails street cop known for his ability to get the job done. He had no aspirations of promotion to detective, much less as a sergeant, and did not think much like a supervisor. 'Thumper' thought his job was basically to protect people who could not defend themselves and throw bad guys in jail, and he was very good at doing that!

Today's lineup consisted of:

Sam 'Thumper' Robinson, the Acting Watch Commander, and East El Camino Valley Unit.

Roberta 'Bobby Boobs' Lee, the West El Camino Valley Unit in Car 543.

Jacob 'Heifer Hauler' Murphy, the Central El Camino Valley Unit in Car 541.

Ethan 'Frank' Mitchell, the second Central El Camino Valley Unit in Car 542.

Explorer Tom Stevens is doing Vacation Property Checks in East El Camino Valley in Car 540.

It was a warm Sunday evening in June. At about 1600 hours, three men armed with handguns robbed a Mom-and-Pop liquor store in the City of Burlington west of Hudson Falls. The three men were last seen driving out of the city eastbound in a gold Ford Pinto with a partial Jefferson license of 123P.

At about 1730 hours, 'Thumper' and 'Frank' were tied up on a stabbing that had just occurred, the suspect possibly still in the area of the Brush Popper Inn in Riverbank.

Jacob 'Heifer Hauler' Murphy was out with a violent mental health patient he took into custody for evaluation at the county hospital in Greenwood.

Tom Stevens was driving a marked patrol car, unit 540, conducting vacation property checks in Evergreen. Tom and Jim Scott did these checks during their respective shifts, and Sergeant Jack Hall requested they place the 'Out of Service' sign in the back window when they drove the marked patrol cars.

Tom and Jim felt terrible that the sign kept falling out of the window and fell to the rear floorboard without being noticed by either of them until after their shift. Both Tom and Jim just hated it when that happened!

During this era in law enforcement, most cops felt that policies and procedures were just guidelines to get the job done and not written in concrete. Tom and Jim had been trained with this same idea. Tom would experience a drastic change of philosophy as his career continued.

Tom had just pulled into the Brentwood Subdivision in the Simpson Heights area of Evergreen. Tom got on the radio and broadcasted, "Hudson Falls 540, I'll be out on a property check at 26133 Delmonico Drive in Evergreen." The dispatcher, Stella 'Green Springs' Bartley, acknowledged the call. Moments later, the call came in from Roberta 'Bobbie Boobs' Lee.

"Hudson Falls 543, I'm following a possible armed robbery vehicle eastbound on State Highway 76 entering Moonglade. The car is occupied by what appears to be three males. Start a backup unit this way."

The Hudson Falls Sheriff's units were tied up and unable to clear. Finally, the Acting Watch Commander 'Thumper' Robinson, came on the air to confirm 543's location.

Deputy Lee came up on the radio with concern in her voice, "Hudson Falls 543, the suspect vehicle is pulling into the Moonglade Market. Copy the tag of Jefferson 123 PAG......I've got three at gunpoint!"

'Thumper' came up and said, "Hudson Falls send 540. I will be breaking two additional units shortly."

Stella, who always had a thing for 'Thumper' dispatched, "540 Hudson Falls respond to back 543 on a felony vehicle stop at the Moonglade Market on Hwy 76. Your call is Code 3."

Explorer Tom Stevens, who suddenly had a lump in his throat, picked up the mic and said, "Hudson Falls 540 en route from Evergreen."

For the first time by himself, in this unprecedented authorization, Tom activated the overhead lights and siren of the patrol car and drove code three from Evergreen to Moonglade, approximately twenty miles away. The whole time he was going, he kept saying, "Remember your training, and do not blow this."

Halfway to Moonglade, Tom removed the lone shotgun key on a ring from his right front gun belt. He unlocked the shotgun rack.

Tom had checked the shotgun before driving the unit, as he had done hundreds of times with other deputies at the beginning of his shift. Moments before Tom arrived, he heard 'Thumper' and 'Frank' clear the Assault with a Deadly Weapon call at the Brush Popper Inn to advise Hudson Falls dispatch that they were en route to 543's location.

As Tom approached the Moonglade Market, he shut down the siren but kept the overheads of the patrol car on. He pulled into the market and parked next to Deputy Lee in a perfect felony stop position. Tom had grabbed the shotgun from his unit and racked a round into the chamber, reminding the bad guys that there were now two 12-gauge Remington 870 shotguns pointing at them, ready for action.

'Thumper' and 'Frank' arrived within five minutes, and the three suspects in this gold Ford Pinto were taken into custody without incident. Due to the calm professionalism of Deputy Roberta 'Bobbie Boobs' Lee, no suspects or bystanders were hurt during this arrest. The suspects admitted to the armed robbery in Burlington earlier that evening and told 'Frank' that they were going inside the Moonglade Market to commit another armed robbery to support their drug habit. Sergeant Hall's squad agreed never to discuss Tom's response to this call again despite receiving praise from all involved squad members for his professional and timely efforts.

The Baker and the Donut Maker

Gabe Smith was a fifteen-year burned-out L.A.P.D. Copper from the Hollywood station. He was tired of dealing with all the 'low-life' in Los Angeles. Gabe was tall and lean and looked weathered with wrinkles already profoundly set on his face at forty years of age. Gabe had that California tan, and his face looked like a saddle bag from a pony express rider's mount. Gabe Smith had been in Hollywood most of his life.

While attending Hollywood High School, Gabe was a runner for Capitol Records on Vine Street in Los Angeles. His parents lived in a small wooden bungalow-style home on Sunset Boulevard near Paramount studios. When he graduated high school, he worked for Fisher Body at the General Motors plant in Van Nuys before being picked up by L.A.P.D.

Gabe's wife of twenty years, Amy Murphy, was a bubbly red-haired, at least when they met, petite Irish lass with deep blue eyes and a welcoming, warm smile. Gabe was crazy over her, and even after all these years of dealing with Hollywood's dirtbags, she could still put a smile on his face when he saw her.

When she got out of high school, Amy Smith learned her baking skills when she went to work for Helms Bakery on the border of Culver City and Los Angeles. After five years with Helms Bakery, she left the company and went to work for Van de Kamp's Holland Dutch Bakeries in Hollywood, where she met her husband, Gabe. Even when she and Gabe were dating, she talked about opening her bakery and being her own boss. That opportunity came available when, after scrimping and saving, Amy raised enough money for her bakery and donut shop in Hudson Falls.

When Amy told Gabe that they were moving to Jefferson and specifically Hudson Falls to achieve her dream of opening her bakery, Gabe did not push back at all. He was looking forward to leaving law enforcement and enjoying retirement life. Little did he know. Amy broke the news to Gabe that she wanted him to stay in law enforcement to guarantee an income and provide medical insurance for the family. Being a good husband, Gabe reluctantly agreed and subsequently went to work for the

Greenwood County Sheriff's Department in Hudson Falls. However, his heart was no longer in law enforcement. Amy told Gabe that she would need his help with the new family business.

Amy's Bakery and Donut Shop is located in the Emerald Valley Shopping Center at the southeast corner of Enterprise Street and Via Rojo Ave in south Hudson Falls on the way to Emerald Valley. Open 24 hours a day, Amy had taught Gabe how to make donuts, and she did all the baking for the shop. Gabe worked the midnight shift at the sheriff's office and came into the business around 8:30 A.M. to make donuts until around 3:00 P.M. every day. Amy would come to work around Noon and bake pies, cakes, and assorted pastries until 10:00 P.M. These hours brought customers into the business all day long for fresh donuts and baked goods. A retired Fire Captain from Greenwood worked the midnight shift because he liked hanging out with the cops, including Gabe and his squad mates, who would stop in throughout the night for coffee. The Fire Captain's wife worked dayshift at the bakery to help Amy.

Gabe worked the midnight shift by design. It was the slowest call for service shift in the county, which meant minimal contact with the citizens. Gabe also had a warped sense of humor that many did not understand or appreciate. Jim Scott, however, became a fan of Gabe Smith from the get-go. Like Tom Stevens, Jim Scott had an excellent reputation with the deputies at the Hudson Falls Station. Jim rode with Gabe whenever he could and performed all the duties of a two-person car, including the radio and all reports. Gabe would regale Jim with stories of L.A.P.D. Hollywood Station and Jim would eat it up like the customers with the freshly made glazed donuts at Amy's.

As Gabe's and Jim's friendship grew, Gabe realized that he had a golden opportunity to improve the quality of his life and enrich the quality of this fine young man riding with him, whose only desire in life was to be a peace officer. So, Gabe told Jim he wanted him to take over as the primary officer in the car. In other words, Jim would do everything while Gabe watched and evaluated. This evaluation came from the vehicle's front passenger side with his ball cap pulled down over his eyes and then napping with his head propped against the passenger window. This evaluation program went on for about two months, and both Gabe and Jim became more confident in Jim's abilities.

One night when Gabe did not get a chance to sleep before his shift at the sheriff's office, he told Jim to do what he usually did on patrol because he was crawling into the back seat to get some sleep.

As Gabe took off his gun belt and placed it on the rear floorboards, he told Jim, "If anything significant comes up, you wake me up and let me know."

Being the helpful sort, Jim agreed and said, "No problem!"

At about 3:30 A.M., Hudson Falls dispatch broke radio silence with, "543 Hudson Falls."

Jim Scott calmly picked up the mic and said, "543. Go ahead."

Dispatch continued, "543 Hudson Falls, Back the Howerton Station Unit on an armed robbery just occurred at the Mobil Gas Station located at 14785 Vera Cruz Blvd." Dispatch added, "Suspects are two Hispanic males with handguns, of medium height and weight, with dark hair and eyes. The suspects were last seen driving westbound on Vera Cruz Blvd. at a high rate of speed. 543, your call is Code 3."

Jim confirmed with dispatch, saying, "Hudson Falls 543 is en route from Moonglade."

Jim reached down to the Federal Interceptor siren control box in one smooth motion. He turned the selector one click to the right from manual to the wail, immediately activating the lights and siren on the patrol car. Gabe, who had fallen deep asleep, suddenly awoke after hearing the screaming siren in his ear.

He said, "What in the hell are you doing?"

Jim replied, "We are headed to back a Howerton unit at an armed robbery that occurred at the Mobil station in Spoondrift."

Gabe, in exasperation, said, "I told you to wake me if something big came up!"

Jim just said, "I have this!"

Gabe sternly replied, "Pull over and let me drive!"

The two responded to the Mobil station without locating the suspects. No one in the gas station was hurt. Gabe Smith learned a lesson;

Jim returned to working the radio and taking care of all the reports. Gabe was not mad at Jim, and the two remained friends for the remainder of Gabe Smith's time in Hudson Falls.

Unfortunately, Gabe could not continue working the double-duty hours he had been doing for three months without a break. The long hours and not seeing Amy for significant personal time started to wear on the marriage. After twenty-two years of marriage, Gabe Smith filed for divorce. Amy's Bakery and Donut Shop was sold to a Japanese couple from Iowa. Amy moved to Santiago Springs to work as a baker for a large resort hotel. Gabe Smith returned to Hollywood, where he worked as a bartender at a burlesque nightclub near Hollywood Boulevard and Vine Street.

Decisions, Decisions, Decisions

Time flies when you are having fun! Two years passed in a blink of an eye. Jim Scott, Tom Stevens, and Robert Henry had remained friends and spent considerable time together. All three would soon graduate high school, and all were anxious to start their lives. The only problem was that all three wanted to be cops, but that would mean waiting another three years until they were twenty-one. Besides the experience at the Hudson Falls Sheriff's Station for Tom and Jim, both shared their off time with Robert and his life in Greenwood. Likewise, Robert spent the last two years as the Captain of the Greenwood Police Explorers, but he came to Hudson Falls and lived in Tom and Jim's world when he was off. Besides spending time with each other, each spent a lot of time in inner thought about the path they would soon be taking.

Robert had left Vaughn's Market in Greenwood and accepted a job as an armed uniform security officer for the Greenwood Entertainment Center. The City of Greenwood Police Department was advertising for the position of Police Cadet. The Police Cadet was a civilian position. The employee would work at the police department in a support role until they were twenty and a half years old when the police department would send the Police Cadet to a local law enforcement academy. Upon completing the police academy, the Police Cadet would be promoted to Police Officer with the Greenwood Police Department.

On the other hand, the Greenwood County Sheriff's Department was advertising for the position of Sheriff's Aide, which was a non-sworn position providing support services throughout the department at various county sheriff's stations. However, the Sheriff's Aide position paid a better salary than the Police Cadet. Robert never applied to the Greenwood Police Department for unknown reasons. He did, however, apply for a Sheriff's Aide position.

Former station commander of the Pine Ridge Station, Captain Elijah 'Eli' Henry, was an old buddy of Captain Liam Allen from the Hudson Falls Sheriff's Station. When Captain Liam Allen found out that 'Eli's' nephew, Robert Henry, had applied for the job as a sheriff's aide, Captain Allen ensured that Robert was hired and assigned to the Hudson

Falls Station. Robert remained with the Hudson Falls Sheriff's Station working dayshift until he applied for a position as a Deputy Sheriff.

Tom had applied for the Greenwood Police Department Police Cadet position and the Greenwood County Sheriff's Department Sheriff's Aide position. Being a man who liked to have all his bets covered, Tom had also seen a United States Air Force recruiter about a law enforcement job in the Air Force. Being blessed, Tom hit the jackpot and received a telephone call from each potential employer in the first week of June.

Tom selected the Greenwood County Sheriff's Department. He was hired and assigned to the Civil Bureau in the Pine Ridge Station, where he would serve civil papers until he was old enough to apply for a Deputy Sheriff position.

Jim Scott chose a different path. Jim signed up to become a United States Army Special Forces Green Beret. Once he told Robert and Tom what he had done, Jim left for Fort Bragg in North Carolina. Jim left the State of Jefferson a strong and healthy two-hundred-twenty-pound high school varsity wrestler and football player, and the next time Tom and Robert saw Jim, he was a lean one-hundred-seventy-pound ready-for-anything machine!

All Good Things Must Come to an End

About a week before Tom Stevens received information that he was hired as the new Sheriff's Aide in the Civil Bureau of the Pine Ridge Station, he made his final transport of a prisoner to the Greenwood Sheriff's Station as an Explorer Scout. He did not realize it at the time, but with that transport came the knowledge of a life lesson he would never forget, 'Humility,' and how to keep your mouth shut!

It was a beautiful Spring morning in Hudson Falls. The air was crisp, and the temperature was about sixty-five degrees with no wind. Before arriving at the sheriff's office, Tom stopped at the local donut shop and picked up a large cup of freshly made coffee. Tom finished the cup as he pulled into the station parking lot. Tom, who typically did not work dayshift, was filling in for Jim Scott, who was called in to work the campground at Lake Hudson. The day shift sergeant was 'Big Bill' Johnson, and the briefing concluded about twenty minutes prior. All the patrol deputies were now at Denny's getting breakfast.

Tom asked the sergeant if he needed anything, and 'Big Bill' replied, "Yeah, I have two to go to Greenwood for misdemeanor warrants."

Tom replied, "I'll take care of it."

Tom checked out an available black-and-white and ensured the car was clean and gassed and everything was in order for the transport. Once that was completed, Tom went into the jail, confirmed that all the booking paperwork was ready, and gathered the two prisoners' property.

The paperwork was placed on the patrol car's front seat, and the bagged property was placed on the right front floorboard of the patrol car. When Tom returned to the jail, he brought each prisoner out of the cell. He searched each prisoner for weapons or contraband. He secured each prisoner with handcuffs to the rear and applied a single-leg iron, one end attached to each prisoner for transport. The suspects were walked out of jail under the eye of 'Big Bill' and placed into the back seat of a pre-searched patrol car.

After Tom called in his transport information to dispatch along with the patrol car's mileage, he was on his way to the central county jail in

Greenwood. When Tom arrived at the Greenwood Station, he pulled into the 'Pit,' which is the location where all prisoners are loaded and unloaded from transport. Tom walked the two prisoners and their paperwork and property to the elevator inside the courthouse and jail elevator. The two suspects were delivered to the booking desk of the central county jail without incident.

After that, both prisoners were taken and placed into temporary holding cells pending additional inbound staff work by the jail deputies. Tom took the jail elevator back down to the receiving area next to the 'Pit,' where his patrol car was parked and waiting for him.

As Tom approached his patrol car, a young man standing on the other side of the 'Pit' next to the 'Identification Section' entrance called out and asked, "What are you doing?"

Tom replied, "I've just dropped off a couple of prisoners at the jail, and I'm heading back to Hudson Falls."

The young man, who seemed interested, said, "No kidding! Oh, by the way, my name is Leland."

Tom replied, "Tom Stevens."

Leland was dressed in plain clothes and seemed about the same age as Tom Stevens. He had a fantastic mustache, as Tom did, and he seemed like a new kid who was just hired and was looking for a friend at the agency.

Leland asked Tom, "What else do you do?"

Like most young men his age, Tom needed to brag about all they do, helping the deputies, writing reports, working with prisoners and evidence, and performing the duties of a reserve deputy sheriff. Leland seemed to take it all in, and since he was so receptive, Tom was encouraged to continue to share his and Jim Scott's escapades at the Hudson Falls Station. However, for some reason, the voice of God stopped him when it came to the story of backing 'Bobbie Boobs' on that felony car stop in Moonglade.

Tom told his new friend that he had to get back to Hudson Falls, and the two shook hands. Leland thanked Tom for sharing everything he and Jim Scott did at the sheriff's office in Hudson Falls.

As it turned out, Leland Parker was not a non-sworn twenty-two-year-old Sheriff's Aide. He was a thirty-five-year-old Chief Deputy of Community Relations with an excellent memory for detail.

A call was made to Captain Liam Allen. When Chief Parker spoke to Captain Allen, he shared that he, too, had teenage boys, and he knew they may not always tell the truth, especially when they had an audience hanging on every word. However, Chief Parker wanted to ensure that if any of the stories Tom shared were true, the practices would stop immediately!

By the end of the day, 'Big Bill' called Tom Stevens into his office at approximately 5:30 P.M. and asked him if he had met anyone new when he was in Greenwood.

Tom had to think for a moment when the sergeant asked, "At the jail?"

Tom replied, "Yes, sir. A new kid named Leland."

That is when the life lesson came about. When 'Big Bill' told Tom that Chief Leland Parker was not impressed with his comments, Tom learned that you should always be careful what you say to people you don't know. Not everything is as it appears. Most importantly, be humble.

We are not to be arrogant or prideful. You are not the only one that makes the world, or the Greenwood County Sheriff's Department, tick!

After Tom and Jim left the Hudson Falls Sheriff's Station, it would be five to seven years until the Explorer program was expanded to the Hudson Falls Station. No others since Tom and Jim have done what those two did as Explorers.

Never Disgrace the Uniform

Tom Stevens and Robert Henry started looking to apply for a sworn law enforcement job in Jefferson in the summer of 1977. They found that the Jefferson Highway Patrol only accepted applications from white males every two years. Affirmative Action has similarly affected the Santiago Springs Police Department and the Lakeland County Sheriff's Department.

Tom and Robert applied to the Greenwood County Sheriff's Department for two reasons, GSD was their hometown agency. Unlike many other large agencies, GSD was taking applications every three months. As Tom and Robert arrived at the testing location, they realized it was a large auditorium with hundreds of people scheduled to take the written examination. Tom later found out that three thousand people were expected to take the exam over the next five days at two locations in the county.

During the next twelve months, several additional tests, from physical strength and ability to background, were administered to the potential candidates. As a result, sixty-five candidates were selected for the Southern Jefferson Basic Peace Officer Course. Furthermore, this three-month academy would be held at the Greenwood County Sheriff's Academy located off Hot Springs Road in Greenwood.

The academy was a live-in facility. Accordingly, if you were a GSD deputy, there was no exception. The sheriff's office provided tactical staff for one academic session, and the Greenwood Police Department provided the tactical team for the next academic session. In the 47th Basic Class, Tom's class drew the Greenwood Police Department for their tactical staff.

Greenwood City College administered the curriculum for the sheriff's academy, and the college had office staff assigned to the academy full-time. Additionally, the grounds were considered a jail facility staffed with correctional officers who supervised inmates called 'trustees.' These 'trustees' lived in quarters opposite the compound where the students were housed.

Trustees cooked the food for inmates and staff at the academy and served as the groundskeepers. Moreover, the sheriff designated the academy as a resident deputy post. Two apartments were kept on the grounds for deputies who were in the process of divorce and needed an economical place to live and eat. The cost was one dollar a day, and if you lived in the apartment, you also served as facility security to back the correctional officers when inmates started to act up. Problems with inmates rarely happened because this was such a sought-after job for an inmate.

The biggest crime this crew committed in recent times was the creation of a still in the riverbed behind the inmate barracks. The 'hooch' they made was created with the left-over fruit served to the recruit deputies for breakfast each morning. All the trustees at the academy were charged and placed back into the general population in county jail. At the same time, a completely new trustee staff was on the scene within two days.

The 47th Basic Academy started with sixty-five students, and after three hard and long months, they graduated twenty-seven deputies and police officers.

At the academy graduation, Sheriff Sam Baldwin delivered the commencement ceremony speech. "I don't care how long you work for me, an entire career, ten years, ten days, or ten minutes; I just require you to do the best you can and never disgrace yourself or the uniform!"

Ten minutes after the graduation ceremony, the 47th Basic Class President submitted his resignation from the Greenwood County Sheriff's Department. The next day, he walked across the street and went to work for the Greenwood Police Department. The Vice President of the class would later become a Chief Deputy with GSD under another Sheriff.

Tom Stevens always wondered if the sheriff was only doing damage control in his speech or if it was just a coincidence. Either way, Tom Stevens and Robert Henry never felt prouder in their life! They were both Greenwood County Deputy Sheriffs.

The Sicilian

Robert Henry was assigned to the Hudson Fall Sheriff's Office on dayshift. It was obvious that he was Captain Liam Allen's boy. Robert Henry would be a 'made man,' and Joe Toarmina wanted no part in it. Let's only say Joe and the Captain did not see eye to eye on most things, and Joe did not want any part of this new kid. Joe had spoken to his wife, and she agreed it was time for a change, so Joe put in for an opening on Sergeant Jack Hall's evening shift.

Tom Stevens was assigned to the Hudson Falls Station, and his first Field Training Officer was Joe 'The Sicilian' Toarmina. Tom first met Joe when he was an explorer, but Joe worked the dayshift, and Tom was rarely around the sheriff's office on the dayshift. Joe remembered Tom, congratulated him on becoming a deputy, and welcomed him back to the Hudson Falls Station.

Joe was born in the Parkside Projects on Detroit's east side, where he spent his early childhood. Raised with the toughness and dedication of 'Rosie the Riveter,' he and his brother learned concrete ideas and standards from their mother, a factory worker's daughter, without a man's assistance or interference.

After the briefing, Sergeant Hall told Deputy Stevens, "Toarmina is always tasked as the first FTO for new deputies assigned to this station. He is very experienced, and you can learn a lot from him."

The sergeant continued, "Keep your mouth shut and act like a sponge to absorb everything you can from him."

As most new deputies do, Stevens asked around the station about 'The Sicilian' to find out as much as possible about his first FTO and what he was getting into.

Stevens established that Joe Toarmina joined the Marine Corps fresh out of high school in Detroit in 1958. This was considered the old corps, of which Joe was very proud. After basic training in San Diego, Joe was stationed at Camp Pendleton in San Diego County, California. Joe would also complete additional training at the Marine Corps Air Ground Combat Center known as Twentynine Palms in San Bernardino County,

California. During this time, Joe became very familiar with the area now known as the State of Jefferson, particularly Greenwood County.

Additionally, Stevens found that as a teenager, 'The Sicilian' spent his winters growing up in the hood of Dresden, Michigan, and his summers working on his grandparents' tobacco farm in Williamsburg, Kentucky.

As a result, 'The Sicilian' received experience and real-world training from these diverse living conditions. To be sure, when he left the Marine Corps in 1962, Joe returned to Dresden, where he went to work as a milk delivery man for a local dairy in downtown Dresden. Dresden is located approximately twenty-five miles southwest of Detroit and was founded by German immigrants. Dresden means 'People from the Forest by the River.'

Long before Joe's return, Dresden had experienced institutional racism and entrenched segregation. This formula continued with a mass exodus of whites to the whiter suburbs and the auto industry's deindustrialization, shutting down operations in Detroit and the surrounding areas[3]. In addition, there were no chain grocery stores or restaurants in Dresden during this era due to the very high crime rate. Joe worked as a milkman in downtown Dresden for five years and was only robbed once.

On Tuesday, July 25, 1967, at around 2:30 a.m., the Vice Squad of the Dresden Police Department raided the very popular and heavily attended 'Blind Pig' called the 'Burning Embers' at the intersection of 4th Street and Duncan Avenue in Dresden. At this time, the Dresden Police Department mainly consisted of white police officers known for enforcing the law with a heavy hand. Accordingly, several people were arrested at this after-hours joint, and as the last prisoner transport van left, a shot was fired through the rear window of an unoccupied patrol car still parked at the scene. This single act ignited the large crowds into committing mass vandalism, commercial and residential burglaries, and arson.

At the end of five days, Dresden would never be the same. The area had experienced the most extensive civil disturbance the city had ever seen. The riots took twenty-three lives, injured dozens of people, and resulted in five hundred fires in addition to one thousand arrests.

---

[3] https://detroithistorical.org/learn/encyclopedia-of-detroit/uprising-1967

By Friday, July 28, 1967, many of the 'mom-and-pop' stores that had not been burnt to the ground started calling many vendors begging for their products to be delivered. Under the threat of random sniper fire over the past couple of days, Joe Toarmina was the only driver representing numerous businesses and vendors willing to go into the affected area to deliver fresh dairy products to the citizens in need. The delivery was done under the escort of two trucks of troops from the National Guard.

After the Dresden Riots of 1967, Joe moved his family to Greenwood County, Jefferson, and purchased his wife, Susie's dream house in Hudson Falls. Joe and Susie Toarmina had been married for sixteen (16) years. Susie teaches a class on successful police marriages at the sheriff's academy.

Sometimes It's Good to Be a Cop

After both deputies checked out and inspected their assigned black-and-white patrol unit, Joe told Tom, "Put us in service, kid!"

Greenwood County Sheriff's Department changed radio designators during the past two years.

Tom grabbed the Motorola microphone with his left hand and, for the first time, proclaimed, "Hudson Falls, 3 David 30, Toarmina/Stevens 10-8 in unit 76-043."

The dispatcher at the Hudson Falls Station, Stella 'Green Springs' Bartley, quickly replied, "3 David 30 10-8 at 16:15 hours."

As 3 David 30 started to head west toward their assigned zone, Joe started with some basic concepts.

First, he told all his trainees, "This is the biggest zone in the station. It is just under three hundred and fifty square miles. When you call for a backup in Zone 30, it can take up to thirty minutes to arrive even when they come to you; Code Three!"

Joe continued, "More experienced deputies work this zone because you need to know how to talk to people. Once you have been a cop for a while, you know how to talk, rather than fight, your way out of situations!"

Tom asked about some of the problem areas in the zone and the types of people who lived there.

Joe continued, "Your professional reputation is everything in this job! Without a good reputation, you have nothing."

Tom shared some similar points with Joe he had been taught in the academy.

Joe added, "I have talked with many 'coppers,' and most told me they got into this business to help people. They wanted to represent good over evil!"

Tom chimed in, "That sounds like me. That's why I got into this business!"

Joe said, "Don't ever be a lazy cop! Don't kiss calls off! Instead, do the best job you can for the citizens we serve. They deserve it. After all, they call us for help and are our customers. You will succeed in this career if you play by these simple rules!"

Stella 'Green Springs' came across the radio "3 David 30 clear to copy a Verbal Disturbance -Boyfriend vs. Girlfriend."

Tom replied, "3 David 30, go ahead."

"3 David 30 respond to the 26400 block of Soapstone Ave near the Maze Stone Village reference a Disturbance Boyfriend vs. Girlfriend. Suspect Bill Moreno reportedly destroyed all the property within the house. Contact Ashley Bartlett. The complainant will take you to the location."

"3 David 30 en route."

Joe told Tom that this was going to be his first call. "Keep your head and pay attention to both parties. Consider all possibilities." Joe told Tom, "I have a history with Moreno."

Bill Moreno was a used car dealer transplant from Santiago Springs. He was forty-two years of age and looked like a cross between Gene Simmons and Mac Davis. He always wore a gold necklace and a large gold medallion around his neck that had great sentimental value. It probably was the only thing that did have sentimental value in his life. Moreno portrayed himself as a self-made man from the mob. Still, he was extremely gun shy of a particular deputy from Dresden with the last name of Toarmina, who went by the nickname 'The Sicilian.' Joe had investigated several complaints at Moreno's car dealerships, which resulted in several civil allegations filed with consumer affairs. In addition, Moreno had a minor criminal history back east.

Tom contacted the complainant, Ashley Bartlett. Upon their arrival at the scene, they encountered a twenty-three-year-old beach bunny who looked like a swimsuit model. She was driving a new yellow Chevrolet Corvette that Moreno had just purchased. She told Deputy Stevens that she and Moreno lived together in this rented mansion and had been arguing all day about his indiscretions. Suddenly, as a result, he finally blew up and started breaking everything inside the house. Moreno was con wise and understood Jefferson's domestic violence laws. Therefore, he never laid a hand on Ashley. Moreno only destroyed the property in this mansion. His name was the only one on the lease. In the meantime, Ashley could provide no documentation or dominion that she lived at this location.

When Deputy Toarmina and Deputy Stevens contacted Bill Moreno, he was cooking his breakfast at the stove in the kitchen. Ashley was correct; Moreno had effectively destroyed everything in the mansion, except for the pan he used to cook his eggs and one small plate he placed the eggs on.

Moreno said, "Good evening, Deputy Toarmina. I see you have a new partner!"

Joe replied, "What have you been up to, Moreno?"

Moreno said, "Nothing more than cooking a little dinner."

Deputy Stevens asked, "What happened here?" as he pointed around the house.

"Oh, nothing; now and then, I get tired of my décor and require a remodel."

"After all, there is nothing illegal about destroying your own property, is there, Deputy Stevens?" said Moreno after reading his nametag.

Bill Moreno was quite smug and sure of himself. However, after Tom and 'The Sicilian' explained their limitations to Ashley and what they could and could not do for her, she decided to take the deputies' advice and return to her family in Del Monico.

The deputies stayed on the scene for several minutes, chatting with the all-knowing Moreno giving Ashley plenty of time to head back to her family home.

It was well worth the look on Bill Moreno's face when 'The Sicilian' waved and said, "Good luck with Ashley!"

Just then, Moreno realized that Ashly had just left in a $32,000.00 sports car he had recently purchased for her!

In the movie, *Only the Lonely*, John Candy once said: "Sometimes it's good to be a cop!"

How true. How true!

'Flatulent Fisher'

Deputy Tom Stevens continued his training program with the Greenwood County Sheriff's Department at the Hudson Falls Station. He had been scheduled to ride with Roberta 'Bobbie Boobs' Lee, but she transferred to the day shift to be with her new love interest, William 'Big Bill' Johnson, the dayshift sergeant. Roberta thought no one knew about her affair with 'Big Bill,' especially Mary, Johnson's wife. Mary was known by most 'coppers' in the valley as the woman who worked midnights at the local Denney's and the one who pulled a butcher knife on the good sergeant after he unknowingly called out the name of one of his girlfriends in his sleep.

As she was chasing him around the living room, she claimed she would 'cut off his balls and send them to Captain Liam Allen of the Hudson Falls Station so he could keep an eye on them since 'Big Bill' couldn't keep them in his pants. After this incident, Sergeant Johnson started calling his girlfriends by male nicknames. He called Roberta 'Sam.'

After the evening shift briefing, Sergeant Hall introduced Tom to his new training officer Deputy Tucker Fisher. Fisher transferred to Greenwood County Sheriff's Department from the Hudson Falls Police Department, where he had been a reserve police officer for the past nine years. Tucker's regular job was investment banking, but the cop bug bit him early!

Tom remembered seeing Tucker working around town with Hudson Falls P.D. and how professional he always looked and acted. That is to say, Hudson Falls Police Department still required officers to wear dress hats when out of the car. Moreover, Tom remembered seeing Tucker wearing an 'Eisenhower' dress jacket with the dark blue uniform directing traffic downtown during one of the parades.

Once hired, Tom learned that the Greenwood County Sheriff's Department issued .38 caliber round nose (38 Special) ammo to all new deputies. In addition, if you were assigned to the jail, you were given a four-inch Colt 'Police Positive' like the one used in the opening of the *Superman* television series.

If you worked patrol, you were assigned a four-inch Smith & Wesson Model 10. In addition, you were also issued a twelve-round ammo dump pouch. Many deputies purchased speed stripes for their pouches, and some still used the 12-round loop leather slide ammo holder, which showed the exposed rounds on their gun belts. Finally, a standard breakfront holster was issued for both weapons.

Deputy Tucker Fisher carried a six-inch Colt Python in a Bianchi 'Judge' breakfront holster. Most deputies could not afford the combination of this gun and holster around this time on deputy sheriff pay.

Tucker also had a state-of-the-art new law enforcement tool called speed loaders on his Sam Browne belt. His ammo pouch held three-speed loaders. Interestingly, John Bianchi was a reserve deputy sheriff when he started making holsters in his garage before creating the Bianchi Leather empire.

Tucker, a firearm instructor, also carried a five-round, 12-gauge, military green canvas ammo pouch attached to his shotgun each shift. In addition, two boxes of rifled shotgun slugs were always kept in his briefcase. Tucker Fisher, who was too new to the squad to establish a nickname, was always ready for war!

Deputy Tom Stevens called him 'Too Cool' Tucker!

Cops are very competitive by nature. They compete for the most arrests, the most citations, the most calls for service, etc. The latest competition among Sergeant Hall's squad was who could produce the loudest, most obnoxious, and longest-lasting fart over the public address system of their patrol car in front of the most witnesses. Of course, the respective player would get additional points if the witnesses were visibly appalled by such actions.

The preparation for this competition began each day in the station's parking lot. After the daily tradition of 'testing,' your siren to a predetermined composition suggestive of a song, various degrees of flatulence could be heard throughout the neighborhood. Unfortunately, the surrounding neighbors complained about the oratory, and Sergeant Hall had to tell everyone to 'knock it off.'

The competition continued for several weeks, and the final two contenders were 'Thumper' Robinson and Tucker 'Too Cool' Fisher.

In the meantime, there had been farting into the patrol car's public address system in neighborhoods, parking lots, sporting events, shopping centers, and even when backing other agencies on calls. But unfortunately, none of these meager attempts would compare to the winning entry.

After briefing and a quick unit check, Tucker told Tom, "Put us 10-8."

Tom picked up the mic and said, "Hudson Falls 3 David 10, Fisher/ Stevens 10-8 in unit 75-127."

Dispatch replied, "3 David 10, 10-8."

As Tucker drove out to Zone 10, he asked Tom, "Did you notice that 'Thumper' wasn't at the briefing this afternoon?"

Tom replied, "Yeah, he took the day off to see that new Sylvester Stallone movie, *Rocky*."

Tucker said, "Exactly, he is taking his wife downtown to see it. So, he will witness firsthand who is the king of farts on this squad!"

Tucker then pulled into the parking lot of the 7-Eleven store in the 100 block of South Basswood Street and tossed Tom the keys saying, "You drive. I'm going to fill up on soda and beer nuts (additional ammo), waiting for my moment."

The movie started at 1810 hours. It was now 1745 hours. Hudson Falls only had a single-screen walk-in theater downtown, and people were beginning to line up around the building east on California Blvd and then north on Cedar Street. There were approximately two hundred people in line, and Terry believed that the buildings downtown would create the perfect echo chamber for the percussions of his classical and timeless fart. Tucker realized that he had always conducted his flatulence while in the driver's seat, so he told Tom to pull over and let him drive. Tom complied.

Tucker had preset the volume control on the public address system to full. As 3 David 10 was slowly driving in the number one eastbound lane of California Blvd, Terry yelled out, "There he is!! There is Thumper and his wife!" The patrol car proceeded slowly, and as it passed Hawthorn Street, Terry reached over and grabbed the public address microphone, raised his right buttock above the seat, shoved the microphone under his ass, tightened his sphincter to the best of his ability, and then suddenly as 3 David 10 passed the Hudson Falls Theater, Tucker let it go with all his might!! Unfortunately, the taco and cheese enchilada combo plate with an extra taco he had for lunch at La Pinata restaurant in El Camino and the Big Gulp soda and beer nuts had not had time to solidify at the expected and standard level.

People around the theater looked up and thought they had heard a wet thud rather than a good old-fashioned fart. When 'Thumper' looked up and saw the fleeing patrol car, he realized that Tucker 'Too Cool' Fisher had shit himself! 'Thumper' Robinson, knowing what had happened, burst out laughing uncontrollably, which had a similar effect on people around him.

More importantly, Tucker Fisher realized what had just happened! He yelled, "I just shit myself!"

Tom, who now was beginning to smell Tucker's efforts, confirmed, "No Shit!"

"Sadly, plenty of shit!" Tucker then activated the yellow 'excuse me' light on the unit's overhead lights and sped away towards his home in East Hudson Falls.

As the two deputies continued eastbound on California Blvd to the Evergreen area, the scent became too intense!

Feverishly trying to roll down the passenger window, Tom declared, "You need to see a doctor!!"

Greenwood Sheriff Department uniform pants are made of high-quality wool, which helped secure the material inside the pant and seat area. Regrettably, for Tucker, this fortification also redirected the liquid and solid material up his back and around his sides which was now starting to leak out onto his bullet-resistant vest and Sam Brown duty (not doody) belt.

The 1975 Plymouth Satellite they were driving had black vinyl seat covers which came as part of the state bid process. The county realized after this purchase that perhaps this was not the best choice of material. To illustrate, stark reality appeared after sending these patrol cars out to the field and realizing that temperatures in these cars with this black vinyl interior routinely reached 130 degrees Fahrenheit.

'Low bid wins' are not always the best way to purchase equipment. However, the county ordered rugged plastic seat cushions installed in all patrol cars to correct that problem. These seat cushions were navy blue. Way to go, 'County Fleet.'

Tucker's soupy mess was starting to spill out onto the plastic seat cushion and eventually onto and between the black vinyl seat covers of the patrol car. Now, this is not, nor will it be, the last time someone has shit in a patrol car; however, deputy sheriffs are generally not the ones doing the shitting!

As Tucker came sliding into the driveway of his residence, Tom went on air and said, "Hudson Falls 3 David 10, Unit Service at the Fisher residence."

Dispatch replied, "3 David 10, 10-4."

As Tucker exited the car, you could see the liquid and partially solid fecal matter draining out under the cuff of his uniform pants. Tucker Fisher got cleaned up and showered, being scolded by his wife inside the house. Luna Fisher was a manager at the Hudson Falls Department of Motor Vehicles Office.

She and Tucker had been married for twelve years. Specifically, she told Tucker that he was the one that was going to take this mess to their local cleaners as the wool uniform pants had to be dry cleaned.

Tucker also cleaned up the patrol car by himself and, later that evening, conceited the 'Farting King' competition to 'Thumper' as the winner.

Tom told Tucker about Sheriff Baldwin's speech at his graduation ceremony when he said, "Never disgrace yourself or the uniform." Tom added maybe the sheriff should have added: "or soil your uniform."

Tucker laughed out loud and told Tom, "You know, kid. You are going to do just fine here!"

In the blink of one brown eye, Tucker went from 'Too Cool Tucker' to his new nickname, 'Flatulent Fisher.'

"Shoot Back!"

3 David 20 had been assigned to a possible fight at the Adahy Indian Reservation with a man down at the baseball diamond near the center of the reservation. Sheriff's units had been sniped at many times on the reservation without anyone ever being hurt. This evening, the responding deputy, Jacob 'Heifer-hauler' Murphy, would receive clear, concise communication with confirmation! (The Four 'C's'.)

At approximately 1843 hours, 3 David 20 reported he was 10-97 (arriving on the scene). Moments later, every law enforcement officer in central Greenwood County on the channel stopped what they were doing and listened as they thought they heard a twelve-year-old little girl scream, "THEY ARE SHOOTING AT ME!!!, THEY ARE SHOOTING AT ME!!!, THEY ARE SHOOTING AT ME!!!"

Radio traffic stopped for a moment or two when suddenly the voice of GOD came over the radio and said, "SHOOT BACK!!!" It was later determined that the voice of GOD was Sergeant Jack Hall!

Jacob had tried to unsuccessfully dig in the sand to hide under the driver's side door of the patrol car. All available Hudson Falls units responded to the reservation, and when they arrived, they found Jacob sitting against the left rear wheel of his unit. He was unhurt but visibly shaken. No rounds struck the patrol car, but several ricochet marks were found in the dirt near where the unit was parked.

Unfortunately for the agency and the deputy, those rounds hit their emotional mark. Within weeks, Deputy Jacob Murphy left the Greenwood County Sheriff's Department and became a Missionary in South America.

Queen One

Vernon Duane Powers came to Hudson Falls in 1969 as the new Chief of Police. Known as 'Duke,' no one ever called him 'V.D,' and if you did, you only did it once. He came from the City of Costa Mesa, where he retired as a Homicide Captain. He was one of the original eight officers the City of Costa Mesa hired when their new police department was created in 1954. He was old school, and he brought a sense of professionalism the City of Hudson Falls Police Department had never known. Hudson Falls P.D. would quickly learn the error of their ways!

Chief Powers stood six foot two inches tall and weighed three hundred fifty pounds. He always wore an Eisenhower jacket with six gold embroidered stars above the stripe on the left sleeve. He also wore a round LAPD-style hat with scrambled eggs on the front when in dress uniform. He looked a lot like the bus driver from the television show *The Honeymooners*, Ralph Kramden, but no one had the backbone to tell him that. He was bald with no other facial hair and reminded most people of an English Bulldog. Yet, during his tenure with Hudson Falls P.D., he created one of the county's most professional and well-respected police departments.

The Greenwood County Sheriff's Department being the primary law enforcement agency in the county, created record-keeping processes and radio designators for each agency in the county. For example, Kitchen Creek Sheriff would use A-Alpha, Duncan Sheriff would use B-Boy, Pine Ridge Sheriff would use C-Charles, Hudson Falls Sheriff would use D-David, etc. These designators would be used as the first digit in report case numbers and radio transmissions so that anyone could immediately know where the report or unit came from. Subsequently, if you heard "3 David 10" on the radio, you would know it was an evening shift patrol unit from Hudson Falls Sheriff working in Zone Ten.

The City of Hudson Falls Police Department was issued the designator Q-Queen. It was unknown how the assignment was made. Still, once Chief Powers told his colleagues at the sheriff's office how unacceptable this was and where he kept 'his goat,' Hudson Falls P.D. would be forever known as the 'Queens of V.D.' at least when the agency administrators got together.

Deputy Tom Stevens made $345.90 every two weeks as a Greenwood County Deputy Sheriff. There was no possibility for overtime or extra duty shifts. However, a friend of Tom had recently lateraled over to the Hudson Falls Police Department from a small mountain agency. With a bit of overtime, Tom's friend brought home a recent check for $625.00. Hudson Falls Police had five pay ranges, and if you were a lateral, they would bring you on at step three. That meant that you could be a topped-out-in-pay policeman in two years. So, as many young deputies in Jefferson did, Tom applied to the smaller Hudson Falls Police Department.

Tom was notified by Chief Powers' executive assistant that the Chief wanted to meet with him at 7:00 p.m. at the chief's residence. This meeting would be the Chief's Interview portion of the hiring process. The assistant gave Tom the chief's home address and told him to dress appropriately for the evening. Tom was very nervous and did not know what to expect. First, he thought, would there be other chiefs at this meeting? Would he be offered dinner? Would this be a cocktail party to see how much he drank in a social environment? Should he take a date? Tom then contemplated what he should wear. Should he wear a suit, a dinner jacket, or a traditional tuxedo?

Tom decided to wear a traditional suit that he had purchased for the meeting. He arrived at the chief's house at 6:45 p.m. He slowly walked to the front door and heard the national news on the television. Tom then rang the doorbell. Chief Powers answered the door within fifteen seconds and called, "Stevens, I presume?" The chief wore a multi-colored horizontal striped bathrobe with brown fuzzy house slippers. He had a massive slice of pizza in his right hand, which he folded over as they do in New York City, and he was still chewing his last bite as he greeted the deputy.

Tom replied, "Yes, sir."

"Come on in. Are you hungry?" The chief then gestured toward two large pizza boxes sitting on the breakfast counter in his kitchen.

Tom said, "No, sir, I'm good!" Atop one of the pizza boxes was a brand-new Hudson Falls Policeman Badge with the number 637 on the bottom.

Chief Powers then asked Tom, "When can you start?"

Tom replied, "Well, sir, I would have to give the sheriff's office a two-week notice."

Powers said, "Fuck the sheriff. I need you now!!"

Amy, the chief's wife, was in the living room just off the kitchen. She was a very slight lady, maybe five foot tall and ninety-five pounds. She told her husband, "Now, Vernon, let that boy give his department proper notice. You know you would require the same!" Powers said, "OK, dear."

Powers then asked Tom, "When can you start?"

Tom told Chief Powers that he could start on Sunday, April 15.

Both men shook hands, and Chief Powers welcomed Tom Stevens to the Hudson Falls Police Department.

Before leaving, Chief Powers shared some law enforcement philosophies with his new policeman. Tom later shared with his family that the chief told him he would only hire married men over twenty-five if he had his choice. But unfortunately, Tom was neither married nor twenty-five. He also told Tom not to even think about living with a woman he was not married to because he would be fired. Finally, he concluded with the comment that as long as he was Chief of Police, a woman would never be in the department as a law enforcement officer!

Deputy Sheriff Tom Stevens resigned from the Greenwood County Sheriff's Office, and after giving two weeks' notice, he went to work for the Hudson Falls Police Department.

Pacific Northwest
Savings and Loan Robbery

It was a mild May afternoon this fourth Friday of the month as Officer Tom Stevens drove into the parking lot of the Hudson Falls Police Department. Rupert Holmes's *Pina Colada* song had just finished playing as Tom turned off the radio on his black 1978 Pontiac Trans Am. Tom liked working the evening shift and always came to work about a half-hour early so that he could take his time dressing out in the department's new locker room.

The Hudson Falls Police Employees Association purchased full-size lockers for the officers, and the department provided the space for them and a weight room. In addition, the Association bought and owned the lockers so those police administrators could not arbitrarily open and inspect them without permission or a search warrant.

Tom stood in front of the full-length wall mirror and ensured his gig line was straight. Accordingly, he then left the locker room and went into the briefing room, Tom was the only one there, and he saw the door to the agency Emergency Operations Center (E.O.C.) was open. Heavy radio traffic was coming from one of the consoles. Sitting at one of the consoles was Sergeant Blake Lampley, the department training officer who filled in as a part-time emergency manager.

Sergeant Lampley asked Tom, "Did you hear what they are working in Greenwood?"

"No, sir, I just got here," Tom replied.

"There was an armed robbery at the Greenwood Branch of Pacific Northwest Savings and Loan." Sergeant Lampley explained, "Take over with three to five suspects. Deputies were fired upon when they arrived, several were shot, and the suspects fled![4]"

Sergeant Lampley continued, "Several units are pursuing in Northwestern Greenwood County, and an 11-99 (Officer Down) has been called at

---

[4] https://www.youtube.com/watch?v=OQXXcFmMVNE
Norco Bank Robbery Documentary Part 1 of 3

the bank." Knowing that Tom came from the sheriff's office, Lampley asked, "Do you know where it is located?"

Tom replied, "I sure do," not wanting to appear stupid to Sergeant Lampley.

Sergeant Lampley said, "Check out a unit and head to Greenwood. Keep your unit radio on the sheriff's Greenwood frequency and your handheld on Hudson Falls Police primary."

Tom went to the Logistics Room and checked out his patrol car (unit 118), Remington 870 Wing-master shotgun with four rounds of .00 Buck, Motorola handheld radio, and Sirchie fingerprint kit.

Unit 118 was a Black-and-white 1977 Dodge Monaco with a brand-new blue and red lightbar parked on the west ramp of the station. Hudson Falls P.D. had a contract with two local car washes in town so officers could wash their cars as needed instead of sheriff's deputies waiting for trustees from the Duncan Road Camp to be delivered to the Hudson Falls Station to clean their vehicles.

Officer Stevens inspected the recently washed patrol car and ensured he had extra shotgun ammo, both .00 Buck and rifled slugs. He came up on the radio, "Hudson Falls, 3 Queen 90 Stevens 10-8 to Greenwood unit 118."

Dispatch replied, "3 Queen 90, 10-8."

Stevens drove northbound on Enterprise Street towards the Las Ramblas Expressway en route to the City of Greenwood. Considering the delay, he responded Code 2 with the yellow flashing excuse me light activated in the rear of the patrol car's lightbar."

As a result of the shooting in the City of Greenwood, all other Greenwood County Sheriff's Stations sent their available units to the city to assist. Thus, all other Greenwood County Sheriff Stations were operating at minimum staffing.

As 3 Queen 90 traveled on the Las Ramblas Expressway towards Greenwood, Tom heard the Hudson Falls Sheriff Dispatcher say, "3 David 30 clear to copy a disturbance verbal pending physical?" Deputy Joe Toarmina responded, "3 David 30, go ahead."

"3 David 30 respond to the Brush Popper Inn reference a verbal disturbance pending physical between three patrons." "3 David 30, the primary suspect is an Indian male 5-10 300 black hair in a ponytail and brown eyes. The suspect is wearing a navy-blue tee shirt and blue jeans and sitting at the end of the bar."

Deputy Toarmina replied, "3 David 30 en route from Grove."

As Tom Stevens was approaching Interstate 997 on the Las Ramblas Expressway, units at the Pacific Northwest Savings and Loan in Greenwood broadcast that no additional units were needed at the bank and effectively canceled the 11-99 (Officer needs help: Mayday).

Greenwood Sheriff's Units were still pursuing the suspects on the ground and were last headed toward Lassen County.

Officer Stevens notified Hudson Falls Police Dispatch that the 11-99 was canceled in Greenwood, and he was now going to assist 3 David 30 with a disturbance pending physical at the Brush Popper Inn in Riverbank on his way back to the city. Riverbank is a small farming and ranching community in unincorporated Greenwood County southwest of Hudson Falls.

The Brush Popper Inn is a country-western bar located in the heart of the community with its dirt parking lot and wood boardwalks. Café doors meet the customers as they enter the fifty-year-old business. Once inside, there is a vast carved mahogany back bar with stained glass and a larger-than-life color portrait of John Wayne as Marshal Rooster Cogburn behind the bar with two Winchester rifles secured on each side of the portrait.

As Deputy Joe Toarmina arrived on the scene and entered the bar, Merle Haggard sang from the jukebox inside. Joe thought how appropriate *The fighting side of me!* was to inspire all these patriotic folks into a frenzy in anticipation of Friday night at the fights.

Joe contacted the bartender and asked her, "What's the problem, Betty?"

Betty said, "The guy at the end of the bar has gotten more and more argumentative with my regular customers, and I just want him out."

Deputy Toarmina saw the suspect immediately and could tell he was unsteady on his feet. He looked like a regular he knew from the Adahy

Bar on Main Street in El Camino named Tommy Mojado. Joe wondered how he ended up out at the Brush Popper Inn.

"What's up, Tommy…. they say you are causing trouble here!"

"Fuck you, Toarmina, leave me the fuck alone!"

Joe had tried to talk to the drunk Indian when Tom Stevens arrived on the scene and entered the bar. Joe finally told Tommy that he was going to jail if he did not "get up and leave immediately!"

Joe added, "By the count of three! One two three!'

'The Sicilian,' who was five foot eight and one hundred sixty-five pounds, jumped on Tommy's back and declared, " You are under arrest!"

The drunk three-hundred-pound Indian danced the deputy around the barroom floor.

The crowd realized that the main event had just started, and they were going to get their money's worth. Tommy Mojado did not know that this bar was in 'The Sicilian's' beat, and everybody loved Joe 'The Sicilian'! Tom Stevens, who was five ten and two hundred thirty pounds, had already started towards the two contenders.

Joe, still on Mojado's back attempting to choke him out, called out to Tom, "Are you going to help?"

Tom replied, "Oh, I reckon!" and he smiled a toothy grin.

At this point, Tom came running full speed at the two men and tackled them both, and all three of them came crashing out the swinging doors of the bar onto the wooded boardwalk and eventually came to rest after a short bit of exercise in the dirt parking lot of the bar. As this was happening, the customers were yelling, "Kick his ass, Joe!"

Tommy Mojado was taken into custody without further incident, and no one got hurt. Tom asked Joe if he was going to charge Tommy with battery on a peace officer, and Joe said, "He can sleep it off at the Hudson Falls Station."

Tom told Joe to call him when he heard more about the robbery and shootout in Greenwood. Joe said to him that he would call him later.

As Joe cleared the scene, he was cheered on by the crowd from within the bar. Tom cleared the scene and returned to the city. He thought what a great cop Joe Toarmina was.

At 2330 hours, Tom was parking his patrol car on the west ramp of the Hudson Falls Police Station. He got the last spot as two other officers were in the jail, and the sergeant took up the remaining site. The end of the watch was at midnight, and Tom would take this time to finish up his reports from this evening and call Joe to find out the details of Greenwood.

Joe was turning his paperwork in to Sergeant Hall when Tom made the call.

Joe said, "Here is what we know so far. Five suspects conducted a takeover and armed robbery at the Greenwood branch of the Pacific Northwest Savings and Loan at Alder Street and Beech Road. Do you know Brody De Franco?"

Tom replied, "I have heard of him."

Joe continued, "He was the initial deputy. He was on the scene right when the call came out, and the deputy started taking fire! Four suspects with assault rifles exited the savings and loan and unloaded on the deputy! He was able to return fire, but he was hit. As other units arrived on the scene, they, too, started taking rounds. After a brief gun battle, the suspects exited their getaway vehicle, carjacked another vehicle, and drove northbound on Alder Street with an armful of weapons and ammo."

Tom asked, "Why did they leave their original getaway vehicle?"

Joe said, "Apparently, during the shootout, the driver was struck by a round in the back of the head. Unfortunately for him, the vehicle operator is now deceased due to his head injury.[5]"

Tom interrupted, "Sweet!"

Joe continued, "As the suspects fled from the bank, numerous patrol units from various agencies began to pursue, and a rolling gun battle

---

[5] https://www.youtube.com/watch?v=cdbdfAc2E2g
Norco Bank Robbery Documentary Part 2 of 3

all over Northwestern Greenwood County ensued. Most of it was in the area of Greenwood, but eventually, the suspects headed toward Lassen County. The suspects stopped in an area known as Bonanza Creek near the national forest. The pursuit went for thirty-five miles.

"The suspects were followed by ground units from Lassen County Sheriff's Department. Leading the pursuit was Deputy Drake Anderson from Greenwood Sheriff. The suspects stopped and set up an ambush for the approaching deputy. Lassen County tried to warn Anderson, but our radios were not compatible. The bastards killed Anderson on the spot! They fled into the forest."

Tom asked, "What is happening now?"

Joe explained, "Lassen County has set up a perimeter in the area. Lakeland County Sheriff is sending a hundred-man Special Enforcement Team to assist. Due to nighttime arrival, they will continue the pursuit at daybreak."

Tom said, "I was listening to most radio traffic, and my question is, who was in charge? Who was running this thing?"

Joe agreed, "These shitbags handed us our asses!"

Tom added, "Supervision, equipment, communication, management, and control all sucked! So far, we have one suspect dead, one Greenwood County Deputy Sheriff dead, five other peace officers wounded, fourteen police vehicles damaged or destroyed, and numerous civilians shot at."

Tom proclaimed, "This is unacceptable. This is 1980, for heaven's sake!! Our response to these calls needs to change, or we as a profession will lose every time." Joe agreed.

Tom concluded the conversation by thanking Joe for the update and asking himself, "Why don't we train our first-line supervisors how to supervise these events properly and how to take command?"

At around 11:00 am on Saturday, May 24, 1980, Joe called Tom at home.

Joe said, "Hey Tom, here is the latest on Greenwood."

Tom replied, "Lay it on me."

"Lakeland County canceled the ticket of one of the four remaining shitbags. He was away from the others along the forested ridgeline and refused to follow instructions. Gee, imagine that! $20,000 was recovered in the original getaway van."

"Wow...anything else?"

Joe said, "Yeah, the other three had been shot or injured during the robbery or the chase. As a result, the suspects were arrested without incident. The bad guys were carrying an AR-15, an HK-91, and an HK-93[6]."

Tom concluded the phone call with, "Times are changing!"

---

[6] https://www.youtube.com/watch?v=HDQrvW5-Pdc
Norco Bank Robbery Documentary Part 3 of 3

Nick's Place

Nick's Place is a dinner house and cocktail lounge located west of downtown Hudson Falls across from the Greenwood County Fairgrounds. The building is a converted farmhouse from the 1920s. The interior was early American, George Washington era, with dark wood and a large mahogany back bar with brass and copper trim and antique mirrors. The bar seated fourteen, with a waitress stationed at each end of the bar. In one corner of the bar was a piano for Sunday and Monday nights and in the other corner of the bar was the bandstand and dance floor for the live band that played during the rest of the week.

Four booths and two high boy tables on the bar side separated the cocktail lounge. On the dance floor side of the cocktail lounge were four booths and eight tables, including a sizeable round conversation table which sat six next to the dance floor. Separating the dining room from the cocktail lounge was a handsome two-sided river rock fireplace with mantels on each side. The business kept the fireplace lit most of the time for the ambiance.

George Williams had recently purchased Nick's Place from a wealthy local investment group. This group had purchased the business as a fun place to hang out but soon realized, as many others had in the past and the future, that the restaurant business is hard work, and if you are not going to do the work yourself, you better have honest people run it for you. George Williams was an individual who honestly had the Midas touch. Everything he touched turned to gold.

The previous owners called the restaurant Broadrick's and, as such, ordered appropriate guest checks with the name Broadrick's and a character of said person on the back of each tab. These owners thought they would be in business for the next thirty years or had a cousin in the printing business because they ordered over 100,000 guest checks with Broadrick emblazed on the back. George being the savvy businessman he was, refused to throw away these guest checks, and subsequently, Nick's Place used Broadrick's guest checks for several years.

George Williams hired Greg and Tammy Price to manage his new restaurant. The Prices came from Milwaukee, Wisconsin. Greg was a large man, approximately six foot five and three hundred fifty pounds, with jet black hair combed straight back; He was the night manager who always wore dark slacks and a button-down white dress shirt open collar with both sleeves folded to the elbow.

Greg was usually back in the office despite his intimidating presence when things got rough. Tammy was the restaurant manager with many years of experience who ran a well-oiled machine. She was friendly and pleasant and would bend over backward for her employees. Tom Stevens met Greg Price one night in a liquor store on the east end of town. Greg loved cops, and he told Tom to come on down any time for dinner or drinks.

"Where's the fight?"

As Tom Stevens pulled into the Nicks Place parking lot, he grabbed the mic from the center console of his patrol car and said, "3 Queen 50, show me out on a Bar Check at Nicks Place." Dispatch replied, "3 Queen 50, 10-4."

As Tom entered the restaurant from the California Boulevard main entrance, he found Marcie Romano at her usual waitress station, placing an order with her favorite bartender, "Uncle Al."

Tom asked Marcie, "Where's the fight?"

She stepped back, looked around the bar area, and proclaimed, "What fight?"

Tom trying to use whatever boyish charm he had left in him, said, "There has to be more than this going on in here," to arouse admiration from the Italian beauty.

Marcie replied, "You scared me!" as she hit Tom on the upper arm.

Tom had met Marcie several weeks earlier when he took Greg up on his offer to come for a drink. Marcie was a cross between Snow White and the original Wonder Woman Lynda Carter. She was five foot seven and weighed approximately one hundred-forty pounds with curves in all the right areas. Marcie had piercing green eyes and dark curly brown hair to the middle of her back.

Tom and Marcie had been dating for several weeks by this time. She was still trying to learn the cop language that all new girlfriends or wives struggle with as they understand what their men and women are saying to each other at the beginning of the relationship. Tom was mesmerized by her! Marcie loved to hear about all the cop stories that Tom and his friends would tell, and her standard practice would be to speak to tell Tom, "OK, go ahead.........Stop! OK, just a little more.........Stop!......OK, just a little more.........Stop!" until the story was over. She could only handle a little bit at a time!

Besides all the common attributes men admire in their women, Marcie possessed skills that Tom found terrific. She was a natural interviewer.

People would tell her the darndest things. For example, a customer was at the bar sitting next to Marcie's waitress station; suddenly, she admitted to having genital warts. This admission came after Marcie only asked her how her boyfriend, whom Marcie knew, was doing. Marcie also knew all her customers by name and something about them.

Marcie could also go out on the floor, take thirty drink orders from thirty different people, and come back to her bartender, 'Uncle Al,' and call them out in the correct order. She would receive all thirty drinks back from the bartender, return to the dance floor to each customer, and give them the proper drink without writing anything down. Marcie did this all night, never working with a bank from the job. As a result of this talent, Marcie made a lot of money and paid cash for a brand-new burgundy Mercury Cougar. Eventually, Marcie became fluent in cop-ease, and she could sit through an entire story without stopping!

Officer Tom Stevens was in love!

Orange Corvette

Laurie Reynolds was the wife of a dairyman and rancher in the western portion of the Hudson Falls, El Camino Valley. Laurie and her husband had been married for seven years, and most of that time was rocky. Family members had called the cops several times to the home for verbal and physical disturbances. Laurie had threatened to leave her husband on several occasions, but they always seemed to work it out before that point. Laurie, blond-haired and blue-eyed, stood five foot three inches and weighed one hundred and one pounds. She was a pure country girl who resembled Barbara Mandrel and wore a pair of jeans very nicely. Laurie drove a brand-new orange Corvette that she liked to park on the sidewalk near the front entrance to Nick's Place. Laurie's orange Corvette and parking habits would eventually lead to her downfall.

One Saturday evening, at about 9:30 P.M., Laurie came into the restaurant and asked for a table. Coming in for dinner was unusual for Laurie as she was just a regular on the dance floor, drinking with various male admirers each time she came in. This night she asked for a booth in the dining room. Marcie brought Laurie her regular glass of white wine, and the wait staff took her order for a New York Steak cooked rare with a fully loaded baked potato. When the waitress brought Laurie her food, she asked Laurie if she needed a steak knife.

Laurie smiled and said, "No, thank you," because she brought her own.

Laurie reached into her purse and produced a large steak knife like the ones used at Longhorn, and using her cloth napkin, she wiped the blade one time. The waitress smiled and said that if she needed anything else to let her know, Laurie said she could use another glass of wine. Marcie brought another white wine to the table and asked Laurie how everything was.

Laurie replied, "Resolved."

Marcie, not having the time to enquire further, returned to the bar and picked up some new drink orders.

As Marcie was standing at her waitress station, two Homicide Detectives from the Greenwood County Sheriff's Department entered the bar and approached Marcie. Marcie had met both detectives through her boyfriend, Tom Stevens. One of the detectives said to Marcie, "I see a new orange Corvette parked out front on the sidewalk." Marcie replied, "Yeah, it probably belongs to Laurie Reynolds."

The detective asked, "Is she here?"

Marcie said, "Yeah, she is in the dining room."

The two detectives went into the dining room and placed Laurie Reynolds under arrest for the murder of her husband. The detective looked down at the table and saw the steak knife Laurie was using for her dinner. It did not match the rest of the silverware used at the restaurant, but it did resemble the set of steak knives at Reynold's home, where she had stabbed her husband thirty-three times and fled to Nick's Place, apparently to have her last meal as a free woman.

The Fashion Show

Many restaurants work with local businesses, such as ladies' clothing stores and jewelry stores, to help boost their sales. Ladies' fashion shows were quite common. Models would walk through the dining room as if it was a runway in Paris, displaying dresses and jewelry available from the local merchants. These events were also suitable for restaurants because they would generate business. Today, men would get a chance to be exposed to the latest in fashion!

Ronnie Boyd was a very successful stockbroker in the valley with many clients. He was a slight man who only stood about five foot six inches, but he was always impeccably dressed in the finest suits, such as Armani, Louis Vuitton, and Hugo Boss. His shirts were made for him at the Custom Shop in Costa Mesa, and his ties were often Dior or other top designers.

Ronnie was a member of a group of local businessmen who would make it a point to stop off at three or four upscale cocktail lounges on the way home each night to have a drink or two and to try and drum up some business. Ronnie often started much earlier in this process, perhaps 2:00 P.M. in the office, and by the time he reached Nick's Place, he was always three sheets to the wind!

Most people liked Ronnie. Ronnie had only one problem, an extraordinarily high and whiney voice the more he drank and got excited.

Ronnie's wife, Marjorie, whom he always called Maggie, was a local socialite who still liked being in his company despite being married to Ronnie for over twenty years. She wanted to be with him and go to the local cocktail lounges and socialize. Ronnie disagreed with Maggie's desires, and he would stay out longer and longer, leaving her at home to stew.

Today was Friday, and as luck would have it, around 7:30 P.M., Ronnie was at Nick's Place just a little longer than he should have stayed. Maggie had decided that it was spring cleaning time, and Ronnie's closet was the first to be purged! So, Maggie had loaded her Mercedes with several armloads of Ronnie's suits, sportscoats, dress shirts, slacks, and ties, and she went hunting for him at his regular hangouts.

Ronnie drove a bright red Cadillac El Dorado with a white roof. Finding the vehicle parked right out front of Nick's Place was not hard. Maggie swung around and parked in the lot near the restaurant's back door. Ronnie was in his glory right in the middle of the bar, demonstrating his prowess in dancing the Hula to a new Polynesian food waitress from Buffalo, New York, who could care less but was pleasant to the bar customer.

Suddenly, the back door of the bar and restaurant swung open, and Maggie, with fire in her eyes, yelled, "You son of a bitch! If you like it so much here, you can move in!" Maggie started throwing Ronnie's clothes all over the bar, and she then started towards the dining room.

Ronnie let out a yell in that whiny voice only he had, "Maggieeeee, what are you doing?" Maggie went to the car and started with the next round of dress shirts and slacks. By the time she was done, most of Ronnie's wardrobe was scattered throughout the restaurant and bar for people to review and consider.

Finally, Ronnie said, "Now, Maggie, I don't know why you are so upset. I told you I would be home soon." Maggie stormed out the back door, and Ronnie followed in hot pursuit! As the couple headed out the back door, Marcie told Ronnie, "Don't worry, Ronnie, I will round up your clothes!"

Marcie started laughing and told 'Uncle Al,' "I never thought I would be saying that to Ronnie Boyd!"

'Uncle Al' said, "You know, I think I like the nighttime fashion shows better than the lunch version. There is more action!"

"Man-Made System, Man Can Beat It!"

Ralph Ortega was a retired sergeant from Hudson Falls P.D. who was now the top Honda car salesman in the valley. Honda had just opened its dealership, and they couldn't keep the new cars on the lot. As soon as the truck would unload, the cars were sold. People always wanted to buy from Ralph based on his community involvement and law enforcement reputation.

Ralph was sitting at the bar in Nick's Place with a middle-aged construction worker, Reggie, bending his ear. Ralph's only break was that his attention from Reggie shifted to Marcie every time Marcie walked by.

The Hudson Falls Police Employee's Association had an early meeting that night, and several members decided to adjourn to Nick's Place for some drinks. Tom Stevens came in with several of the gang and naturally gravitated to the large round conversation table off the dance floor. Marcie saw the crew from the P.D. and knew what they drank.

She brought the drinks over and kissed Tom on the cheek. After a couple of rounds, Tom noticed Reggie's attention on Marcie and did not like it. Reggie was now putting his arm around Marcie as he and Ralph talked with her. Ralph was watching the group from the P.D. from the corner of his eye, knowing what would eventually happen.

Marcie walked past Reggie, and he put his arm around her. Tom, along with six members of Hudson Falls P.D., stood up, looking to whoop some ass, ready for a fight or to back Tom's play as if it was a well-choreographed and practiced dance move being performed to The Eagle's *Life in the Fast Lane*, which was playing on the jukebox. However, they were just drunk enough not to know why.

Ralph grabbed Reggie and waltzed him out the restaurant's back door. Accordingly, Marcie was able to grab Tom by the arm and walk him to a private corner of the restaurant. Marcie proclaimed, "What do you think you are doing?" Tom started to reply when Marcie interrupted him and said, "I have been doing this for some time, and I do not need you to protect me from my customers!" She added, "I would not tell you how to handle your calls. You do not tell me how to sling booze!"

The good sergeant saved Reggie from an ass-whooping and Tom from disciplinary action from the P.D. Tom saved nothing but face thanks to Marcie! One good thing about Marcie, once she yelled at you, it was over and forgotten! Tom went back to the table with his tail between his legs.

The live music started at 9:00 P.M. The cops from the P.D. were on their way to becoming well-oiled when the boys from the county came in to join them. Of course, the county crew always brought a couple of badge bunnies with them.

Every police or sheriff's department has rules and regulations called policies and procedures. Unfortunately, each of these policies or procedures has someone's name attached!

At about 11:00 P.M., Officer Darius Taylor was dancing with one of the bunnies when the band started to sing one of his favorite songs. In his exuberance, he fell into the bandstand and the drum set. Suddenly a four-inch blue-steel Smith and Wesson Model 19 slid across the dance floor. Deputy Robert Henry proudly recovered the weapon and held it high as a trophy. Greg Price, who heard the noise, came out of the office to the dance floor to see the commotion. Once Greg saw it was the cops, he felt better and ordered a round on the house for the group.

Monday morning, the interim order came down from Hudson Falls Police Administration: Carrying of Firearms Off Duty in Public Drinking Establishments.

Tom Stevens and his friends were very proud! This was the first policy named for them. Even though it was Taylor's gun, they were all there as a team! For six months afterward, when a group from the P.D. came into Nick's Place, Marcie would come by with her bar tray, and they would all check their guns with her. The guns were kept behind the bar in a locked storage room. Like most cops, policies were considered a guide. As a result, no one was actually carrying their firearms while in this public drinking establishment. As Tom Stevens would say, "Man-made system, man can beat it!"

The Bookie

Tom Stevens had an unforgettable night planned for his girlfriend, Marcie Romano. Specifically, he was planning to ask her to marry him officially. It was all set; he would take her to Bobby McFadden's Mixed Bag in Santiago Springs, where he would pop the question after the salad before the main course. Tom and Marcie arrived, and Bobby McFadden's was packed as always. The two went inside to the front desk to confirm their reservation. Afterward, they went into the bar and ordered a round of drinks.

After a few minutes, the hostess entered the smoke-filled cocktail lounge to escort Tom and Marcie to their seats in the dining room. The restaurant was overcrowded, and when the opportune time arrived, Tom asked Marcie to marry him. Marcie, who knew Tom would ask that night, succumbed to emotion and began to cry. A businessman at the table next to Marcie (having had just enough to drink) didn't hear the proposal but saw the aftermath and the crying. As a result, he offered to kick Tom's ass to defend Marcie's honor. After peace was restored through discussion and diplomacy, the businessman bought Tom and Marcie a congratulatory round of drinks. This, of course, was after Marcie told Tom she would love to marry him!

After a couple of months of adjusting schedules, Tom and Marcie drove to Las Vegas. They were married in the civil service at the Clark County Clerk of the Court's Office at around 02:00 A.M. The officiating county employee was sitting outside the office, apparently on a break, sitting on the park type-bench out front. He was smoking a cigar and reading the racing form, and he tried to hide it when Tom and Marcie walked up. Tom always told their friends they were married by a bookie in Las Vegas. Thanks to Marcie's mother and stepfather, the two honeymooned for two nights at the historic El Cortez Hotel in downtown Las Vegas.

When they returned from Las Vegas, Tom moved in with Marcie into her small tung and groove wooden bungalow-type house built around the turn of the century that opened with a skeleton key. This house sat on an acre of land surrounded by a chain-link fence in the middle of Moonglade, a community west of Hudson Falls. Previously, Marcie had shared the home with her grandmother, who had left to spend her remaining years with a cousin in Seattle. A long-time neighbor of Marcie, who also happened to be a ranking member of a local outlaw motorcycle gang, offered as a wedding present to kill anyone who gave Marcie or Tom any trouble for a case of beer. Like the beer, that offer was kept on ice.

In the meantime, a couple of years went by, and during that time, Tom's mother and stepfather had significant marital problems. As a result of Tom's mother's infidelity, the marriage ended in divorce. Likewise, Marcie had left Nick's Place to stay home to care for her young family. Tom's sister, Sharon, had visited Tom and Marcie several times in Moonglade, frequently coming out to ask for money. Sharon was not the highest caliber of person, and her associates were often even less. At night, Marcie stayed home alone with baby Gunner while Tom was working as a patrol sergeant on the P.M. shift in Hudson Falls, fifteen miles away.

One night, Tom was contacted by a seasoned sheriff's office vice and narcotics sergeant named Randy Curtis. Randy asked to meet Tom at a local safe house. Upon Tom's arrival at the safe house, Randy showed him a piece of paper with a hand-drawn floor plan map. Randy asked, "Does it look familiar?"

Tom replied, "It's a map of my house in Moonglade!"

Randy continued, "A confidential informant of mine contacted me yesterday and told me that your sister had contacted him to solicit a burglary of your house." Randy showed on the map where Sharon had highlighted the areas where Tom kept his firearms and Marcie kept her jewelry.

Randy added, "Your sister told my informant that she would split the profit with him 50/50. My informant told her he wanted nothing to do with breaking into a cop's house and to get lost!"

Tom thanked Randy for the heads up and made sure he told the informant he had made the right decision. Tom asked Randy if he could have the map, and Randy handed the weathered map over to Tom.

To be sure, Tom realized what could happen if he was to confront his kid sister over her conspiracy, so he decided to tell his mother. After all,

Mom had raised him and her with the same moral values and knowledge of right from wrong! Tom met with his mother, told her what had occurred, and showed her the hand-drawn map. His mother shook her head and moved her hands in a dicing motion, claiming, "I don't have time for this! She is your sister; you talk to her!"

Tom could not believe his ears at her response, much less the lack of concern for her daughter-in-law Marcie who may be home with the baby when this asshole decided to commit the act. Tom's parting words to his mother were, "Tell Sharon if anything happens to my Marcie or Gunner, she will not have to worry about the criminal justice system! Her life will not be worth living!"

Tom Stevens never spoke to his sister or his mother again.

"Get Rid of Her in Week 6!"

Noah Evans was Tom Stevens' beat partner at Hudson Falls P.D. who had lateraled from the Yucca Flats Police Department about a month after Tom left the sheriff's department. Noah joined Hudson Falls P.D., a poster cop with jet-black hair and a peaches-and-cream complexion. He was seventy inches tall and weighed one hundred seventy pounds. His chiseled good looks were accented with an 'Oil Can Harry' type mustache perfectly trimmed in the center of his upper lip. Noah was not handsome; he was just a pretty man! He was married to a mousy little woman with as much personality as a house plant, but that was ok with Noah because she and her family owned a string of Radio Shacks in the El Camino Valley, and he had enough personality for both!

The San Jose Police Department had developed a comprehensive training program for new officers called the Field Training Program. This plan would become the gold standard for training recruits across the country. Additionally, San Jose submitted this document to the Jefferson and California Commission on Peace Officer Standards and Training for approval as a statewide standard of training proficiency. The commission in both states had recently approved the program, and each respective agency within the states had to resubmit San Jose's plan reconfigured to meet their own agency's training needs and program standards. To ensure compliance, Tom Stevens had been temporarily reassigned to the training section where he had just completed this task for the Hudson Falls Police Department. Tom and Noah were selected as the first Field Training Officers for the Hudson Falls Police Department. This appointment came when two recruits graduated from the Greenwood County Sheriff's Academy.

Laura Harris was a middle-aged, well-educated white woman with strawberry blond hair and a charming personality. She had lost her teenage son to a drunk driver several years ago, and police executives were sure she would never be able to deal with a drunk driver professionally. Laura Harris was the City of Hudson Falls' first female officer in the agency's history since 1910. She, like Tom, filled out a uniform a little too well, and neither she nor Tom was a poster cop. Furthermore, Tom knew that all the ladies at city hall were rooting for Officer Harris.

Chief Powers had retired within the previous six months and became a city council member. Moreover, Chief Powers' number two-man,

Joseph Arnold, became the Chief of Police, and Tom Stevens was sure Chief Arnold was going to carry on certain beliefs and traditions.

After Tom met Officer Harris, he thought she was a good person and requested that he be her Field Training Officer (FTO). In those days, Field Training Officers were selected by agency management based on their promotability and considered the agency's future. Field Training Officers stayed with their respective trainees for the entire length of the training program. Accordingly, FTO candidates did not put in for the job.

After reminding Tom about all the difficulties he was about to take on, along with agency traditions and mindsets and an admonition of cultures, the HPD administration agreed to have Tom as the Field Training Officer for the first female Police Officer for the Hudson Falls Police Department.

Andrew Addison was a tall, slim, good-looking kid who had worked a couple of years as a cadet for the police department. Like his new Field Training Officer, Noah Evans, he was a very agreeable type who was a poster cop. In talking with Tom, it was clear that Noah Evans was of the same mindset as the current and former Chiefs of police regarding females in law enforcement. So, from the moment of Noah's appointment, it was a competition with Tom to see who would put out the best, "Oh wait, can't say policeman anymore, can we, Tom?" Police officer!

A month after the appointment of the two new hires, it was clear that both new officers were doing well in the new FTO program. Each had difficulties. In academics, Officer Harris was leading due to her higher education. Officer Addison was doing better tactically but slower in report writing.

Chief Arnold saw Tom in the hallway and met him by the station's back door. The Chief asked Tom how Officer Harris was doing and before Tom could finish, the Chief told Tom to "Get rid of her in week six!"

Tom replied, "I will get rid of her if she needs to be removed," without thinking and hesitation! Tom Stevens did not realize until later how this conversation put a bullet in his career with the Hudson Falls Police Department. Two and a half months later, Officer Laura Harris completed and graduated from the Hudson Falls Police Department Field Training Program. Officer Addison also graduated from the program after being extended by two weeks.

The Missing Member

It was a fantastic February evening with about two hours left in the P.M. shift when Laura Harris got the hotshot call from dispatch, "All units and 3 Queen 40; a Stabbing Domestic just occurred at 300 South Harvard Street. The victim is on the front porch, and the Fire Department will be staging in the area. 3 Queen 40, your call is Code 3." Tom Stevens and Noah Evans were having a cup of coffee at Amy's Donut Shop in the south end when the call came out, and both picked up the call as backup. Laura was the first on the scene, and she located the victim's wife, a twenty-year-old Mexican beauty named Maria, who worked as a waitress at a small diner downtown. Maria was visibly shaken and crying.

When Tom arrived, he found the girl's husband, Hector, lying in a prone position on the front porch of the fifty-year-old two-story craftsman home. The homeowner had divided the house into two apartments. Maria and Hector rented one of the apartments. Hector was holding his crotch and screaming in pain. He looked like his balls had literally exploded, and blood was everywhere.

After checking with witnesses in the area and determining the suspect was gone. Tom notified dispatch, "Hudson Falls, 3 Queen 50 Units are Code 4 10-6. Send in the Fire Department for a Hispanic male in his mid-twenties with a stab wound." Dispatch confirmed the information and sent it to the fire department. When Noah arrived on the scene, Laura asked him to stay with the wife for a minute while she talked to Tom. Noah had no problem with this as he always had a wandering eye for the waitress from downtown.

Laura told Tom, "This call is not what you think it is. These two were supposed to celebrate their second wedding anniversary tonight. He went out drinking with friends instead, and when he came home, he wanted to have sex with her. Unfortunately for him, he was unable to maintain an erection. The two argued, and he reached into a kitchen drawer and grabbed a pair of pinking shears amid the argument. He then said something about not being a real man and using the pinking shears to cut off his dick."

Tom said, "You have to be kidding me!"

Laura added, "Maria told me Hector staggered onto the front porch and threw his severed member into the flower bed. Hector collapsed where the responding officers found him."

Tom organized the three cops and remaining firemen, not involved in treating Hector, into a search party for the missing 'member.' Noah was the lucky finder of said 'member.' He said, "It was hard and difficult to locate due to the flowerbed recently stocked with new bark. When I looked down, Noah said, it was mixed in with the bark and leaves with a little blood trail at the severed end."

Firefighters gathered the member and transported it along with Hector and Maria to the hospital, where after extensive and lengthy surgery, the penis was reattached.

As Laura and Tom walked back to their patrol cars from the Emergency Room, Laura told Tom, "Boy, he sure showed her, didn't he?"

Tom replied with a snicker, "I wonder what Maria is thinking?"

Laura replied, "Will there ever be a penis between us again?"

Tom interrupted, "Will I need to buy my husband Hector an Erector Set this Christmas?"

Laura added, "Tom, you are one sick bastard!"

The Marlboro Man

Jeremy Bronson was a customer of Marcie Romano at Nick's Place. Jeremy was as handsome as Noah Evans was pretty. A rugged guy who looked just like the Marlboro Man in the cigarette commercial. Jeremy owned a large commercial landscaping company that kept his six-foot-three frame lean and tan. All the ladies loved him.

Jeremy met the love of his life, Jennifer Stone, at Nick's Place, and soon they became regulars on the weekend to dance the night away. Jennifer worked for a local divorce attorney as a paralegal. She had brown shoulder-length wavy hair with a fresh and innocent look. Jennifer always smiled and was always upbeat. The two dated for several months and eventually married. The young couple seemed very much in love and happy together.

One evening Noah Evans received a call from dispatch of a possible suicide at a sprawling ranch house near the base of Emerald Valley. The reporter, Jennifer Stone, was hysterical. She told dispatch that she found her husband in the master closet with a headshot wound.

When Noah arrived, the investigation revealed that Jeremy and Jennifer rarely fought, but there was a significant blowup over Jeremy's business expenses that night. Jennifer pushed Jeremy during the argument, and in a fit of rage, he strangled her, causing her to pass out. Jeremy thought he had killed Jennifer.

Not able to live with what he had done, much less without her, Jeremy wrote a suicide note describing and apologizing for what he had done. He went into the master closet and loaded a Mossberg 12-gauge shotgun with one round of buckshot, put the barrel into his mouth, and pulled the trigger, thus only leaving a bloody stub with a lower jaw above his formerly white but now blood-soaked dress shirt collar.

When Jennifer woke up, she found her husband's remains in their closet and phoned the police. Unfortunately, Jennifer had yet to tell Jeremy that she was seven weeks pregnant and that the couple would have their first child.

A Different Path

Four years as a Green Beret had changed Jim Scott. Four years changed all three friends. When Jim returned home from Fort Bragg, he was fifty pounds lighter than when he arrived. He also had a new young wife, Lizzy, whom he met at a local bank outside the base. Tom Stevens had married Marcie Romano, and they were expecting their first child. Robert Henry was in the process of a divorce from his wife, Charlie. Robert was still at the Hudson Falls Sheriff's Station, but Tom had lateralled over to the Hudson Falls Police Department. Jim and Lizzy moved into the house Jim had lived in that belonged to his grandmother, and Lizzy was able to get a job with the local branch of the First Interstate Bank as a teller. Tom felt that Jim had changed and was acting more reserved and standoffish.

Once he caught his breath after returning home, Jim announced to Tom and Robert that he planned on attending the Rio Hondo Police Academy in Los Angeles County. Tom and Robert tried to recruit Jim to their respective departments, but Jim was set on making it himself. So, for the next six months, Lizzy remained in Hudson Falls, and Jim moved to Los Angeles County to attend the police academy. The three friends remained in contact during the six months, and Tom and Robert helped Jim whenever they could, both with academics and looking out for Lizzy. Finally, graduation day came for the academy. Tom, Marcie, Robert, and Lizzy drove to Los Angeles for the ceremony. Unsurprisingly, Jim was number one in defensive tactics and officer survival skills. The five friends spent the weekend in Los Angeles, and before they returned to Hudson Falls, they took in a Dodgers game at Chavez Ravine.

Despite the recruitment efforts of Tom and Robert, Jim applied for and went to work for the El Camino Police Department. The three friends now worked for separate and distinct departments in the El Camino Valley. Jim remained with the El Camino Police department for three years. During this time, he and Lizzy became more distant despite her trying everything possible to please her man. It appeared to Tom and Robert that Jim was unhappy with the white picket fence life he had been living for the past two years. Finally, after two and half years of marriage, Jim put Lizzy on a bus and sent her back home to North Carolina. Neither Tom nor Robert saw what was about to slap them in their face!

It was a Saturday night, and somehow Jim, Robert, and Tom had the night off. Marcie was naturally working at Nick's Place, and the boys were drinking beer and playing cards at Robert's apartment. After about a couple of hours of reminiscing about how the three met and changed each other's lives, Jim proclaimed that he was leaving the El Camino Police and had applied to the Joshua Woods Police Department in San Bernardino County, California. Tom and Robert started laughing, believing that Jim must have been joking!

Joshua Woods was a mining town once owned by the United Steel Corporation, founded in the 1930s and run as a company town until early 1970 when United Steel shut down its operation and left. While United Steel owned the desert town, with a population of just under 2,500, law enforcement was provided by a resident deputy from the San Bernardino County Sheriff. Since a private company owned Joshua Woods, it was never incorporated as a city. When United Steel left, along with ninety percent of the town's residents, so did the resident San Bernardino County Deputy. After about five years, the three hundred remaining residents came together, and they incorporated the City of Joshua Woods.

Since then, the City of Joshua Woods has grown to a population of about 70,000 with its fire and police departments and complete public works and city government. The majority of the city's population were probationers from Los Angeles County. They moved there under the cloak of starting over again but were just re-establishing their criminal operations. Based on FBI statistics for the previous five years, Joshua Woods had the distinction of having the first homicide of the new year, usually within the first five minutes. No police officers lived in the city, nor did any firemen. Both groups of employees drove fifty miles to get to this oasis in the middle of the desert in the Inland Empire.

The Joshua Woods Police Department is like the Oriental Casino of Tombstone, nothing but the dregs, roamers, and derelicts. JWPD only hired rejects from other departments. Joshua Woods would hire you if you have been fired from another agency and were on your last leg of being a cop. Jim Scott was not kidding and had actually applied for this organization and was scheduled for a chief's interview this coming Tuesday at 10:00 A.M.

Jim arrived at the Joshua Woods Police Department at about 9:30 A.M. on Tuesday. In the parking lot was an Action News van from Los Angeles.

They were there to do a documentary-type story on the history of police brutality in the Joshua Woods Police Department. Action News had a reputation for doing hatchet jobs on local governments whenever they had the opportunity.

Francesca Moretti, an anchor on the six o'clock news, was in the lobby with her cameraman, demanding to see the Chief of Police. Chief Hank Hoover was a retired Los Angeles County Sheriff's Captain who last had commanded the North Hollywood Station. He was a no-nonsense dinosaur from the 1950s who was not a fan of Action News.

At about 9:45 A.M. Chief Hoover entered the police department via the main entrance. He walked past Francesca without comment and into the records office, which backed up to the glassed-off front lobby, and said to a patrol sergeant looking for something in Records, "Get that platinum bitch out of my lobby before I have her arrested for trespassing!"

The sergeant escorted Francesca Moretti and her cameraman out the front door to their van in the parking lot. About fifteen minutes later, the Records Supervisor came to the front window and said to Jim, the Chief will see you now. A uniformed officer walked Jim back to the Chief's office.

Usually, Chief Hoover, who looked like a twin brother of the actor Edward Asner, would never look at a crystal-clean candidate such as Jim Scott for a 'coppers' job in Joshua Woods, but the two seemed to get along. Jim may have exposed the crazy Green Beret side, and the chief thought it would be a great addition to his team. Nevertheless, toward the end of the interview, Jim asked the Chief if he believed in P.R. (Public Relations). The Chief sat back in his chair, put his right hand to his chin, thought a moment, and said, "Yeah, I believe in P.R. 24 (A type of Side Handle nightstick). That's the kind of P.R. I believe in." The Chief let out a thunderous belly laugh and asked Jim if there was anything in his package he needed to know about, and when Jim said there was not, Chief Hoover hired him on the spot. Jim gave notice to the El Camino Police Department and was working in Joshua Woods as a policeman in less than three weeks. Jim moved to Barstow, where he rented a small one-bedroom apartment. Tom and Robert helped him move to his new digs.

When Jim showed up to work his first night, he was assigned to 'Blackjack' Bradshaw as his break-in officer. Joshua Woods did not have a formal training program, as most of its officers had been on the job for years. The first order of business was that 'Blackjack' took Jim to Madam Delilah's House of Ecstasy for a quicky. This was a traditional social jester for all new officers or special guests. Let's say that Madam Delilah had a special relationship with Chief Hoover and his boys.

The City of Joshua Woods was about five square miles, and they fielded fifteen patrol cars a shift. You did not see another cop unless you requested a backup. There was no such thing as a routine patrol. You went from call to call all night long. 'Blackjack' told Jim that the cops were looking for a new motto on the sides of their patrol cars, 'Working the Hoods in the Woods.' He said he thought the Chief was almost convinced. Jim rode with 'Blackjack' for three shifts when he was released on the city.

It was a warm Saturday night in July when Jim got the third hot shot call of the evening, "Car 143 respond to Granite Park at 100 S. Hackberry Avenue reference a 245 PC Assault with a Deadly Weapon. The suspects are three black males 20-23 years of age, wearing dark clothing. The weapon used was a tire iron. Suspects fled north on Hackberry in a grey 1963 chevy lowrider with primer spots on the rear. No license plate was seen."

Jim replied, "Dispatch car 143 is en route from the east side."

When Jim arrived on the scene, he found a young Hispanic male, approximately nineteen years old, holding his head with a white towel. There was minor bleeding from a small cut on the left side of his forehead. The young man's name was Robert Lopez, but he went by Bobby. Bobby was a student at Cal State San Bernardino. His father, Robert senior, was a 'Big Time' corporate lawyer in San Bernardino. Bobby mentioned that probably three times. Bobby was driving a new white Honda Accord with a Cal State University parking permit sticker on the right rear bumper.

The investigation revealed that Bobby had come to Granite Park to buy some 'meth,' and the deal went sideways. The suspects had taken a tire iron and hit Bobby a couple of times, then broke out a taillight and the right-side windows of his car just for the heck of it. Jim had called for medical aid, and as the fire department was finishing up with Bobby,

Jim's new boss, Sergeant Desmond Testa, arrived on the scene and asked Jim what he had. As Jim explained what had happened, the sergeant suddenly stopped him and went over to Bobby, and asked him, "You drove from San Bernardino to my city to buy dope, and this is what happened to you?" When Bobby anxiously agreed, Sergeant Testa told Bobby to "Get the fuck out of this city and never come back!" The sergeant looked over at Jim and said, "Officer, issue that man a citation for a defective tail lamp, and while you are at it, check his immigration status!" So went the life of a policeman in the City of Joshua Woods.

Jim, Robert, and Tom lived their lives to the fullest and started to drift apart. Jim remained with the Joshua Woods Police Department for four years. Jim called Tom on a Wednesday afternoon and told him that he had sold everything and was moving to Alaska. Jim said he was coming by the Hudson Falls Sheriff Station on Saturday at 3:00 P.M. to say goodbye. Tom had to tell Robert. Jim arrived right on time on Saturday, driving a brand-new red Jeep. After the friends spoke for a while, Jim said he had to get going. He was burning daylight! The three long-time friends hugged, and Jim drove away.

That was the last time that Tom saw his best friend!

The Poster Cop

Daniel Blocker started his law enforcement career as a reserve police officer with Hudson Falls Police Department. Daniel was five foot ten and one hundred sixty pounds with perfect hair like Jim Reed on Adam-12. He could also have done commercials for any dentist's office in town because he had perfect teeth! He was young and eager and always wanted to ride with Tom Stevens.

Daniel was married with a couple of kids and made a great living as a Master Mechanic for the local Ford dealership. He worked hard all week, and on Friday and Saturday nights, Daniel would come out and ride with Tom on Friday nights and Noah Evans on Saturday nights. Both Tom and Noah liked Daniel, and they decided they would put him through the Field Training Program as a Reserve Officer. It would take a little longer, but he would receive the same training as a regular officer.

Unfortunately for Daniel, like many others, he divorced his first wife. After five years as a reserve officer for Hudson Falls P.D., he decided to go to work for the Greenwood County Sheriff's Department. After Daniel had graduated from the sheriff's academy, he was assigned to the new John Sampson Detention Center, where he could expect to be for the following five years. Greenwood County Sheriff's Department realized what an asset they had in Daniel because he was soon used as the poster cop. He was in all the recruiting efforts showing him working in the jail, and attending recruitment fairs and other community-related events.

Daniel also married a second wife, Wendy, considerably younger than him and his first wife. Wendy would argue with Daniel constantly, and he would call his friends for advice on improving his marriage. Robert Henry remembered that Daniel had called to ask for advice on how to prove to Wendy how much he loved her. Daniel was desperately trying to make the marriage work.

Daniel had just received word from command staff that he would soon leave the jail due to his excellent work in the recruiting arena. He would be assigned to the Greenwood Station, but he was also told that Sheriff's Administration had been watching him. They had big plans for his future. That afternoon, Daniel came home and told Wendy, and they again began to argue about unrelated marital issues. Finally, Daniel left home, slamming the back door into the garage. He went to his new Ford F250 Truck, sat in the driver's seat, pulled out his agency-issued firearm, and ate his gun. Despite all the help from his friends, Daniel thought he had no other way out of the pain he felt. What a tragedy that Daniel thought he had no other options.

"This Isn't What it Looks Like!!"

Andrew 'Andy' Harris is a weathered Fire Captain for the Greenwood County Fire Department in Station 27. He is a recent widower and a thirty-year veteran of the department. Andy is well respected by his employees and in the emergency services community.

Chris Garcia is a forty-year-old Fire Engineer who works for Andy. Chris, a high school-educated man, had been single most of his life until recently when he ordered a bride from Russia named Sasha Petrov. Sasha is a tall slim raven haired twenty-six-year-old beauty with crystal blue eyes. Sasha was becoming fluent in English, and she happily married Chris three months before this warm Tuesday in May. Life here in America was great until today, Sasha would soon realize.

"3 Queen 50 clear to copy a Disturbance: Woman with a Sledge Hammer!"

Tom Stevens replied, "Hudson Falls, go ahead."

Dispatch continued, "3 Queen 50 See the man regarding a domestic disturbance, a woman with a sledgehammer, on Avenida Los Padres just east of Aspen Street. The reporting party in a blue Ford F250 will wave you down."

Laura Harris picked up the assist by advising dispatch, "3 Queen 40 to back 3 Queen 50."

As Tom arrived, he saw Andy waving him down in the middle of the street. Tom knew Andy from his days with the sheriff's department. Tom asked, "Hey Andy, what's happening?"

Andy told Tom, "Chris called me at home in a state of panic. He told me that he brought an eighteen-year-old fire explorer named Tiffany home."

Further investigation revealed that Tiffany and Chris had been fooling around for about a month. Chris told Tiffany that Sasha was out shopping and that she would be gone all day. Chris invited Tiffany to his home. As Chris planned, things got hot and heavy, and Chris and Tiffany ended up in the large glass shower off the owner's suite. Both bodies were well-soaped up. Chris' manhood gave Tiffany its full attention when suddenly Sasha flung open the bathroom door. Sasha yelled something in Russian to both of the shower's occupants that probably wasn't, "Honey, I'm home!"

In a moment of brilliance, Chris proclaimed, "This isn't what it looks like!!"

Sasha stormed off towards the garage where Chris stored his two prize jet skis. Chris followed her when suddenly he stopped to call his friend and boss Andy. Tiffany was not new to this sort of thing, and she was rinsed, dressed, and gone before Andy's arrival ten minutes later.

As Chris was on the phone with Andy, he heard his beloved jet skis turn into a collection of Legos and toothpicks. When Chris got to the garage, he found Sasha swinging a ten-pound sledgehammer as if she were swinging for Yankee Stadium's fences. When Andy arrived, Chris was in the garage with the sledgehammer, and Sasha was in the owner's suite crying on the bed. Andy concluded his recap of the incident to Tom by saying, "I just don't want this incident to ruin Chris' career or bring anything down on the fire department."

Laura Harris arrived on the scene, and after a quick briefing from Tom, she made contact with Sasha in the bedroom. Tom contacted Chris in the garage, and after confirming what Andy had told him, Tom and Laura met to review what each had learned. Tom asked Laura, "Do you want to have some fun?" Laura replied, "Of course!" Tom said, "Follow my lead!"

After securing all the weapons in the home, the two officers contacted Chris in the garage. Tom asked Chris, "Ok. We have heard each side of this story. Did you say, 'this isn't what it looks like?'

Chris replied, "Yes, I did."

"Ok, Chris, time to answer the burning question everybody wants to know, what was it?"

The answer never came.

As Laura was leaving the residence, she reminded Sasha about those beautiful things they have in America called divorce lawyers! Laura said, "Welcome to America!"

Greenwood County Fire Department did not officially hear about the call from Hudson Falls P.D. Chris' career remained intact. Tiffany left the fire department explorers and became a stripper in San Diego. Andy Harris thought, "I have to find some smarter friends!"

"This isn't what it looks like!" has gone down in history as the dumbest response to the woman you are cheating on when she catches you naked in a shower with another woman.

"Is This Your First?"

"3 Queen 50 clear to copy a call?"

Officer Noah Evans told his trainee Jan Ricci to "Pick up that call."

While driving northbound on Aspen Street from California Blvd, Ricci grabbed the mic with his right hand and said, "Hudson Falls, go ahead."

Dispatch replied, "3 Queen 50 respond to a Medical Aid Call – Woman Giving Birth at the Lazy Daze Trailer Park 310 North Enterprise Street Space #8."

Dispatch continued, "Hudson Falls Fire has an extended response time. They are assisting El Camino Fire with a fatal multi-vehicle collision on the Las Ramblas Expressway." She added, "Hudson Falls Ambulance also has an extended E.T.A. due to Heavy Calls for Service." Finally, "3 Queen 50, your call is Code Three."

Ricci replied, "3 Queen 50 en route" He immediately turned on the lights and siren and headed toward Enterprise Street from Park Hill.

Evans told Ricci, "Your job is to get us there without getting us killed, understand?"

"Yes, sir," Ricci replied.

Jan Ricci was the eldest son of Betty Ricci. Jan was named after Jan and Dean of the 1960's rock and roll group she loved so much. She considered herself something of a big shot over at the city of Hudson Falls Finance Department.

Betty wanted her son to work as a police officer for the City of Hudson Falls. This would be an excellent temporary job to get his feet wet as he attended law school. Betty firmly believed Jan would work at one of Hudson Falls' most prestigious law firms.

Jan Ricci was a handsome kid who looked like he had just come from Malibu beach. He only had one problem; he was as dumb as a box of rocks. Another turd in the punch bowl was that his mother had used her influence at city hall to get her baby boy hired. This was Ricci's second rephase in the Field Training Officer Program. Unless he made significant changes and showed considerable improvement, his career at Hudson Falls P.D. would not be extensive.

Lazy Daze Trailer Park was a sixty-year-old travel trailer park used primarily by immigrant farm labor families. Space # 8 was on the park's southeast corner off the main entrance. Before the patrol car arrived on the scene, Dispatch announced, "3 Queen 50, the R/P advising that the victim is in the bedroom and the baby's head is cresting." As the patrol car came screaming onto the property, everyone on the outside scattered to parts unknown. This happened every time a police car entered the complex. Most residents believed the Border Patrol was there to bust them for immigration violations.

As the two officers entered the forty-year-old travel trailer, they heard the screaming and moaning sounds of a young Hispanic girl coming from the rear of the trailer. The trailer had a small portable heater in the living room, and the smell of grease from last night's tacos and refried beans were thick in the air.

As the officers passed the kitchen, they saw a ceramic painting of Santa Maria De Guadalupe on the wall. They found a woman lying in a prone position in the back bedroom with her legs spread wide open and screaming something unintelligible in Spanish to her husband. He left her to retrieve the officers. Above her on the wall was a wooden cross with a miniature metal replica of Jesus Christ. You could hear the residents talking from other trailers in the packed trailer park and children crying and fussing!

In broken English, the girl's husband asked the officers if they could help his wife! After all, he called the fire department for help, not the police department, yet the cops were the only ones to show up. Unfortunately, Ricci did not project mastery of the situation currently involved. Noah was the father of a little girl and had already assisted in the births of three other babies as a policeman.

Evans had a calming effect on the expectant mother as he told her, "Everything will be all right, let's deliver your baby." Evans also told Ricci to relax as he was breathing heavily with the new mother. Evans thought Ricci would hyperventilate. However, Ricci didn't need to say it; he had never seen anything like this before other than the 1950 Navy childbirth training film he saw in the police academy.

Within minutes, the baby boy was born without problems. Evans cleared the baby's face, nose, and mouth and marveled again when the baby took its first breath and started crying! Ricci proclaimed, "You did it," to Evans, who immediately gave credit to the new mother. Evans set the baby on the mother's stomach as he heard the ambulance arriving on the scene.

Shortly after that, the superficial mucous membrane, afterbirth, and the placenta were discharged onto the bed. Ricci thought it looked like a giant purple man-o'-war jellyfish covered in blood. He felt he would pass out but did not want to fall into that discharge pile or onto the mother and baby. Evans then started the right of passage for all trainees who deliver a newborn; he told Ricci to take off his car coat and hand it to him. Ricci complied without hesitation or knowledge of what was about to happen.

Evans spread Ricci's car coat open on the bed. He picked up the placenta and other discharge and placed them in the center of the officer's coat. Evans zipped the coat up and, using both hands, tied the car coat into a nice bundle of afterbirth to be examined by hospital staff as necessary.

Father, the mother, and the new baby boy were transported to Hudson Falls Hospital without incident. Jan Ricci looked in disbelief as the ambulance left the scene towards the hospital. Evans, who had already cleaned up, for the most part, told Ricci that he could now add childbirth to his law enforcement resume!

Ricci, complaining, asked, "What about my car coat?"

Evans replied, "Maybe your mom can buy you a new one!"

The new mother was so thankful that she named her new baby boy Jan Noah Rodriguez!

"Piss, Poor Policemen"

Tom Stevens and Noah Evans knew why they had been summoned to the chief's office. Noah had seen a two-bit thief and drug dealer named Mickey Bagshaw driving his purple Chevy Monte Carlo eastbound on California Blvd near El Camino Avenue. Evans had busted Mickey for shoplifting two months ago. Noah also knew that Mickey failed to appear in court, and a bench warrant was issued for his arrest. Noah, westbound on California Blvd, hung a U-turn to stop Mickey. As Noah started to call in the stop, Mickey changed lanes without signaling.

Noah and Mickey were in the number one lane eastbound on California Blvd at Basswood Street. When Noah 'lit them up,' Mickey stomped on it, and the pursuit was on! Tom, Noah's beat partner, heard the call and was westbound on California Blvd from Black Walnut Avenue. Mickey fled eastbound on California Blvd to northbound Aspen Street. The pursuit continued northbound on Aspen Street past Avenida Los Padres. Tom joined the chase at California Blvd and Aspen Street and started to call in the chase allowing his partner, Noah, to focus on driving and catching the bad guy.

The pursuit continued northbound on Aspen Street to Red Oak Avenue, where Mickey turned eastbound and drove to the cul-de-sac dead end. Mickey exited his vehicle, which was still rolling, and ran to the yellow house at the dead-end, his mother's home. The purple Chevy Monte Carlo rolled into a yellow Chrysler Newport that belonged to his mother, causing minor damage to the Monte Carlo but nothing to the Newport.

Mickey was under the mistaken belief that if he made it inside his mother's house, all bets were off, and he would become untouchable – to his surprise. Noah was the first to hit the front door with full force causing damage to the frame. Tom was close behind, and when both officers entered the house, they were met by a hysterical mother and a cowering Mickey on the loveseat in the living room. Mickey decided to fight his way out, and after a bit of *E Thumpus Gordas*, Mickey was taken into custody. Mickey's mom called the Hudson Falls Sheriff's Station during the scuffle. She claimed two Hudson Falls cops broke into her home and were beating her son for no apparent reason. Hudson Falls Sheriff sent two cars, code three, to assist. Mickey was arrested for the shoplifting warrant, the pursuit, and some dope found on his person and in his vehicle.

Hudson Falls Sheriff had their nose a bit out of joint because they were not advised of H.F.P.D.'s intentions before the event. It was not critical, but it made it up to the Sheriff's Station Commander, Captain Liam Allen.

The last thing Chief 'Duke' Powers liked was a phone call coupled with a lecture from a sheriff's captain about how he should manage his police department! So, Hudson Falls Police Department wrote a check for the damages caused to the front door of the suspect's mother's residence.

The appointment with the chief was at 10:00 A.M. Tom Stevens arrived at 9:45 A.M., and Noah Evans was already sitting outside the chief's office. Both officers were dressed in class 'A' uniforms. Tom thought it had been six months since he had met Chief Powers at his home when the job was offered. Tom knew this meeting would not be as cordial as the last one. Indeed, Law enforcement had been a paramilitary organization. In those days, Hudson Falls P.D. held military customs in high esteem.

Suzanne, the chief's secretary, looked up from work on her desk, smiled, and said, "You both may go in."

As both officers entered the chief's office, Tom, the senior officer, said, "Officers Stevens and Evans reporting for duty as ordered, sir!"

Stevens and Evans stood at attention in front of the chief's desk. Chief Powers did not stand nor greet the officers. He did not offer them a seat or tell them to stand at ease. Seconds before Chief Powers started his address, Stevens noticed how big the chief's desk was. It was an executive-style mahogany desk with three significant bookcases behind it. Numerous awards and photos were on the shelves and walls of the office. These were framed crime scene photos taken when the chief was a Homicide Captain with the Costa Mesa Police Department in the early 1960s. The office was imposing and intimidating at the same time.

The one thing that drew Tom's attention to the center of the chief's desk was a large coffee table-type ashtray. This ashtray was a vintage orange and green ceramic or California pottery mid-century modern piece shaped like a colossal kidney bean. The ashtray had not been emptied for a day or two and was packed with approximately thirty cigarette butts. When Chief Powers started the ass-chewing, he started with being disappointed and went down what seemed like an endless list of procedural mistakes Evans and Stevens made during the arrest of Mickey Bagshaw. This was not an open discussion; this was an old-fashioned ass-chewing that would have made Inspector Todd from *Beverly Hills Cop* proud. Tom would glance down at the ashtray on the chief's desk and notice that every time the chief made a point, he would become angrier, remembering his conversation with the sheriff's captain. He would pound the desk with a closed fist. Every moment moved that fist closer to the ashtray set atop three stubby legs.

As Chief Powers reached the final item on his checklist, he concluded by saying that, in his opinion, the officer's antics consisted of those from 'Piss, poor policemen!' and with that, during his final pounding of the desk caught the corner of that ashtray. He flipped it up into the air five inches scattering the contents across his beautiful mahogany desk, into his half-full cup of coffee, into his in-and-out basket, onto the floor, and across his LAPD Blue uniform shirt!

Two cigarette butts wound up stuck behind his badge. Both officers, who were still standing at attention, began to react. Noah's body started to tremble slightly despite his best attempt not to laugh. Tom bit his lower lip so hard it began to bleed out the corner of his mouth.

The last thing Evans and Stevens heard from the chief was, "You two get the fuck out of my office before I fire the both of you!!"

One of the good things about Chief Powers was once he chewed your ass, it was over. He did not hold it against you and treated you the same as before the discipline. Later that day, Evans and Stevens tried to lay low after the briefing. They were loading up their patrol cars on the west ramp.

Chief Powers, who always parked on the station's east side in a designated spot, came out the west ramp door and said, "You two have a good shift."

Moments later, you heard, "3 Queen 20 Evans Unit 114 10-8."

And then, "3 Queen 50 Stevens Unit 118 10-8."

Dispatch replied, "Hudson Falls copies both units 10-8 at 1633 hours."

Blue Light Special

Patrol schedules at Hudson Falls P.D. ran for three months at a time. Tom Stevens was about to start his following schedule on midnights, beginning in January and running through March, the coldest time in the El Camino Valley. Midnights start at 00:01 A.M. and end at 08:00 A.M. Tom, like most cops, was good for the first three-and-a-half hours of the midnight shift, but at 03:30 A.M, Tom's eyes felt like they wanted to bleed!

The first three hours of midnights are busy with domestic disturbance calls, loud parties, and bar fights. Undoubtedly, between 02:00 and 03:30 A.M., seventy percent of the local bar patrons pilgrimage to the three twenty-four-hour coffee shops open in town. Specifically, the only place open at 04:00 A.M. were the two donut shops and two seven-eleven stores. But, of course, no drunks ever showed up at the donut shops because they knew that was where the cops hung out. Moreover, by 03:30 A.M., most people had finished their breakfast and had started to head home.

Cops from each of the four valley agencies would meet at the donut shops to socialize and drink as much coffee as they could hold to help wake up to make it through the remainder of their shift. By 04:30 A.M., it was usually nap time. Cops traditionally met behind shopping centers or other closed businesses. They would park adjacent to one another, facing opposite directions, driver's door to driver's door.

Tom's beat partner was tied up in the H.F.P.D jail this morning processing an uncooperative drunk driver. It was Tom's first night back from his weekend, so he was exhausted. Tom cleared his last call, a barking dog, and headed toward the heart of his beat. Behind K-Mart at Enterprise Street and Via Rojo Street was a storage area built against the building. This area consisted of two other walls made of cinder blocks, six feet tall, with a staircase design on the one long side. The open side was a little bigger than a one-car garage. K-Mart was not the original tenant of the building. This storage area was not part of K-Mart operations and has never been used other than by the cops to write their reports or to catch a quick break.

When Officer Stevens entered the K-Mart parking lot, he drove around the building one time to ensure the building was secure. As he pulled around, he backed into the storage area until the car was completely concealed from view. Fortunately, all the employees had left for the night. Officer Stevens has used this site many times in the past.

As most cops do, Tom left the engine running, turned down the radio just a notch, and pulled out the open pack of Marlboro 100's box from his right front uniform shirt pocket. Next, Tom removed the red Bic lighter and lit the cigarette, taking a slow drag. In like manner, he positioned the cigarette between his left index finger and middle finger. After that, he moved it down to the web of his hand between the white cigarette paper and the gold filter paper. Finally, Tom placed his left arm on the open windowsill of the driver's door. Deputy Tucker Fisher taught him this trick years ago, saying that the cigarette would burn down and wake him up if he fell asleep. Tom then leaned his head back against the headrest and closed his eyes.

Officer Dexter Hill was a two-year veteran of Hudson Falls, P.D. To illustrate, he was a man with a tiny brain but a good heart. Hill was a prankster who knew where all the cops would occasionally take a break. When he pulled around behind K-Mart, he parked about fifty feet away from the storage area where Tom was parked. As he approached on foot, he could hear the engine running from Stevens' patrol car. Hill, who had not yet completely lost his mind, peeked around the corner of the block wall and confirmed that it was, in fact, a police car with the engine running. Tom would later find out that Hill did not even know if it was a Hudson Falls Police car or a Greenwood County sheriff's cruiser.

As Dexter Hill walked back to his patrol car to shut it off, he thought how funny this would be and how he would make a cop piss his pants this cold January morning.

Tom was settled back enjoying his snooze when, thanks to the grace of God, he heard a slight noise as Dexter Hill started to use the stairway blocks to climb to the top of the block wall adjacent to the parked patrol car. As soon as he heard the noise, Tom instinctually unstrapped his swivel breakfront holster, which held his six-inch blue steel Colt Python .357.

Suddenly, Dexter Hill jumped from atop the six-foot block wall onto the hood of Tom Stevens' patrol car. Dexter Hill's face was distorted when he pressed his face against the patrol car's windshield, screaming like a wild animal. He looked like an armed robber with women's stockings pulled over his head to conceal his identity. As Tom Stevens raised his gun to the windshield, he could somehow see the Hudson Falls Police Department Patch on Dexter Hill's uniform shirt. That coupled with the reflection of Hill's badge as it glistened in the cloud-free cold moonlight. In a split second, Tom broke leather.

Hill believing he was about to meet his maker, screamed, "Tom, it's me, Dexter!"

Hill rolled to his left and right off the right front fender of Tom's unit onto the ground allowing only inches between the exterior wall of K-Mart and the passenger side wheels of Tom's patrol car.

Tom heard nothing when Hill identified himself. Tom dropped the unit into drive and quickly pulled out of the storage area, only just missing running over Officer Hill. When Tom pulled out of the storage area, both officers had experienced an insulin dump.

Dexter had jumped up and dusted himself off, saying, "I'm ok!"

Tom, who still had his gun in his hand and was coming back to confront his attacker, said, "To hell, you are, you son of a bitch! What in the fuck were you thinking? I almost shot you!"

After several minutes the insulin level in both officers came back to normal. Officer Hill apologized to Officer Stevens for his stupid prank. Indeed, he realized he probably should not have done what he did. In the same way, Tom realized that he had to find a new place to rest, and from now on, he would meet with someone else to take a break. Besides, Tom also realized that if Hill thought this was a good idea, he needed to find a new beat partner.

The adventures of Dexter Hill made their way around the station. This incident became known as the night Saint Michael (the Archangel and patron saint of the policeman) had an early morning 'Blue Light' special at K-Mart for Officers Dexter Hill and Tom Stevens.

Red Tape

Cyrus Pappas started his career as a dispatcher for the El Camino Police Department. Eventually, he was promoted to policeman in El Camino. After eight or so years, he lateraled to the Hudson Falls Police Department. Cyrus was known for two things; he was an outstanding officer for making drunk driving arrests and getting Greenwood County Correctional Officers in fights.

Every time you heard Pappas come up on the radio, "Hudson Falls 1 Queen 60 is 15, 19, One time for Deuce," he had one prisoner in custody for drunk driving. He returned to the station, setting the stage for his following production number.

On the way into the jail for booking, Pappas told his prisoners to tell everybody in jail that Pappas had saved their life by arresting them for drunk driving. He would let them go in four hours with just a ticket if they did this. Afterward, Pappas would ply them with guilt until they agreed to say they were getting off easy. To be sure, every drunk driver taken into custody at Hudson Falls P.D. was released in four hours or when sober, along with a notice to appear or ticket.

Pappas had discovered another star. As soon as they hit the jail's back door, D.W.I. suspect John Bailey began singing the praises of Officer Cyrus Pappas to anyone who would listen. Pappas would take his appropriate bows and confirm with the booking officer that Mr. Bailey would be released in four hours with a citation! Pappas would look over at Mr. Bailey and give him a big wink and a smile as the booking officer completed the process.

As Sergeant Wayne Esposito (the watch commander) passed by, Pappas would ask him, "Did you hear Sarge? I saved another life tonight!" Esposito would grumble, "Yeah, you are my hero!"

Another version of Pappas's shenanigans came when agencies were not so concerned about civil liability, and violence was considered a routine part of police work. If Pappas were taking a prisoner to the county lockup, he would tell them about a little-known secret.

During the trip, he would say, "If you could kick the booking officer's ass, they would let you go."

You would be astonished how many people fell for that old gag. No new charges were ever added to the suspect's booking sheet. But the suspect and the sheriff's office correctional officers were entertained when they got to jail. Pappas would always warn the jail staff that something may be coming with a grin on his face.

Karma is a beautiful thing. Pappas brought in a white male on a felony warrant on his last trip to the county jail. This trip was uneventful until he entered the facility. His attention was immediately drawn to a new D.W.I. blood nurse assisting the Jefferson Highway Patrol with their prisoner. Pappas handed his prisoner over to the booking officer and meandered to meet the new nurse.

Loreen, or 'Candy' McCall as her friends called her, came from a four-generation law enforcement family from Los Angeles County. She was not buying anything Officer Cyrus Pappas was selling! After several unsuccessful minutes passed, Pappas took his leave after busting a couple of C.O.'s balls on his way out. To Pappas' misfortune, he never picked up his handcuffs left for him on the booking desk, as is standard practice. Pappas realized this four hours later. Being somewhat concerned, Pappas called the jail and confirmed that they had the cuffs.

Now it is known that all cops like to pick up souvenirs from other cops, such as pens or handcuffs. So, all good cops have their handcuffs engraved with their names. All others will soon learn.

As payback for his jail antics, the correctional officers found Pappas's handcuffs and decided to 'wrap them up for safekeeping.' This process used red construction warning tape tightly wrapped around the handcuffs, forming a circular sphere. The correctional officers used yellow sheriff's crime scene tape and tightly wrapped this tape again, continuing in the shape of a round globe. The next level was duct tape. This process took approximately two hours until the handcuffs were concealed in a circular sphere larger than a basketball. The final covering of the globe was silver duct tape with Pappas Hudson Falls P.D. written on it with a Black Sharpe.

When Pappas arrived at the Duncan Jail, he walked in as his cocky self and proclaimed that he was there for his cuffs!

The three correctional officers standing at the booking desk said, "No problem," as they reached under the desk, pulled out the immense basketball, and tossed it to the officer.

"What's this?" asked Pappas.

The lead correctional officer said, "Next time you leave the Duncan Jail without your cuffs, you will remember that all you have to do is cut through the red tape!"

Let Sleeping Dogs Lie

It was a cold winter Monday night in early February. When Tom Stevens arrived at the station around 11:30 P.M., it was already forty degrees downtown. It was expected to get even colder throughout the night. Darius Taylor and Hong 'Ben' Lombardi were in the locker room, dressing for their shift.

Hong Lombardi, whose full name is Hong Kong Lombardi, is the son of an Irish mother and an Italian father. Hong's father named his son after the city where he spent his favorite military leave in the U.S. Army. The son, who now goes by the name 'Ben,' was as tough as nails. Wouldn't you be hard as nails if you were raised in an Italian neighborhood with the first name of Hong?

Lombardi and Taylor were first in the briefing room, followed soon after by Tom. Finally, Cyrus Pappas came shuffling into the briefing with only moments to spare. As Sergeant Wayne Esposito droned on in briefing, the three officers noticed that Cyrus Pappas looked exhausted.

As the three officers walked outside to the police parking lot, the three teammates joked and asked Pappas if he would make it through the shift without passing out.

Pappas declared, "I'm ok, don't worry about me!"

Moments later, the entire midnight crew was in service. Tom headed out to his beat on the east end. He checked all the strip malls and businesses along California Blvd., and all was quiet. So, he decided to drive into Beat 10 and check on his wife Marcie at Nick's Place. When Tom pulled into the parking lot, he found only one patron's car parked there. He knew Nick's Place would be closing early tonight.

As he entered the bar, Marcie walked over to Tom and kissed him on the cheek. Peggy O'Donnell, a forty-five-year-old blond professional gal six feet tall and one-hundred-and-ninety-pounds, was sitting at the bar. Peggy worked for the county administrator's office in Greenwood. She was dressed in business attire and had just been given the last call as she ordered her fifth martini for the night. Peggy was a regular of Nick's Place, whom one would call a classical barfly. She was in the mood for love in all the wrong places or maybe just to get laid, and tonight she had her eye on Greg, the night manager. This love affair with Greg started a month ago when Greg made the mistake of agreeing to dance with her one Saturday night when the band was rocking the house.

When Peggy saw Tom, she smiled and said, "Hey Tom, when are you going to leave Marcie and come be with a real woman?" Marcie said, "Peggy, Tom couldn't handle you! You are way too much woman for him!"

When Peggy heard this, she let out a big belly laugh that could be heard throughout the bar.

Greg finally emerged from the back office, and when he saw Tom, he yelled out, "Hey Tom, how goes the battle?"

After a few minutes, Greg told Peggy, "Time to leave!"

Peggy said, "Only if you walk me out to my car!"

Greg looked over at Tom Stevens and asked, "Tom can you handle that?"

Tom Stevens told Greg, "You caught it. You clean it!"

Peggy chimed in and said, "Greg, will you clean me in a bubble bath or shower?"

Greg grouchily replied, "Come on, Peggy," as they both walked out the back door to the parking lot. Several minutes had passed, and Tom Stevens looked down at his belt to see if he had turned on his radio when he exited the patrol car. Radio traffic was slim to none. When Greg re-entered the bar via the back door, he walked over and got behind the bar. He grabbed a bottle of Anisette and poured it into his open mouth for at least a count of ten. Anisette is a licorice-flavored liqueur that is consumed in most Mediterranean countries. It is colorless but contains a large amount of sugar which was not good for Greg's diabetes.

Greg proclaimed, "I learned from a cop in Green Bay that if you drink this, the cops can't tell if you have been drinking!"

Tom thought how stupid the cops must be in Wisconsin, or Greg was using the Anisette to clean the taste of Peggy's martini-soaked tongue from his throat. So, Tom stayed until Marcie was finished closing up, and they both went to Denney's for an early breakfast.

After breakfast, Tom returned to his beat to check businesses and other hot spots. Radio traffic in the patrol car was minimal, along with the county radio traffic. It was 03:00 A.M. when Hudson Falls P.D. Dispatch decided to do a safety check of all units out of sheer boredom. Supervision would also use this trick to ensure all the cops were still awake. All Hudson Falls P.D. units answered the safety check promptly, except for 1 Queen 30 Officer Pappas. Pappas did not reply until the third call from Dispatch, and even then, his response was strained.

It was now 03:30 A.M., the temperature was at thirty-four degrees, and Tom had wandered over to Beat 30 to find and check on 1 Queen 30. Tom was driving southbound on Seven Palms Drive when he looked over to the golf course and saw what appeared to be a police car parked in the middle of the third fairway. As he approached, he caught 118 on the lower right-hand side of the trunk lid and knew that this was Pappas' patrol car. Pappas, who did not smoke, was sound asleep with the engine running. The heater was near full blast, and all the widows of the cruiser were rolled up. Tom stood outside Pappas's car for several moments, and there was no movement. Finally, Tom thought to himself, of all the times members of the squad suffered through the practical jokes of Officer Cyrus Pappas, this was a golden opportunity for payback!

Immediately, Tom contacted the other two officers on the squad. The three met at Amy's Donut Shop on Enterprise Street and Via Rojo Street. After Tom briefed the others, they returned and found Pappas still sound asleep in the patrol car. Hong Lombardi, who had a plan, stopped by his house, which was on the way, and picked up a 12 ft by 12 ft canvas painting drop cloth from his garage. Subsequently, when the three officers returned, they quietly unfolded the drop cloth. They placed it atop the patrol car covering all the windows. Pappas only moved slightly during the application. As all three officers quietly retreated, they did their best not to laugh!

Consequently, the call came to the watch commander at about 07:15 A.M. from the groundkeeper at Seven Palms Golf Course. He wanted to know why a partially covered police car was parked in the middle of his third fairway with the engine running. No squad member ever claimed knowledge of the incident. Pappas never played a practical joke on his zone partners again. Unfortunately, the groundskeeper was drinking buddies with the chief of police, and this little 'sleepover' cost Pappas three days off without pay.

Where the Dicks Hang Out

Detectives of the Hudson Falls Police Department work on general cases with an average caseload of one-hundred-and-ten cases per month. However, Detective Tom Stevens was having a pretty good week! He recovered two stolen refrigerators, two microwave ovens, and two dishwashers, with four suspects in custody for commercial burglary. Earlier that week, he had arrested two fourteen-year-old juvenile suspects. In interviews, the suspects bragged about what they had done and shared how they would expand their operation by murdering in the future to accomplish whatever they wanted. They thought they would create a *Crime Story*-style criminal empire by doing strongarm robberies.

The strangest case of the week started Wednesday morning with a prolific burglar named Manuel Hernandez, who had quite a unique modus operandi. Manuel Hernandez was not new to the El Camino Valley. Hernandez worked as a groundkeeper for a private Christian school in El Camino and lived in the maintenance shack on their lands. He had been capering and committing residential burglaries in the El Camino Valley for many years. The uniqueness of his crimes consisted of two parts. First, he always wore a flowing white bridal veil while committing the crime. Secondly, before leaving the residence, he would squat in the middle of the living room and defecate in a large pile. Hernandez's third habit was not as unique as many thieves have the same pattern. He would always keep a small trophy from each victim. In addition, Hernandez usually would select a home occupied by a senior citizen.

Furthermore, he considered himself a pretty slick thief who enjoyed the deed even more if the residence was occupied at the time of the crime. That is to say, several times in the past, the homeowner woke up or came upon Hernandez in the act of stealing items wearing his prized wedding veil. To that end, that is how the bridal veil was tied to Hernandez. One victim caught Hernandez squatting in mid-pinch of his victory shit in the center of their living room. Consequently, the sheriff's office had approximately thirty open cases with this M.O. and Detective Tom Stevens, twenty.

One cold January morning at about 3:00 A.M., a Hudson Falls P.D. patrol car turned southbound onto Butternut Avenue from westbound Quartz Ave. Manuel Hernandez saw the black-and-white, turned around, and started to walk southbound on Butternut Avenue at Honey Locust Ave. Hernandez left the sidewalk momentarily to stash a pillowcase. The pillowcase was full of stolen items from a residential burglary he had just committed. Due to the distance, the cop could not see where exactly Hernandez had tossed the bag, only that he left the sidewalk and moved toward the building out of his vision. The beat car stopped Hernandez on Butternut Ave south of Honey Locust Avenue.

Hernandez was stopped in the area north of a senior mobile home community. He was arrested on outstanding traffic warrants and transported to Hudson Falls, P.D., for booking. At the time of his arrest, Hernandez was found to have an injury to his right upper arm with a homemade and applied bandage. He had a long white flowing bridal veil under his tucked-in checkered flannel shirt and possessed a small ceramic fawn pug statue in his left front pocket. The jailer at Hudson Falls P.D. called Detective Stevens at home to let him know who was in custody and the items checked into his property. Detective Stevens placed a hold on Hernandez and his property pending his arrival later that morning.

At about 6:00 A.M., Tom sat at his kitchen counter sipping his third cup of coffee. A commercial for Preparation H came on the television in the kitchen just before the morning traffic and weather report. Tom was suddenly enlightened that this beautiful product would relieve painless bleeding during bowel movements.

Detective Stevens arrived at the Detective Bureau at quarter-to-eight that morning. He walked to the jail and met up with the jailer, who showed him the bridal veil and the ceramic pug figurine in Hernandez's possession. The detective took control of the two items and returned to his office to write a property receipt as evidence. Tom knew that the pug was a trophy from a recent job. At about 8:30 A.M., the residential burglary call came into dispatch from a mobile home in Ponderosa Pines. The homeowner woke up to discover the crime and the deposit in her living room.

Investigation revealed several items were taken from various locations within the home. The ceramic pug was part of a matched set belonging to the victim's great aunt. The pug Hernandez had, as determined later, was taken from a bookcase off the dining room in the center of the home. The other one was kept on the nightstand in the victim's bedroom. When Detective Stevens arrived on the scene, the seventy-nine-year-old female victim showed him where she had kept the two pieces. Detective Stevens then remembered the Preparation H commercial he saw on television earlier that morning. The detective examined the pile of excrement in the living room and observed what could be traces of blood. Detective Stevens took a swab of the suspected blood for future analysis.

When Detective Stevens returned to the office, he was greeted by Sergeant Henry Martinez, who proudly proclaimed in the form of a question, "Hey, is this where the dicks hang out?"

This was funny the first time Henry used it, but Sgt. Martinez had beaten the line worse than Rodney King!

Martinez said, "Hey Tom, one of my beat cars got a call of a suspicious bag found near the entrance to a business on South Butternut Avenue. It possibly contains the items taken from the residential burglary you are working on."

Detective Stevens replied, "That's great, Sarge! Can you have your guy bring the items and bag to the Detective Bureau? I will go ahead and inventory the items for evidence and confirm these are the stolen items from my burglary."

The items found at the business on south Butternut Avenue were stolen from the residence down the street. Detective Stevens notified supervision and dispatch that he would be transporting the prisoner to Duncan Sheriff for booking. The detective knew that with the injury to his right arm, Manuel Hernandez would need an 'Ok to book' from a doctor. Stevens drove Hernandez to the El Camino Valley Hospital Emergency Room for the 'Ok to book.'

Dr. Dan Taylor was the attending physician in the emergency room this afternoon. Tom met Dr. Taylor several years ago when they worked the midnight shift. Dr. Taylor must have been a cop in another life because he seemed to always be in sync when law enforcement hit the emergency room. Detective Stevens completed the paperwork for the charge nurse before the doctor saw Hernandez. Detective Stevens told Dr. Taylor about the charges pending against Manuel Hernandez and asked him to play along with his lead. He also said that Hernandez's injury might require a couple of stitches. He would like to have a fresh sample of Hernandez's blood on a piece of gauze used to treat Hernandez for comparison with the sample taken from the scene.

Manuel Hernandez was sitting on the side of the bed in examination area three. Detective Tom Stevens was standing next to the pulled curtain entry point when Dr. Dan Taylor entered the area and introduced himself to the detective and the suspect.

As Dr. Taylor removed the home-applied bandage from Hernandez's right arm, he asked, "How did you injure yourself?"

Hernandez, without thinking, replied, "I cut myself on a broken window."

Dr. Taylor started to clean the injury, and as he did so, he broke the news that Hernandez would need four stitches.

Once Dr. Taylor started the procedure, Detective Stevens said to Manuel Hernandez, "Ok, Manuel, let's recap; I have you in possession of a stolen pug ceramic figurine. You were stopped with a long white bridal veil stuffed under your shirt. Your M.O. is legendary. You live in El Camino but were stopped in the 900 block of South Butternut Avenue in Hudson Falls in a residential retirement community with no apparent business or purpose at 3:00 A.M. Additionally, a patrol officer saw you stash a pillowcase with stolen items near the front entrance of a business. I will dust all pieces of the glassware and ceramic items you took and compare them with your fingerprints.

And finally, I will take a sample of the blood I took from the scene and compare it with your blood taken just now from your treatment, and ok to book!"

In a brief attempt to defend himself or throw the detective off guard, Manuel Hernandez said, "You have nothing on me, detective. I always wear gloves when I caper, and besides, I didn't bleed anywhere in that house!"

Detective Tom Stevens replied, "Let me clarify; I will prove that the blood found on that piece of shit in that old lady's house came from the same piece of shit in this examination room!"

Dr. Taylor chimed in and said, "Oh, that will be easy to prove!"

After the examination, Detective Tom Stevens transported Manuel Hernandez to the Duncan Sheriff's Station and Jail for booking on one count of residential burglary. Through additional investigation, interviews, and recovery of further evidence, Detective Stevens cleared twenty residential burglary cases in the City of Hudson Falls, and Greenwood County Sheriff, thirty of the Hudson Falls Station. Even the City of El Camino cleared some cases in their jurisdiction.

Detective Tom Stevens had a terrific week.

The Rule of Three

Tom Stevens did well at the Hudson Falls Police Department. He was promoted to sergeant when he was twenty-six years old. He worked in most assignments as a supervisor, including Patrol, Investigations, Training, and Administration. Tom was an up-and-comer who made the promotional list for lieutenant yet always came out number two on the list. Tom would joke that he felt like Avis always coming in number two to Hertz.

The last promotional test for lieutenant was finally Tom Stevens' time. Tom tested in the number one position, followed by another person, and Tom's good friend Laura Harris in the third position on the list. Most law enforcement agencies have alliances with influential people and management groups formed at all ranks within the organization. Hudson Falls P.D. was no exception.

Unfortunately for Tom, the chief of police did not necessarily support or like the group of managers and supervisors that Tom had aligned himself with at the police department. For that reason, the chief brought Tom Stevens into his office during the next promotional cycle. He announced that he would not promote Tom to lieutenant and added that he needed a female in his upper ranks. Consequently, the chief stated that he would invoke a little-known personnel rule within the City of Hudson Falls Human Resources rules and regulations known as 'The Rule of Three.'

'The Rule of Three' allowed the chief of police to pick from the top three candidates on the promotional list. Subsequently, Laura Harris was promoted to lieutenant.

Tom and Laura had been good friends for many years since Tom broke her in as a new copper. She was well-qualified for the position, and Tom knew she would do an outstanding job. But unfortunately, Tom was in a dark period during this time of his life, and he could not understand how he was not promoted.

'The Rule of Three' had never been used in the eighteen years Tom was with the agency, but there was nothing Tom could do. Tom nearly allowed his feelings to consume him, and consequently, his friendship, which was based on respect and admiration for Laura, ended. Laura tried desperately to save the relationship, but Tom would have no part. Tom would eventually realize his mistake and tell his wife Marcie that his greatest regret in law enforcement was losing Laura Harris as a friend.

Community Services Bureau

The chief of police that promoted Laura Harris retired a little over a year later. The new chief, Warren Thompson, was selected by his predecessor from within the agency and, again not aligned with the same management group as Tom Stevens. Chief Thompson had called Tom into his office. After a lengthy discussion, Thompson declared that despite their differences in the past, he knew what Stevens could do. He wanted to create a new proactive street crime enforcement team that Stevens would supervise. The twist was Sergeant Tom Stevens would report directly to the chief of police. This was unheard of and, as one could imagine, not well received by the different management layers between sergeant and chief.

The new Community Services Bureau was created. This bureau consisted of a one-hundred-five-member volunteer services section that opened and staffed three substations in the community seven days a week from 0800-1700 hours. In the same way, volunteers were also involved with Citizens on Patrol, Crime Prevention, Crime Scene Investigations, Traffic Control, and other duties as assigned. The number of hours these members volunteered equaled over seventeen million dollars in savings for the City of Hudson Falls if the city were to have paid sworn officers to do these jobs.

The Hudson Falls Police Department Volunteers would receive national and statewide recognition for their accomplishments. The cherry on top was when they received praise from Congressman Sony Bono and President Bill Clinton. Indeed, after years of watching law enforcement mistakes, Sergeant Tom Stevens developed and organized the City of Hudson Falls Volunteer Services under the Incident Command System or ICS. He learned ICS from his friends at the Jefferson Division of Forestry.

The remainder of the Community Services bureau consisted of the Special Enforcement Team (SET), which worked on projects directly from the chief of police. The original SET members were two future chiefs of police for the City of Hudson Falls; Grant Turner and Francis 'Frank' Phillips. The majority of SET's activity involved working with landlords to remove the criminal element from the apartment or rental property and improve the residents' quality of life using the broken window theory of law enforcement and other crime prevention techniques.

The last group assigned to Tom was a part-time gang unit known as FIST or Formalized Intervention at Street Thugs. FIST was a county-wide task force that worked together in their enforcement actions. Being originated by the Greenwood County Sheriff's Department, on the street, the team was known as the Green FIST. SET and FIST trained with the Los Angeles Police Department CRASH unit out of Hollenbeck. This training was a couple of years after the LAPD scandal. Constantly challenged, none of the Hudson Falls cops could master the Hollenbeck burrito challenge of eating a five-pound burrito in one sitting!

Tom and Chief Thompson had several meetings and discussions. They decided that Community Services would work for the Administrative Commander that Tom had ties to, as indicated on the organization chart. SET would still receive its direction from the chief of police through the Community Services Bureau Sergeant.

The Silver Fox

One crisp Wednesday morning in the fall, Sergeant Tom Stevens got a phone call from the Detective Sergeant at the Burlington Police Department. Burlington is a city approximately fifteen miles west of Hudson Falls with a significant history of trains, skydiving, and crime. Sergeant Robert 'Bob' Fox had dreaded this phone call to his old friend. 'Bob' was an academy classmate of Tom at the Greenwood County Sheriff's Academy Class of Forty-Seven.

Tom and Bob worked an outer perimeter security detail for a week in the hot mountain sun while the 'Silver Fox' was visiting the Lance Bigelow estate in Emerald Valley. This fun-filled adventure took place one summer in August, right after Tom and Bob graduated from the academy. Bob became known as 'The Silver Fox' of Burlington at the time. The two sergeants kept in touch despite life's daily distractions.

Bob said, "Hey Tom, I hear you had a major FIST operation in Hudson Falls last month! I read the story in the *Press Herald*."

Tom replied, "Yeah, we had a good day. Gang problems and shootings should go away for a while. What can I do for you, Bob?"

With a heavy heart, Bob Fox told his friend, "We are losing the city. We need help! Please consider this phone call as an official request for mutual aid."

Bob had a solid work ethic, yet not all members of Burlington P.D. shared in his dedication. The two friends talked about how a shortage of staff and increased crime had taken a toll on the work product and morale of the officers in Burlington. As a result, the City of Burlington requested ten City of Hudson Falls officers to assist. Burlington would pay the Hudson Falls officer's salary at that time and one-half overtime.

Additional logistical and administrative details were worked out. On a Friday afternoon, Tom, his Special Enforcement Team, and eight Hudson Falls' FIST team members were sitting in the briefing room at Burlington P.D. about ready to go into service for the first time.

First, the Patrol Captain greeted the boys from Hudson Falls and thanked them for their assistance. He turned the briefing over to Detective

Sergeant Bob Fox and a twenty-minute wonder patrol sergeant named Stanley 'Stan' Daniels. He looked like he had just left supply with his new sergeant chevrons.

Bob held up a wanted flier of a homicide suspect named Orangelo (pronounced: Or-ran-gel-lo) Jones. Burlington P.D. had been looking for Orangelo for the past ten days. After talking about the crime this suspect was involved in and a brief criminal history, Bob added that Orangelo lived in the projects in town. The new sergeant, 'Stan,' joined in the conversation by almost proudly proclaiming that they, being Burlington Police, did not go into the projects because the residents, shoot at them!

Bob looked at his colleague Stan in disbelief!

Each member of the two Hudson Falls Teams looked back at Sergeant Tom Stevens, sitting in the back row, with the same question: "Are they serious, or are they just fucking with us?"

Before the briefing, Sergeant Stevens divided his teams into two-person units. He broke the news that Burlington P.D. requested his teams to drive Hudson Falls patrol cars during this operation. Burlington P.D. units were worse than those shown on the television show *Hill Street Blues*! At this time, the Hudson Falls officers realized how good they had it.

After the briefing, all units headed toward the projects where Burlington P.D. refused to go because of their safety. Two FIST units saw Orangelo talking to a group of friends near the basketball court. Once eye contact was made, Orangelo took off, running towards his mother's apartment. LaQuinta Jones's apartment was on the second floor on the east side landing. Orangelo ran up the stairs and slammed the door behind him.

As trained by the LAPD, a two-person FIST unit responded to back up the officers in foot pursuit. Two other FIST two person-units responded to the apartment building for perimeter security. Their purpose was to prevent ambush by firearms or by refrigerators being tossed off the roof onto responders or their vehicles.

The initial two officers kicked in the front door. As quite common, Orangelo's baby's Momma tossed her four-month-old baby daughter toward the officers. Per their training, the officers stepped aside and refused to catch the baby and allowing it to land on the furniture in the living room behind them.

Before this specific training, officers would always catch the baby. Then they would be attacked by residents of the apartment and often killed, holding a baby and trying to defend themselves.

Orangelo was found hiding under a bed in a back bedroom.

For the previous ten days, Burlington detectives had been looking for Orangelo, who was arrested for homicide without incident. Orangelo was transported to Burlington P.D. for booking within forty-five minutes of Hudson Falls' specialty teams being given the assignment.

About thirty minutes later, LaQuinta Jones and a handful of her friends and family went down to the Burlington Police Department to protest her son's arrest. Lemongelo (pronounced: Lea-mon-gel-lo) Jones, Orangelo's younger brother, was with his mother.

After a traffic warrant for Lemongelo was found, he was arrested. LaQuinta Jones, a thirty-nine-year-old black woman, built like an inverted triangle, with one very blue and one very dark brown eye, realized that she was no longer dealing with the Burlington Police Department. So, she proclaimed, "All you Popeye Chicken-eatin' mother fuckers should go back to Hudson Falls."

Tom, in turn, went to the local Popeye Chicken franchise and contacted the manager. Tom requested ten Popeye Chicken 'overseas' style hats that their front counter employees wore. After the manager complied, Tom met with all members of his specialty teams. He instructed his units proudly to wear their newly issued hats on patrol in the projects when they saw LaQuinta Jones or members of her family. "LaQuinta will realize that we Popeye Chicken-eatin mother fuckers are still in town!"

The Beginning of the End

The Hudson Falls Police Department had assisted the Burlington Police Department for close to a month. Sergeant Tom Stevens noticed the total lack of initiative among the Burlington officers. For instance, the Burlington officers would hang around the station and watch the television. Rarely would a Burlington officer pick up a call for service. Instead, they would always wait for the Hudson Falls, or at the time, recently arrived El Camino Police units, to pick up the call.

Tom had just cleared the south end of the City of Burlington after checking on SET and FIST, who was working a gang shooting south of Branford Ave on Chase Street. The Burlington Sergeant was in the station. As Tom pulled into the back station parking lot, he saw two other Burlington P.D. units parked behind the P.D. building. By now, Hudson Falls P.D were single officer units driving their cars, along with El Camino P.D.

Suddenly, Burlington Police dispatch came across the radio, "Attention any available Burlington unit, we have a report of a stabbing at a residence in the 2800 block of Pinta Court. This is brother vs. brother at a large wedding reception. The weapon used was a pocketknife."

Tom instinctually picked up the mic, "3 Mary 23 en route from the station."

Working the city's north end, Noah Evans also replied, "3 Mary 25 en route from 44th and Diamond Street."

Dispatch replied, "Copy units en route. Additional on the suspect Robert Tuigamala, Samoan Male, 33 years of age, 5'10", 350 lbs, black hair, and brown eyes. The suspect is wearing a blue floral shirt and tan shorts and is armed with a pocket knife. The victim is the suspect's brother Johnnie Tuigamala."

As Tom and Noah arrived in the area, they could hear the music from the live band in the backyard several blocks away. As the units entered the subdivision on Voyager Lane, they found that the entire length of Pinta Court was blocked with parked cars from Voyager Lane to the end of the cul-de-sac. The two officers parked their patrol cars on Voyager

Lane and walked the remainder of the way to the house at the end of the cul-de-sac where the party was taking place. The house was a two-story Spanish-style home with a tile roof. As they approached the house, Noah called in and confirmed the location. Tom Stevens requested two additional units for the large party.

The two officers met the victim Johnnie Tuigamala outside in front of the house. Johnnie told the officers that he and his brother had been arguing about their cousin's wedding all day. Finally, Bobby pulled out a five-inch pocketknife and sliced his brother's upper right arm. Johnnie received minor injuries treated by his wife before the officer's arrival. Johnnie added that Bobby was drunk. He wanted Bobby out of his house. Tom had estimated the attendance of this party to be approximately three hundred people.

Noah asked where Bobby was. Johnnie told him that the last time he saw his brother, he was inside the house in the living room.

As the two officers entered the house, they saw Bobby Tuigamala standing at the base of the stairways. When Bobby saw the officers, he turned and started to run upstairs; all three hundred and fifty pounds of him. Tom and Noah were right on his heels. Once he reached the top of the stairs, Bobby turned and swung at Noah. Noah could deflect the punch, and as he did this, Tom jumped on Bobby's back and attempted to place Bobby in a carotid sleeper hold.

Due to the size of Bobby's neck, the hold applied by Tom had little effect. Finally, after dancing with Tom for several minutes on the landing, Noah could get in position to tackle both the suspect and his sergeant. All three men came tumbling down the flight of stairs. When they landed on the bottom of the stairway, Noah was still attempting to handcuff Bobby, who was not fighting but merely resisting. Tom still had the carotid sleeper in place and was giving his all when suddenly, Bobby looked over at the patch on Noah's arm and asked, "Are you boys from Hudson Falls?"

Tom and Noah answered in the affirmative. Bobby suddenly stood up, Tom still on his back and Noah hanging onto his right arm. Bobby said, "My apologies, sergeant. I thought you guys were Burlington cops!" Bobby held his back and continued, "I didn't realize you guys were from

Hudson Falls. I apologize!" With that, Bobby Tuigamala was arrested on various charges and transported to Burlington P.D. for booking. Tom had never seen anything like this in his law enforcement career!

Four Hudson Falls FIST units responded to the scene minutes after Tom and Noah first contacted Bobby. No Burlington units ever responded to the call.

Six months later, the once respected and time-honored Burlington Police Department collapsed. The City of Burlington became the next contract city for the Greenwood County Sheriff's Office.

"Her Voice"

Sergeant Tom Stevens had just finished tuning up a three-year officer who had spoken unprofessionally and disrespectfully to one of the dispatchers on duty. The officer failed to follow agency policy and procedure by providing certain information to communications timely. He decided to take out his negligence on the dispatcher. After the ass-chewing, Tom sat back in his chair, closed his eyes, and thought, "Cops are such condescending assholes!"

There are two types of employees across all law enforcement agencies in America – Sworn and Non-sworn. Sworn employees are the officers and deputies who carry firearms and can place someone under arrest. Non-sworn employees are civilians working for the agency, such as dispatchers, jailers, crime scene technicians, and community service officers.

In most agencies, civilian or non-sworn employees are treated as second-class citizens. The overwhelming mantra is: If you aren't sworn, you aren't born! Sergeant Tom Stevens thought this attitude unacceptable, and he would never allow his cops to treat any civilian inappropriately!

Shaaron Claridge was a communications dispatcher for the Los Angeles Police Department who worked out of the Van Nuys Division. She is best known as the voice of dispatch from the crime-fighting television series *Adam-12*[7]. Tom Stevens, as a boy, was raised with her voice while he and his stepfather would regularly watch the show. He remembered how dispatch sent help to Officers Reed and Malloy whenever they needed help.

Communication knew where the officers were, and Tom thought them equally as much a part of the team as the two officers in the patrol car. Tom knew that when Malloy and Reed heard her voice, they would know everything would be all right. As a result, they could go home safely to their own families.

---

[7] Shaaron Claridge – Wikipedia Retrieved April 3, 2021
https://en.wikipedia.org/wiki/Shaaron_Claridge

In 1983, the movie *Blue Thunder* starring Roy Scheider was released. Tom took his wife Marcie to see the film. When Shaaron Claridge's voice came over the radio in the movie theater, it was like Tom had just met an old friend exclaiming to Marcie, "It's the dispatcher from *Adam-12*!"

Tom Stevens knew everything would be all right for the cops in the movie because he heard 'her voice!'

Sergeant Tom Stevens's voice was Brooklyn Green. Tom first met Brooklyn Green when he reported to the Hudson Falls Sheriff's Station for his high school ride-along program. Brooklyn Green was an old-school dispatcher/matron/supervisor for the Greenwood County Sheriff's Department with fifteen years of service. Her uniform was tailored with a long-sleeved shirt and a green female tie. Her desk, including a sizeable golden glass ashtray, sat behind the dispatch console. Brooklyn served as the backup dispatcher and supervisor for all office staff.

Later, when Tom became a deputy sheriff, Brooklyn would show him how to do the job as a dispatcher, often leaving him alone at the desk to sink or swim. She laughed, saying she had great confidence in him.

Tom noticed that whenever dispatchers needed a break, they would call Sergeant Jack Hall to cover the desk. When Sergeant Hall sat down at the console, he would take command like Captain James T. Kirk going into battle, no matter the circumstances.

Brooklyn Green was the same at commanding the console as Sergeant Jack Hall. Over the years, whether he saw it firsthand in the dispatch center or heard it over the radio, Tom knew that all the cops who worked with Brooklyn Green would be all right and go home at the end of their watch.

Two years after Tom left the sheriff's office and went to the Hudson Falls Police Department, Brooklyn Green retired from the Greenwood County Sheriff's Office. Her husband, George Green, was a strikingly handsome man with chiseled features and a retired lieutenant with the Greenwood County Marshal's Office. Brooklyn and George sold everything they had, bought a travel trailer, and were off to see the world.

Two years later, George and Brooklyn returned to the El Camino Valley. Tom and Marcie met them in a local Vaughn's Market one afternoon, and as they were leaving, Marcie told Tom how pretty Brooklyn's legs were. Tom hung the nickname 'Great Gams' on Brooklyn Green. George became ill with COPD and started pulling a cork earlier each day. Brooklyn joined Hudson Falls Police Department. She worked for another fifteen years until her second retirement from law enforcement ten years after her husband's death.

Brooklyn and Tom had come full circle. She took him under her wing and taught him the finer points of being a good dispatcher. She faithfully and consistently worked for Sergeant Stevens at Hudson Falls Police Department for many years. In thick or thin, Tom knew that Brooklyn had his back, and he was most comforted not in the backup units that were coming to help but in the fact that Brooklyn Green was on the radio.

Sergeant Stevens knew if he ever wrote a book, he would include the story of the love, respect, friendship, and admiration of a civilian non-sworn dispatcher – Brooklyn Green.

The Turquoise Symptom

The term, 'Turquoise Symptom,' was coined by Sergeant Tom Stevens after years of watching cops respond to heart-pounding and gut-wrenching calls for service. As tradition carried on, when the hotshot call was broadcasted by dispatch, units from all over the area would respond. Many officially, many on their own without telling anybody, and many others were self-deployed, thinking they needed to be there to help. Most went to the scene so they could get right into the action. Many others would go where they felt they should. Often many would simply show up and start to socialize with their fellow sophisticates once the adrenaline dump diminished and subsided.

To add to this problem, bosses, whether sergeants or lieutenants, frequently fail to take command of the incident. Mass confusion ensues due to an emotional reaction instead of a professional response. This first symptom of the Turquoise Menagerie Syndrome began supervisors' dilemmas and crises.

Tom first recognized this symptom during the response to the Norco Bank Robbery in Norco, California, on May 9, 1980, when the Riverside County Sheriff's Department and numerous local Police Departments responded to the robbery of a bank and the tragic death of a deputy sheriff. Sergeant Tom Stevens saw the same situation unfold again last week on Wednesday, July 18, 1984, during the San Ysidro McDonalds massacre and mass murder. Twenty-two persons were killed, and nineteen others were wounded. It took the San Diego Police Department and other law enforcement agencies seventy-seven minutes to neutralize the shooter, allowing for victim rescue.

Tom acknowledged that as law enforcement was responding to both of these events, the areas surrounding the crime scenes began to look like a sea of blue, tan, and green uniforms saturating the response location. Tonight, Monday, July 23, 1984, Sergeant Tom Stevens would experience his first tsunami in the State of Jefferson as that turquoise wave came crashing down his front door in Hudson Falls.

What was originally reported as a possible kidnapping, in the end, was determined to be a lover's spat. Eighteen-year-old Michael Jones went to see his girlfriend, seventeen-year-old Sarah Smith, at the Creekside Lodge in Markleeville in Alpine County, California. It was a slow night, and only a few customers were in the bar at the lodge. It was a typical warm summer evening, and customers were still talking in disbelief about what happened in San Diego last week. Sarah Smith worked as a nighttime clerk when Michael Jones entered the lodge. Michael motioned for Sarah to come over and speak with him in the lobby near the front door.

The conversation was ongoing about their relationship, and their voices were raised during the discussion. Finally, the night manager, Chris Evans, exited the office behind the front desk and glanced in the direction of Michael and Sarah.

Michael wanted to talk with Sarah in private, so he grabbed her by the arm and started to walk her out the front door to his car parked in the front of the lodge. Believing she was trying to resist Michael's actions, Chris returned to the manager's office. Chris took one more look out towards the lobby, and when he could not see Sarah any longer, he went back into the office to call for help.

Michael opened the front passenger door of his car and helped Sarah sit in the front seat. The night manager Chris was concerned and not sure what was happening, so he called the Alpine County Sheriff's Office to the lodge to investigate.

An Alpine County Sheriff's unit was nearby, and as the deputy approached the lodge approximately mid-block, he activated his overhead lights. Michael Jones, whose only criminal history was shoplifting, was on probation and panicked when he saw the red lights of the patrol car. Michael threw the now running car into reverse and sped away from the lodge with Sarah still in the front seat.

The Alpine Sheriff's office pursued the suspect vehicle, a red 1967 Ford Mustang with California plates. Sheriff's dispatch advised that based upon information from the reporting party, the call may be a kidnapping after a verbal disturbance. Chris knew that Sarah was seventeen years old, but more importantly, he also knew that her boyfriend, Michael was eighteen years old and considered an adult in the eyes of the law.

The pursuit continued northbound from Markleeville to the new Interstate 997. Once the pursuit got to the Interstate, a couple of California

Highway patrol cars entered the arena. Michael was not necessarily speeding, as he was only traveling 70 miles per hour. He was not driving recklessly; he was deep in discussion with Sarah, and she was deep in thought and conversation with Michael. The pursuit continued north on Interstate 997 and entered El Dorado County near Tahoe City. Three Eldorado County Sheriff's units, two Tahoe City units, and two more California Highway Patrol units joined in the pursuit.

As the pursuit continued northbound, units entered Placer County. Five additional units from both the Sheriff's office and local police joined the pursuit, headed towards Nevada County, where three more units waited to join in on the action. During the pursuit, Michael Jones never drove in a reckless manner other than speeding five to ten miles over the limit. Both Michael and Sarah had reconciled their differences, and now both were scared and did not know what to do with all of these cops chasing them.

The two young lovers told each other they loved one another and would get through this mess. Michael told Sarah that his Aunt Alice and Uncle Lucas lived in Hudson Falls in Greenwood County. Michael explained that his aunt and uncle raised him, and if anyone could help him and Sarah, it was his Aunt Alice and Uncle Lucas. Meanwhile, back in Alpine County, Sarah's parents had been contacted by the Alpine County Sheriff's Department. They were convinced that the evil Michael Jones had kidnapped their poor and helpless daughter because she would never leave her shift at the lodge. They told the deputies that they wanted to prosecute Michael Jones to the fullest extent of the law. All of this occurred while the two young lovers sped off toward Hudson Falls.

As the pursuit continued northbound on Interstate 997, the units entered Sierra County, where two additional units from the Sheriff's office joined in. The last county on the California side before the Jefferson State Line was Plumas County. Plumas County had three units from the Plumas County Sheriff's Department standing by to assist. As the pack of black-and-whites left California and entered the State of Jefferson, little did Michael and Sarah realize that Michael's luck had just changed, and he was now wanted for kidnapping with interstate transportation of a victim.

Whether it was for the possible federal charges now pending or the fact that it was a slow Monday night, or maybe none of the various supervisors were aware or cared what their units were currently doing, or could it be the always-used stick from cops that the radio was breaking up? They could not copy supervision canceling them with the order to return to their own county. All of the California units involved in the pursuit were now entering the State of Jefferson and now specifically Greenwood County from northbound Interstate 997 to eastbound on State Highway 76 towards the City of Hudson Falls.

Sergeant Tom Stevens was having a cup of coffee with Officer Noah Evans at the downtown 7-Eleven store when dispatch came up on the radio, "Queen 90, Hudson Falls."

Tom replied, "Queen 90, go ahead."

Hudson Falls Dispatch broadcasted, "Queen 90, Greenwood County is advising units from California have just entered Greenwood County from Northbound I 997 to eastbound S.R. 76. They are pursuing a Red 1967 Ford Mustang, bearing California plates of NCL 543."

Dispatch continued, "The vehicle is wanted for kidnapping, and the victim is currently in the vehicle's front seat. The suspect is a Michael Jones WM, 18 Years of Age, 6 ft. 2 in. 175 lbs. brown hair and brown eyes, wearing a red plaid lumberjack shirt and blue jeans with brown boots. Unknown weapons at this time.

Officer Laura Harris was working in Beat 30 on the west end of Hudson Falls. Sergeant Stevens told Officer Evans to head towards the west city limit and standby with 3 Queen 30 to take over the pursuit once it entered the city. Officer Evans in 3 Queen 40 left his sergeant and headed towards the west city limits. Sergeant Stevens contacted Officer Harris on the radio and gave her essentially the exact instructions he gave to Officer Evans in person.

Tom called Sergeant Jack Hall of the Greenwood County Sheriff's Department, who was already out in the field controlling the pursuit and his unit's involvement. Tom told Jack that once the suspect entered the City of Hudson Falls, his units would take over as the lead in the pursuit. Once the suspect left the city, Hudson Falls would be pulling out of the pursuit and transferring command back to the Greenwood County Sheriff's Office. Sergeant Hall agreed.

As Tom was heading westbound on S.R. 76 from downtown Hudson Falls, he could see the red and blue glow of the lightbars of the patrol cars from the Turquoise Tsunami as the wave, and the circus was coming to town. Moments later, Officer Laura Harris broadcasted, "Hudson Falls, 3 Queen 30, and 3 Queen 40 are pursuing the suspect from California eastbound on S.R. 76 from the west city limits." Dispatch replied, "3 Queen 30 and 40 are in pursuit; all units clear the air!"

However, the next broadcast came as a surprise to all involved. Michael was driving the red Ford Mustang and suddenly got a flat tire on the right front wheel, causing him to lose control of the vehicle at approximately sixty miles per hour.

The vehicle skidded onto the dirt parking lot of the Wilson Mobile Home Sales Lot at 2770 West S.R. 76 in the city. As the vehicle was sliding on the dirt parking lot, it struck the left front corner of one of the new mobile homes causing moderate damage and knocking the mobile home off of the temporary concrete support blocks it was sitting on.

As the now twenty-nine police cars descended with officers and guns drawn and all screaming different orders to the occupants of the vehicle, it became difficult for Officer Laura Harris and Officer Noah Evans to remove the victim, Sarah Smith, from the vehicle as many of the officers exited their patrol cars with the lights and sirens still going. Finally, Hudson Falls Police Department officers removed the uninjured Michael Jones and placed him into custody for the kidnapping, evading, and numerous other traffic violations.

As the suspect was being placed into the back seat of Noah Evans' patrol car, the high-fiving and back-slapping started with each officer proudly sharing their involvement with this "case of the year."

Sergeant Hall and his crew were already meeting with the Alpine County Deputy and the California Highway Patrol to confirm information and charges when Tom thought, "I'm sending this circus packing!"

Sergeant Stevens instructed two more of his officers, that showed up on their own, to go around and get the names, agencies, and employee identification numbers from all of the cops on the scene. Tom's officers were told to tell these officers remaining on the scene that they would need to come by the Hudson Falls Police Department to complete a supplemental report for their actions, in this case, to serve as witnesses in court.

The plan worked as Sergeant Tom Stevens knew it would! All of the cops on the scene left quicker than the clerk of a Dunkin Donuts, telling them they were sold out of coffee and donuts.

This Turquoise symptom was resolved.

To summarize, the turquoise symptom is created when a group of law enforcement officers, including police officers and sheriff deputies, respond to the scene of a catastrophic event or incident, whether natural or man-made, wearing their blue, tan, or green uniforms, without direction or control from an Incident Commander. As a result, the response is often emotional rather than professional and self-deployed rather than requested or dispatched. This failure of command and control as well as negligent supervision ensures these law enforcement professionals respond to the scene and merely form a clump of turquoise pending additional direction.

The Menagerie Symptom

The following sequence of events in the failure to establish a command and control by first-line supervisors is what Tom Stevens called the Menagerie Symptom. The Menagerie Symptom, or look at us and see how competent we are, comes right after the Turquoise Effect. We have all seen the Menagerie Symptom on major calls handled by big and small police departments and sheriff's offices throughout the country.

We have often seen when cops respond to the scene or nearby and park all over the place. They park on sidewalks, in people's yards, or wherever else they want to park. Many times, this action limits the ingress or egress from the scene.

This situation may not sound like a problem unless it is you or one of your people who have been shot and needs medical attention, and unfortunately, due to no ingress, we can't get to you to provide the help you need.

We have also seen barricaded suspect scenes where law enforcement officers have responded and are now standing around and doing nothing. An example would be where there are six officers in a medium-sized intersection to block it off. Two officers could easily accomplish the task, but now there are six standing around doing nothing.

Besides being a waste of human resources, the public can tell what we are or are not doing. It is especially not good to see these same officers laughing and joking at a mass casualty scene. This same image is even more embarrassing when we observe locations where cops are on top of each other and appear that they would be shooting each other if a shot would suddenly be heard in the area.

Whether manufactured or natural, catastrophic events or incidents also draw large crowds. It is often apparent when perimeters are set or not set, and the initial supervisors on the scene take crowd control measures.

Failure to have crowd control measures in place and not feeding the beast known as the media will present issues and obstacles in the Menagerie, which quickly could have been resolved at the beginning of the law enforcement response.

Sergeant Tom Stevens has worked with his friends in the fire service and learned both basic and advanced scene management and control techniques. He started working on standard response protocols to train law enforcement to effectively manage the first critical hour of a significant event or incident.

Supervisors must assess the situation[8]. They must conduct a size-up by asking themselves several questions, "What do I have? Location of the Incident? How many suspects? Type of weapons? Type of chemicals?" Supervisors must remember that simple information is challenging to obtain. Stress brings confusion.

Additionally, responding law enforcement must identify the danger zone. This must be done immediately to limit further exposure to danger. Once the danger zone has been identified and determined, that information must be broadcasted to the Communications Center. Tom Stevens had seen numerous times in his career the sector commander driving to the scene and subsequently parking his unit right in front of the suspect's location. The danger zone boundaries should be communicated to the general public in the affected area. No one, including law enforcement and Fire Department, will be allowed to enter the danger zone until authorized by the Incident Commander.

Tom Stevens also realized that law enforcement must control and contain the scene of mass casualty events. First, an inner perimeter must be established. No unauthorized personnel are to have access to the inner perimeter. If plainclothes personnel are used on the inner perimeter, they should be replaced by uniformed personnel as soon as possible. Supervisors should ensure responding personnel takes proper cover, and concealment, or in the event of a Hazardous-Materials incident, personnel should maintain a safe distance. The next step is to establish an outer perimeter. This perimeter is used to limit and control access into the emergency incident area.

One of the most critical tasks that must be accomplished is to identify and secure safe travel routes for emergency vehicles both to and from the scene. This is formally known as ingress and egress. The public and

---

[8] WMD RESPONSE: 7 CRITICAL TASKS - American Public University System. http://start.amu.apus.edu/common/dl/visor-cards/visor_wmd.pdf

Tom had seen time and time again where the responding cops parked anywhere and everywhere they wanted, with the result being blocked roadways and access to the scene preventing the ability to provide emergency medical treatment to law enforcement officers or victims. The outer perimeter prevents or controls access to the inner perimeter.

Finally, a media information area should be established, and a Public Information Officer should be requested. The beast must be fed, or it will find its information elsewhere. All other outer perimeter personnel should be aware of the following locations: The Command Post, the Staging Area, and the Media Information Area.

Moreover, an Incident Command Post should be established between the inner and outer perimeter. However, depending on the type of Incident, it should not be in the line of sight of the scene.

Most importantly, Tom Stevens realized that once initial assignments have been given to the responding resources, a Staging Area must be established. The Staging Area is used to control the deployment of personnel and material. The Staging Area should be found outside the inner perimeter. A Staging Area is never to be within view of the scene and should not be at the Incident Command Post. A unit should be assigned to the Staging Area to assume the duties of a Staging Officer. The Communication Center must be advised of the Staging Area location and the route to be used to gain access to it. It is imperative to inform all unassigned units responding to the scene to report to the Staging Area. Dispatch should be instructed to contact any responding mutual-aid agencies with the Staging Area information.

Finally, Tom Stevens knows that supervisors need to request additional resources. They should assess the need for additional personnel, specialized units, or other agencies. Often, supervisors will not request additional resources because they believe it makes them look weak or unable to accomplish their mission without outside help.

Remember. The Turquoise Symptom is the blending of all the colors of the uniforms responding to the event. The navy blue, light blue, green, and tan uniforms blend, forming a sea of turquoise one might see when they look out at a major incident and see all those unassigned resources just drifting and hanging around doing their own thing.

Without Incident Command, the effect is the creation of a menagerie once all responding staff or personnel have arrived. As the Oxford Dictionary defines the menagerie as a collection of wild animals kept in captivity for exhibition. Law enforcement must want to exhibit our resources. Without command and control, the resources go wherever and do whatever they want—many times, appearing incompetent or incapable of doing the very job they are required and were hired to do.

A failure of Command and the resulting Turquoise Menagerie Syndrome have contributed to post-traumatic stress disorder in numerous responding personnel. Sergeant Tom Stevens believes that failure to respond to significant incidents without knowing about command and control will evolve into cancer that can ruin a community and the resources charged with protecting them. The Turquoise Menagerie Syndrome has also destroyed careers, marriages, and individuals.

Gifts from GOD

Tom Stevens considered himself a man of faith. During his young adulthood, he studied numerous religions, most of which were a variation of Christianity. One thing that Tom objected to regarding organized religion was the application of artificial rules and regulations cloaked under the authority of God. One of Tom's most significant personal achievements that he was most proud of was when he thoroughly read the Bible from cover to cover. After that, Tom realized that he was a follower of Jesus Christ, not organized religion, and a follower of the word of God, the Holy Bible.

Tom was far from perfect. Despite his best efforts, he still had the mouth and language of a street cop! Tom rarely took the name of the Lord in vain, but there was always room for improvement.

Tom's favorite statement regarding the Bible was, "If you want to know how God himself thinks, read the Old Testament!"

Unlike most people, Tom's favorite part of the Bible was the Old Testament. Tom thought it might have been because most people forget about the Old Testament. After all, it is much more intense and restrictive, so people jump to the New Testament. Either way, Tom Stevens knew he was blessed and a child of the Most-High God! Tom often shared his thoughts with law enforcement chaplains, who never really replied but gave him a strange look.

When he saw her, Tom Stevens knew that Marcie Romano was a gift from God. On June 26, 1981, they were married at 2:00 A.M. A marvelous time for a cop to marry! Tom and Marcie ended up having three children together. The oldest is Gunner Stevens, as rough and tough as his name implies. He is all boy but has a soft spot for his mother. Gunner told his dad he wanted to attend the U.S. Naval Academy at Annapolis, Maryland. He planned on becoming the Captain of an aircraft carrier like the U.S.S. Enterprise. Gunner Stevens was born on July 8, 1983.

The middle child is Colt Stevens, born on April 12, 1985. Colt was a large baby weighing in at 9 lbs. 4 oz. He seemed to give Marcie nothing but trouble when he was conceived. To her chagrin, Colt has a strong

Type 'A' personality like his father. Colt had told his mother he would be a cop like his dad ever since he was five years old. Recently, to put his mother's mind and heart to rest, Colt assured her that he would not be a local cop, but he wanted to be a United States Marshall and track down fugitives. Despite Colt's best efforts, Marcie didn't feel any better.

Tom and Marcie's baby was Simone, born on December 20, 1987. Simone 'Candy' Stevens is a mini version of her mother with dark curly hair, green eyes, and freckles across her nose. It is not hard to imagine how she has her father wrapped around her little finger. Recently she proclaimed to the family that she would be a showgirl and General Manager at the Gold Canyon Resort and Casino, where her mom works.

The Stevens are a tight-knit family, and the boys are very protective of their mother and sister. Both are momma's boys, and Simone is a daddy's girl. All the children attend the Fairmont Preparatory Academy in Santiago Springs, and Tom works off-duty jobs to help pay for the private schooling of three children on a cop's salary.

Robert Henry was never at a loss for female companionship. Most females found him charming, including most females who worked out of the Hudson Falls Sheriff's Office. Robert was the first of the three amigos to be married. His first wife, Charlotte 'Charlie' Sullivan, sold real estate in her father's office in downtown Hudson Falls. Charlie and her brother Ben went to Hudson Falls High School with Tom Stevens and Jim Scott, and Ben was on the wrestling team with Jim.

Charlie and Robert were closely approaching their first wedding anniversary when Charlie and her girlfriend came into Nick's Place for a drink and to say hello to Marcie.

After the two girls were seated in a corner booth in the bar, Marcie approached the two and said, "Hey, Charlie! How have you been?"

Charlie smiled and replied, "Fantastic! Marcie, this is my friend Isabella. Issy, this is Marcie."

The two women smiled and shook hands. Marcie asked, "What can I get you two?"

Charlie replied, "Two glasses of Rose."

Marcie said, "Coming up, I'll be right back."

Marcie returned with the two glasses of wine. Charlie talked with Isabella and glanced at Marcie to include her in the conversation. "Robert and I have been together almost a year. I think he wants to start a family."

Marcie and Isabella showed their support for such a plan, and Marcie asked, "How soon?"

Charlie said that Robert had arranged a romantic dinner for them on their wedding anniversary. They would be in their apartment at 7:00 P.M. Charlie and Isabella stayed, had two additional glasses of wine, and split an appetizer. Marcie got busy with the evening happy hour rush, and business clientele were now starting to fill the bar at Nick's Place.

Less than a week later, on Robert and Charlie's wedding anniversary, Robert set a romantic table for two in their apartment. He lit the candles and started to play soft music. When Charlie came home, she was taken aback by the steps Robert took. First, he poured her a glass of white wine, and himself, three fingers of Seagram's V.O., poured neat.

As Charlie sat on the couch sipping her wine, Robert downed his drink in one gulp and told her, "I can't do this anymore! I want a divorce!"

He left the apartment and the marriage without ever looking back. The next evening, he spent time with a local badge bunny getting his wounds and other things licked in an attempt to get over his recent breakup.

Six years later, Robert married his second wife, Emily Anderson, at a large wedding at the Greenwood Country Club. Emily was ten years younger than Robert and was a dental hygienist. She was the daughter of a very prominent corporate lawyer in Greenwood. Robert and Emily were married for six years, and their union resulted in two children. The first was a boy named Thomas, and the second was a girl named Britney.

After their divorce, Emily worked as a dental assistant and married a neurosurgeon in the San Francisco Bay area. Emily's new husband attempted to adopt her children and relieve Robert of his financial responsibility. This had a positive effect on Robert because Robert stopped pulling the cork as much as he would regularly during each of these little trials of life. But unfortunately for all, Robert rarely saw his children after the divorce, as they moved to San Francisco.

When he returned home from the army, Jim Scott brought not only a killer physic but also a new wife named Elizabeth Williams. Jim met 'Lizzy,' as he called her, while banking at a Bank of America outside Fort Bragg, North Carolina. Lizzy was the human form of a 19th-century librarian caricature, and Jim was smitten with her. The only problem with Lizzy was that she was about as fascinating, charming, and personable as a house plant. Despite being a great cook, Jim eventually could stand no more, and after two years of marriage, Jim and Lizzy were through.

Jim Scott remained single until he moved to Lone Pine, Alaska, where he went to work as a police officer. Jim eventually became the Chief of Police of Lone Pine. One day at a city department head meeting, the city manager introduced the new Fire Chief, Amelia Hernandez from Wyoming. Amelia had two children, David, who was thirteen, and his sister Mia who was ten. The Chief of Police took a particular interest in welcoming the new Fire Chief to the community. Jim and Amelia dated for nine months before they were married. They remained married with no children together until they retired from government service.

A New Start

After twenty-two years in Greenwood County law enforcement, Tom Stevens had enough! Marcie always talked about moving to Lakeland County and working at one of the casinos or resorts. Tom was about to make her wish come true. So, after a few trips to Santiago Springs, the Stevens' packed up their belongings and moved to the 'State Capital.' Tom worked a few security jobs in Santiago Springs until he was hired as a civilian manager, lieutenant equivalent, for the City of Santiago Springs Police Department. Tom was the manager for the Records Section and eventually the Communications Section. This civilian position resulted in a twenty thousand dollar-a-year pay cut from his sergeant's salary in Hudson Falls.

For some reason, people from Santiago Springs enjoyed hearing cop stories from Greenwood County. Several months before Tom started work in Santiago Springs, Greenwood County Sheriff made national news by chasing a pickup truck full of illegal aliens northbound on Interstate 997 from the California border. The chase was followed by a news helicopter from Reno. When the truck stopped on the side of the freeway, all occupants in the truck's bed jumped out, running for the fences. Unfortunately, the deputies pursuing did not realize the news copter was overhead filming, so they started to dispense street justice to the illegals via their nightsticks.

Many cops came from back east and down south to work in Lakeland County. Tom Stevens was quite an anomaly coming from Greenwood County to Santiago Springs. Whenever people would ask him what part of Greenwood County he came from, Tom would ask them if they remembered that news report on the illegal aliens on the freeway.

When they said, "Oh yes,"

Tom would reply, "That's where I'm from!"

After spending two years at the Santiago Springs Police Department, the call of the wild became too much for Tom to ignore. He wanted to go back to being a copper again! However, his colleagues told him he could not work for the Santiago Springs Police Department because he would likely be fired! Hands down, everyone said that the best agency for Tom to work for was the Lakeland County Sheriff's Office! That was the only agency to which Tom applied.

Marcie told Tom she would support his decision to return to law enforcement only if he applied to the Lakeland County Sheriff's Office in 2000 and not the Greenwood County Sheriff's Department in 1976. "You can't go back in time!" Marcie said. Tom agreed, and when he got the call to come work for the Lakeland County Sheriff's Office, he felt like he had just got called up to pitch for the New York Yankees!

Sergeant Tom Stevens considered his legacy at the Hudson Falls Police Department versatile. First, he trained the first female officer, who became very successful in her career. He was an original founding member of the National Association of Field Training Officers. Second, he developed and expanded a nationally recognized citizen volunteer program. This program saved the City of Hudson Falls millions of dollars in costs if sworn employees had performed these services. Lastly, he created the Special Enforcement Team, which he initially staffed with two future chiefs of police for the City of Hudson Falls.

He Ain't Horny; He's My Brother

Simon Moore was promoted to sergeant and reassigned from Sector 4 in Santiago Springs to Sector 1 in Rockwell. When first built, it was known as the Rockwell Substation. But as cops will, it was shortened to 'The Rock.' As soon as one of the cops appeared on the radio and proudly announced he would be behind 'The Rock,' the name was changed to North Lakeland Substation or N.L.S.

After sixteen years of donating his time to the agency, Warren Hill started to work full-time with the Lakeland County Sheriff's Office. He, too, was assigned to Sector 1 and worked for Simon Moore. Simon's dry sense of humor and Warren's razor-sharp wit was a recipe for an Internal Affairs or, as the LCSO called it, a 'Professional Standards' complaint.

That complaint came one warm summer evening in July at a small home in south Rockwell, which the cops called Lower Rockwell. Suddenly, an alert tone came across the radio regarding a hotshot call of domestic battering. Dispatch advised that one brother took a baseball bat to another, which resulted in serious head injuries. The father now separated the brothers, and medical assistance was needed. Deputy Hill and his zone partner quickly picked up the call and responded Code 3. Three adjoining zone cars also assisted with crowd control because they knew that all the neighbors would be outside gawking and adding their opinions and comments once the cops arrived.

Humidity was high, and Warren could feel the sweat running down his back under his protective vest. Once he arrived, he found the victim inside a small wooden home with dirt floors. A scantily clad young woman of perhaps twenty years old was crying in the kitchen. The father and brother were in a back bedroom, still in a heated argument. A baseball bat lay on the couch next to the victim.

As the investigation continued, the father, Mathias Robinson, explained that his oldest son Antoine Robinson, who was in the back room, was married to Shanice in the kitchen. But, the father continued, his youngest son Booker Robinson, who was hit upside the head several times with the baseball bat, was the victim on the couch. The father explained that Booker has always admired Antoine over the years and always emulated him in everything Antoine did or pursued. If Antoine played baseball,

Booker played baseball. If Antoine liked Chrysler's 300s, Booker liked Chrysler 300s. If Antoine made an impression of Denzel Washington, Booker made an impression of Denzel Washington.

The family lived together in this small three-bedroom house with no air conditioning. Listening to Antoine and Shanice doing the horizontal Mambo every night, with the windows open to cool the home, became too much for Booker to stand for another night, and subsequently, he felt it was his turn to take a crack at Shanice, as well! Shanice and Booker were going at it on the couch in the living room. Dinner was cooking on the stove. And Antoine and his dad walked in the front door. Booker looked over his shoulder at Antoine and his dad, knowing the ass-whipping was coming. He planned to finish what he had started. Booker enjoyed the thrill of victory and the agony of defeat simultaneously!

After the scene was secured, Lakeland County Fire Rescue treated the victim. Simon Moore's corporal was tied up on a call in Dayton, so Simon responded to check out the call. When he arrived, Simon exited his vehicle without a hair out of place, looking as if he had just come out of a walk-in freezer sucking on a Grape Slurpee from a 7-Eleven store. Deputy Hill excused himself and stepped away from Mr. Robinson to brief Sergeant Moore. As Warren started, Simon switched the Slurpee from his right hand to his left. Moore held up his right hand as if he was stopping traffic and said, "Like Dr. Suess."

Warren paused for a moment and relayed all of the information gathered in the investigation into a perfect work of poetry. Lasting several minutes, another deputy standing by heard the dissertation. He said he would swear that Dr. Suess himself had just finished reading his latest book aloud. As Warren spoke, Simon took another sip of his drink, biting the plastic straw hard. His eyes closed, and his body started shaking as he desperately tried to hold in his laughter in front of the victim's father, who was only feet away.

Suddenly, Mr. Robinson came over to the sergeant and deputy and angrily asked, "What's so funny?" Sergeant Moore told the father that Deputy Hill had just told him a joke, and he apologized for his actions. However, the father did not buy it. The complaint came to Simon's lieutenant from Professional Standards the following day. Both Simon and Warren received a counseling sheet. Booker was transported to Rockwell Hospital, where he recovered from his injuries.

I'll Have Mine With Pepperoni

After completing the month-long orientation training at Central Operations, Deputy Tom Stevens was assigned to Sector 1 to start his four-month Field Training and Evaluation Program. Tom's first Field Training officer was Benny Cucinella. Tom was introduced to Benny during the 300- shift briefing with Sergeant John Moore. Benny was a lateral from the Springfield Police Department, but you would swear he just got off the plane from New York if you talked to him.

After the briefing, Benny and Tom walked to Benny's patrol car, parked at the rear of the North Lakeland Substation. As Benny secured some items in the vehicle's trunk, Tom noticed a large ice chest behind the roll bar cage on the back seat on the driver's side.

Tom asked, "What's this for?"

Benny replied, "A good cop never gets wet or goes hungry!"

Benny opened the ice chest, where he had a wide variety of cold cuts, cheeses, crackers, olives, and chopped veggies with ranch dressing.

Benny told Tom to drive and gave him directions to a dirt road behind the dump in south Rockwell. On this lonely dirt road, Benny began to explain the workings of all the equipment in the center console of the 2000 Ford Crown Victoria patrol car. He started by picking up the Motorola radio mic and explaining to Tom that this was a microphone for the sheriff's radio. To speak into it, you hold it approximately three inches from your mouth, push this button, and hold it down the entire time you talk. Benny reminded Tom to keep the button pushed down for a second before the radio transmission so he would not cut himself off.

Benny did an excellent job painstakingly explaining every radio function, from the off-and-on- switch to each channel's volume. He did the same with the lightbar and sirens. The two deputies listened to the yelp, the wail, and the hi-low. Benny explained how to use these sirens to clear an intersection while responding to a call Code-3. Benny asked Tom if he would like to put them in service.

Tom replied sure, picked up the mic, and said, "Lakeland 311A Cucinella/ Stevens 10-8 unit 572."

Dispatch replied, "311A 10-8 at 1602 hours."

Benny told Tom, "You did very good!"

Tom replied, "Thank you, sir."

As the two deputies started to drive away, Benny told Tom to call him 'Benny.'

Tom replied, "Sounds good, Benny. Thanks."

Several minutes passed when Benny asked Tom, "So Tom, what did you do before becoming a deputy?"

Tom said, "Well, I worked in Greenwood County, where I retired. My wife Marcie always wanted to live in Santiago Springs, so after I retired, we moved here."

Tom realized no good cop would settle for that answer, and Benny did not disappoint.

Benny continued, "What did you do before you retired?"

Tom said, "I was a cop for twenty-two years! I retired as a sergeant who ran a special enforcement team that worked from the chief's office."

Benny, in exasperation, asked, "Why didn't you say something? I would not have bored you with all that radio and siren shit!"

Tom replied, "Benny, you were doing your job and an outstanding job! Who am I to stop you on such a roll?"

Benny laughed and said, "OK, Sarge, let's go fight some crime!!"

Later that shift, 311A picked up a call in Zone 13 for training purposes. Three black males in their early twenties robbed the Domino's Pizza at Chester-Springfield Rd and John F. Kennedy Trail at gunpoint. After that, they fled in a dark-colored sedan southbound on the trail into the city of Santiago Springs. As Tom took the call, Benny noticed that several pizzas were stacked on the counter, ready for delivery. However, the business owner was in fear for his driver's safety and had told Benny that he was shutting down his business for the night. All of his customers were notified they would not be receiving their orders.

By the time Tom had cleared the call, he saw Benny with an armload of large pizza boxes as he put them in the patrol car's back seat. Benny brought out a total of twelve pizzas that, according to Benny, the owner said he would throw away. So, for the next twenty minutes after the call, 311A delivered pizzas to all of the zone cars in Sector 1 and two homeless camps. One in the south end and one in the north end. After that night, Tom realized that Benny Cucinella was his kind of cop!

No Need for a Tape

After the alert tone pierced the silence inside the patrol car, a dispatch came across the air. It said, "Special Attention Zone 12, a report of suicide via shotgun has just occurred on South Ash Park Road south of Rockwell Blvd. Lakeland County Fire Rescue is en route."

Dispatch continued, "Reporting party, Donna Davis, advised she will flag you down. Davis is a white female 35 years of age with a white top and blue jeans. Responding units handle code three!"

Bobby Hernandez was the first to respond, "County 312A is en route from Oak Canyon Road and McKinley Boulevard."

Dispatch replied, "312A copy at 1725 hours."

As Tom Stevens grabbed his mic, he looked over at George Fontana and asked, "Do you want to pick up this call?"

George Fontana said, "You bet."

Tom broadcasted, "Lakeland 313B will handle the suicide from Pine Loop Road and Marion Drive for training purposes."

Tom lit up the lightbar responding Code-3 to the call in the adjoining beat.

George Fontana was Tom's next Field Training Officer. He was a lateral transfer to the sheriff's office from Springfield Police Department.

As they responded, George told Tom, "I've never handled one of these that just occurred."

Tom, who was not trying to be a wise guy, told George, "Don't worry, I'll walk you through it!"

George laughed and said, "Hey, wait a minute, I thought I was the FTO, and you were the trainee!"

Tom replied, "We will get it covered."

When 313B arrived on the scene, Lakeland County Fire Rescue had already checked on the victim,

Edgar Ferrara, who was inside the house in the living room. He sat on the couch with a 12-gauge Remington shotgun between his legs. Edgar Ferrara was an unemployed advertising executive who called his now ex-girlfriend over to his house. After a few moments of arguing with her, he put the shotgun barrel into his mouth and pulled the trigger.

For that reason, the firefighters were now attending to the reporter, Donna Davis, who, until minutes ago, was the victim's girlfriend. She was visibly shaken outside the home by the fire truck. Deputy Hernandez had already interviewed Donna Davis. He discovered that the victim and Donna had been drifting apart due to his apparent drug abuse. The victim had called Donna to the house to ask her if they could start over. She declined due to an experience with a junkie in her past. Edgar put the shotgun in his mouth and splattered his brains all over the wall behind him.

Sergeant Moore came up to Tom and told him that he had called Homicide Detectives, which was standard protocol. They should be there within the hour. Sergeant Moore asked Tom if he needed anything else, and Tom told the sergeant he was good.

Deputy Bobby Hernandez approached Tom. Bobby was a three-year deputy and member of the SWAT team. He was very personable and had a strong desire to learn as much as he could about becoming the best deputy possible.

Bobby said to Tom, "I have never investigated a call like this. Can I hang around to pick up some tips?"

Tom told him, "Absolutely!"

Tom explained some of the standard issues and points that needed to be addressed in the initial report. Bobby asked Tom if he thought the Homicide Detective would let him hang out and observe or help with the investigation.

Tom could appreciate the desire of the young deputy. He took a deep breath and said, "Listen, Bobby, chances are, you are going to get one of the two types of Homicide Investigators. The first will be an old-time seasoned homicide detective who will be happy to take you under his wing. While he conducts his investigation, he will point things out and share his observations and opinions. Or, you will get a condescending asshole who thinks he is God's gift to criminal investigations. How dare you, a common patrol deputy, ask him to educate, much less speak to you for any length of time?"

As Bobby, Tom, and George were standing outside waiting for the Homicide Detective, they saw

Sergeant Moore. He told them that Donna had been transported to the hospital to be evaluated due to her high emotions. Within moments, a red Porsche 911 Carrera pulled up to the scene and parked right in front of the three deputies.

The driver of the Porsche opened the driver's door. Tom saw the striped long-sleeve Lee Iacocca dress shirt with the white cuffs and initials in the same color as the shirt's stripes. Tom looked over at Bobby and said, "You're fucked, kid!"

The detective asked, "Who's call, is it?"

Tom replied, "Mine."

Tom gave the detective a thorough briefing of what the initial investigation had determined.

In the usual condescending fashion, the detective asked Tom, in a demeaning voice, "Did the F.D. run a strip EKG Tape to confirm the victim was deceased?"

Tom, who never had much use for assholes, replied, "Detective, I can guarantee that mother fucker is dead!"

Sergeant Moore, who did not necessarily like this detective, just chuckled.

In a less obnoxious tone, the detective asked, "How can you be sure?"

Tom replied, "If you go inside, you will find the victim on the couch in the living room. He is the one whose head looks like a soup tureen with a lower jaw and eight teeth. It won't be hard to miss. It's that new piece of art on the wall!"

Later that night, at the end of watch at the briefing table, Sergeant Moore read Tom's suicide report when he told Tom, "You did too much."

Tom said, "I just did the investigation as I usually would."

The sergeant asked, "What if this report's information was different from the information in the detective's report?"

Tom answered without hesitation or emotion, "The detectives' report would be wrong."

Sergeant Moore chuckled again, approved the report, and told Tom, "You will do fine here!"

Critical Tasks

Tom Stevens' final field training phase with the Lakeland County Sheriff's Office was in Sector 1 day shift on Sergeant Travis Nelson's Squad. Many considered this squad to be one of the best in the agency. To illustrate, Travis Nelson was a poster cop and a cop's cop! He had lateralled from the Reno Police Department several years ago. He believed he would have more opportunities to put bad guys in jail with Lakeland County.

As a young patrol deputy, Travis Nelson worked on the crime-infested South John F. Kennedy or JFK Trail. Deputy Nelson came across an auto stripper in the numbered streets who suddenly turned when confronted. He shot the young deputy in the gut. The suspect ran off, and Deputy Nelson chased him down within about a block and arrested him. Immediately before calling in, those shots were fired, and Travis Nelson requested an ambulance. The young deputy later became a long-standing member of the agency SWAT team and trainer in Officer Safety and Street Survival Tactics. Agency-wide, the consensus was that Travis Nelson was a true badass!

Sergeant Travis Nelson's corporal was Paul Davis, who worked the streets with the same skill as his Irish ancestors, who walked the foot beat. Paul could mingle with hookers, hypes, con artists, and lowlifes as if he was going to a family reunion. He was a master at developing and working informants, and many of his tips helped numerous vice and narcotics detectives clear the paper from their desks.

Travis Nelson's squad was considered the greatest because their whole purpose in life was to arrest bad guys! In addition, they were very good at it! Travis Nelson did not care about calls pending or response times, and he was often heard saying, "There were calls pending when I started here, and there will be calls pending when I leave here!"

The entire squad had been trained to react to each hot shot call that came over the radio consistently and professionally. Sergeant Nelson also believed wholeheartedly in applying command and control measures on each in-progress call to which his squad responded. After the alert tone, two-zone cars responded to the scene; one was to run with the canine unit if needed, and the other took the initial report.

Sergeant Nelson would set the perimeter and evaluate the need for the canine unit and air support from Air-1, one of three sheriff's helicopters. Other units would switch to the alternative radio channel and receive their perimeter assignments from Sergeant Nelson. All perimeter units would respond to their assigned location, where they would activate their overhead lights and get out of the vehicle to keep an open eye for the suspects.

This process would drive the suspects to the ground, assisting the canine unit in the apprehension. Most times, it would result in the perpetrator's arrest. Once trained and practiced, this process was accomplished as smoothly as any deputy calling in a vehicle stop. The entire process was consistently done on any in-progress or just-occurred crime.

Sergeant Nelson would often say, "You did not want to be the supervisor working when a deputy is shot. Your failure to follow the command-and-control measures that the Lakeland County Sheriff's Office Training Division had dubbed Critical Tasks, resulted in the suspect escaping. You never wanted to be 'That Supervisor'!"

Failure to Educate

Tom Stevens's last Field Training Officer was Asa Williams, a true southern boy born and raised in Apopka, Florida. Asa Williams started his career at the Hathaway Police Department and came to the Lakeland County Sheriff's Office as soon as possible. Marcie Stevens called Williams 'Bad Asa' after the Fabrizio Pizza commercial character. Asa seemed to like the nickname. Deputy Williams admired Corporal Davis, his work ethic, and how he got the job done. He had absolute and unquestionable loyalty to Sergeant Travis Nelson.

Tom and Asa were given the daily task of making the run to Operations bringing the mail and the previous day's reports to headquarters. Asa, who liked Tom from the onset, decided to give Tom some advanced officer training. The two deputies stopped at several locations within Operations, including a brief stop at Fleet. Asa told Tom about the process of how he would receive his first patrol car. Next, Asa said they would meet Emma, the Patrol Division Chief's Administrative Assistant.

Emma was the one who made the vehicle assignments when the cars were available. In the past new and stupidly arrogant young deputies would call and demand Emma to say when they would receive their patrol cars. They were treating this civilian employee as if she was a second-class citizen. These same deputies would ask themselves and their sergeant why they were driving a ten-year-old patrol car with eighty-five thousand miles and a bent frame. Car Pool vehicles were in better condition!

When Tom met Emma Caruso, he was amazed at how much she looked like his wife, Marcie. She was a couple of years younger with the same long dark brown curly hair, pale complexion with freckles on her cheekbones, and piercing green eyes. When Tom met her, he immediately told Emma and pulled out a picture of Marcie to show Emma the similarities. Emma agreed with Tom and smiled in amazement at the photo of her older sister. After Emma and Tom chatted for a few minutes, the two deputies left Operations and started back towards Rockwell.

Sergeant Nelson had been driving southbound on Lincoln Ave near west Adams Street. He looked over at a group of six black males hanging outside Louie's Liquor Store next to Tidwell Apartments. The sergeant recognized one of the six as Antwan James, whom he had arrested in the past for possession, and ADW. As the sergeant completed his U-turn, two of the six fled via a hole in the chain-link fence towards Tidwell Apartments. South Rockwell units heard, "Lakeland, Sierra 11 be out with six black males at Louie's, Adams, and Lincoln" Dispatch replied, "Copy Sierra 11 Adams and Lincoln with six." Within moments Charlie 11, Corporal Davis, arrived on the scene to assist in the investigation. Corporal Davis started running the remaining four subjects as residents of Tidwell Apartments started looking out their apartment windows. When dispatch returned with a hit on Antwan for a probation violation on a shoplifting case, Asa and Tom arrived on the scene. The group started talking smack, saying, "You didn't need to call all these Cracker Motherfuckers."

Tom said, "I'll take him off your hands, Sarge." Travis Nelson nodded his approval. Tom told Antwan he was under arrest for an outstanding warrant for Violation of Probation. After he was searched and the cuffs were applied, Tom said, "I'm sorry, let me introduce myself to you. I'm Deputy Stevens from Greenwood County." Tom continued, "You need to educate me. I was raised in Los Angeles County and worked in Greenwood County. Most of the blacks I dealt with preferred red or blue (referring to the Bloods or Crips). We never had a hard time communicating with each other. We always knew where each of us stood. So, I have a question as I am not from here. I am still trying to learn about Central Florida and Atlanta's charming southern life and quaint customs. Those customs you all brought here when you came to work in the hospitality industry in Santiago Springs. I have a question. I've been called a Cracker Motherfucker by you and your friends here in the hood numerous times. I am not familiar with that term. So I would like to know when you call me a Cracker Motherfucker, is that supposed to have the same effect on me as me calling you a Fucking Nigger? If so, I'm just not feeling it. Sorry."

Antwan James did nothing but mutter under his breath.

The next thing Deputy Stevens said to Antwan was, "Watch your head," as he placed him into the back seat of Bad Asa's patrol car.

Tom turned around to walk back to his colleagues. The remaining three subjects did not have outstanding warrants and slipped through the chain-link fence. They started running toward the center of Tidwell Apartments, yelling, "Fuck you, man! Fuck you, Cracker Motherfuckers."

Tom walked up to his sergeant, corporal, and field training officer. Each was still laughing at the education session and the lack of response from Antwan James, who was usually a loudmouth. Finally, Sergeant Nelson told Tom he could go to work for him anytime! Corporal Davis agreed.

Three days before his last shift with Bad Asa, Tom got an email from Emma Caruso instructing him to respond to Fleet Service and pick up his assigned patrol vehicle. Emma had mentioned that the car was not new, but she thought he would like it. Upon his arrival, he was taken out to the yard and given the keys to unit 1101, a one-year-old Ford Crown Victoria with 15,000 miles. The unit came from Sector 5, the Casino and Resort Area, and was assigned to a female deputy. The car would later be called his favorite by Deputy Tom Stevens, who finally realized, "I'm not in Greenwood anymore!"

"Maynard"

Bernard Rothchild was in Phase Three of his Field Training and Evaluation Program. He had been riding with Warren Hill as his Field Training Officer for the previous three days. Bernard soon realized that you either loved or hated Warren Hill. At this point, he was unsure. Little did he know that his mind would be made up after this day shift. Bernard was a high brow who lived with his parents in Stagecoach in western Lakeland County. Stagecoach is located on the Fleming Chain of lakes and is known as a local status symbol of wealth and grandeur.

Bernard's mother could not understand why her son did not want to join the family law firm. Why, instead, did he want to work at the sheriff's office and with the dregs of society? She told him he would have to park it behind or in the garage once his take-home patrol car was issued. She could not stand the thought of that car parked outside in front of her house! Bernard told all his Field Training Officers and anybody else who would listen that he would be a Sector Captain in the sheriff's office within ten years.

Bernard still introduced himself as Bernard when he met someone new. So, when Warren Hill met him the first time, he said, "Dude, Bernard is way too formal for me. I'm calling you Ben, okay?" So at least for Phase Three, Bernard was now known as Ben.

Aunt Hattie's was a gay bar located along the Promenade corridor between the City of Santiago Springs and Lakeland County. And near Lawson Monroe Catholic High school, where Warren Hill and his lieutenant 'In the dark' Hunter went to school.

Unit 214 received a report of vandalism to a vehicle at the location. Dispatch further advised the caller, Doug Williams would meet the deputies inside the bar. As they responded, Warren told Ben that he might have difficulty locating the bar because it had a conservative exterior. Aunt Hattie's looked more like an architect's office than a gay bar. Warren knew 'Doug with a Rug' Williams before Warren was a deputy when he worked for his father at the Hill Music Company. Warren delivered cigarettes to several 'Ol man Williams' vending machines and bars in the Santiago Springs area in the 1970s.

Upon their arrival, Ben noticed this was the most elegant bar he had ever been to. It looked like the nostalgic Hollywood of the 1930s and 40s. Doug came from behind the bar, gave Warren Hill a big hug, and told him how glad he was to see him! Warren introduced Ben to Doug and told Doug that Ben would be investigating the vandalism. As Ben continued his investigation and report, the Budweiser man arrived for his twice-a-week delivery. He propped the door open to maneuver his dolly more easily. The morning sun's light shone through the open rear bar door. Suddenly she appeared!

The most beautiful creature Ben had ever laid eyes on. She paused in the bar's doorway, and when she did, it appeared that she had just been sent down from heaven to be presented from the God above for Ben's pleasure. She was perfect! She was five foot seven inches tall with curves in all the right places. Her platinum blond hair curled down to her pale white shoulders. Her eyes looked like polished green emeralds, and her full pouting lips were red like a fire engine. She had a small round black mole on her left cheek and wore a white dress identical to Marilyn Monroe's in her classic movie *The Seven Year Itch*.

She dropped her keys on the dance floor as she entered the bar. As she started to bend over, she partially exposed her right thigh to the point you could tell she was wearing white thigh-high stockings held up by a white garter belt. Ben was Johnny on the spot as he bent over to pick up her car keys. He looked at them, and the keyring said 56 Thunderbird.

Ben asked the woman, "Do you have a 56 Thunderbird?"

She replied, "I sure do, a white one in the parking lot. Same color as my dress."

They stood up together and were only inches apart when she said to him, "You are so sweet, Sugar. What's your name?"

Ben distinctly said, "Bernard Rothchild." He could tell she was wearing Chanel No. 5, remembering the fragrance when his mother would shop at Saks Fifth Ave.

Ben was also starting to realize blood flow to certain portions of his anatomy.

The Goddess said, "Oh, Barney! You are so cute; I could eat you up!"

Ben felt the beginning trembling of his body towards orgasm as she spoke his name! Ben did not know what to say. Finally, she excused herself as she turned and walked to the ladies' room. Ben was following her every move.

Moments later, she came out of the ladies' room and called out to Doug, who was still behind the bar dealing with the Budweiser man, "Doug, there is water all over the lady's room floor! How can you expect a lady to use the facility in this condition?" she continued, "Be a dear and come clean it up for me!"

At this point, Doug replied in an exasperated voice, "Come on, Maynard, I don't have time right now! You have a cock; use it! Go to the men's room!"

Maynard turned around and walked toward the men's room. In a baritone voice, you could hear "Bitch!" Ben stood there glassy-eyed, looking toward the restrooms in disbelief. Maynard Monroe was one of the regular entertainers in the evening show at Aunt Hattie's. Deputy Rothchild did not notice her photograph in the marque as he entered the nightclub.

Warren walked over to Ben and said, "I think we have enough! Let's get out of here!" Warren looked back over at Doug and said, "If we need anything else, we will give you a call."

Doug replied, "Thanks, Warren. It was nice seeing you again."

As the two deputies walked back to the patrol car, Ben said to Warren, "I'm not gay!"

Warren replied, "Did I say you were?"

"Well, no."

Warren continued, "In that case, listen up. There are some valuable training points here. First off, always look for an Adam's apple. Second, if the lady has a size twelve or bigger shoe, things are not how they appear! In law enforcement, we call that a clue. Lastly, know exactly what you are dealing with before letting your guard down. Pretty distractions can get you killed, and complacency can hurt you or your partner too! Got it?"

Warren never said anything to anybody about what happened in that bar. No joking, no harassing. As the future Captain drove home to Stagecoach, he concluded, "I think I'm a fan of Warren Hill!"

When he got home, his mother asked, "How did it go at work today?

Ben replied, "Just another day at the office."

From that day forward, Ben never used the name Bernard again at the sheriff's office.

"Hollywood"

Deputy Bill Baxter was a tan and athletically handsome man who was charming and down to earth. Bill was born and raised in Los Angeles, California. He attended the University of California Los Angeles and graduated with a degree in theatre arts. Bill moved to Santiago Springs upon graduation to become a cast member at one of the casino's productions. He hoped to be discovered for his good looks and acting ability.

A Bahamas West Casino and Resort Security manager passed through Human Resources that morning when Bill first applied. When they met, the security manager convinced Bill that he was born to 'Protect the Resort!' Once the manager saw Bill in their security uniform, a star was born! Bill just became the poster cop for Bahamas West Resort and Casino. Bill later met his wife, Cindy, at the Gold City Casino. She also worked as a production manager in the *Give My Regards to Broadway Revue* at the Gold City Theatre.

The Lakeland County Sheriff's Office provides law enforcement services and private security. They are at all casinos, resorts, hotels, and theme parks along the Jefferson Esplanade for on-duty and off-duty contract work. Bill often worked with the off-duty deputies at the resort and casino and naturally developed strong friendships. After a while, Bill got the 'bug.' He convinced his then fiancé, Cindy, that he wanted to join the sheriff's office as a deputy sheriff since nothing had become of his acting career. Bahamas West did its best to keep Bill as a security officer. Still, he left the resort and casino to join the law enforcement academy at Santiago Springs College. Bill and Cindy were married the same week Bill graduated from the academy. The wedding present from Lakeland County came when Bill was offered a position as a deputy sheriff with the Lakeland County Sheriff's Office.

Bill started his career with Lakeland County, working the evening shift in Sector Four, the busiest sector in the county. It did not take him long to realize he was no longer in the controlled environment of the casino. Specifically, the three years of experience in Sector Four helped create a fine-tuned and honed deputy sheriff ready for any assignment in the agency. Bill, now known as 'Hollywood' by his peers due to his college degree, had the opportunity to transfer to Sector One, which was closer to home. 'Hollywood' and Cindy Baxter had purchased a home in the Bent Oak Subdivision in Sector One two years after they were married. The couple often spoke of someday raising a family together.

The open position in Sector One was on dayshift, working for Sergeant Phil 'Rat Bastard' Owens' squad. Phil Owens was a long-time Special Weapons and Tactics operator whose squad had been with him for many years. Owens believed in the Seven Critical Tasks and the Incident Command System. He also ensured his corporal was well versed in them and implementing all aspects. One thing was certain, Phil 'Rat Bastard' Owens would be the tip of the spear when the shit hit the fan!

On Tuesday morning at about 10:00 A.M., 'Hollywood' Baxter was working a traffic collision at Johnson Street and Maple Place, assisting Jefferson Highway Patrol with traffic control in the intersection. As traffic slowly traveled northbound on Maple Place, Bill noticed a gray Ram 1500 pickup truck like his wife Cindy's. As the car got closer, Bill realized it was, in fact, Cindy. As she approached the intersection, she smiled with her long auburn hair flowing out the open driver's side window in the breeze. Bill blew his wife an exaggerated kiss as she turned westbound on Johnson Street towards Birch Canyon Road. She, in turn, blew one back at him! Bill assumed she was going to Vaughn's Supermarket down the street for shopping since this was her day off.

'Hollywood' was on the traffic control detail for about twenty minutes. Approximately ten minutes after clearing the call, dispatch hit the alert tone and made the broadcast,

"Any available unit, report of a possible suicide just occurred at Birch Canyon Park 400 E. Birch Canyon Rd. Unit respond Code 3."

Birch Canyon Park was in 'Hollywood's' zone, so naturally, he picked up the mic and said, "Lakeland 215 is en route."

Sierra 12, Sergeant Phil Owens, came upon the air and advised dispatch he, too, was en route to the call.

Dispatch came on the air with additional information, "Victim is in a gray pickup truck parked near the group camping sites in the park's northeast corner. The park ranger will meet you at the park's front entrance and escort you in."

215 acknowledged the additional information.

'Hollywood' arrived on the scene within moments and met with the ranger at the front gate. He knew exactly where the location of the group camping sites was because he had worked off-duty at the park several times. The park ranger told the deputy that he would meet him back at the location as soon as possible. Specifically, he would travel in a golf cart from the front gate.

Accordingly, when 215 arrived on the scene at the group camping sites, he advised dispatch that he was 10-97 and "Out with the vehicle." 'Hollywood' never called in the vehicle tag as the standard procedure would dictate. Was it because he didn't need to since he recognized the vehicle and calling it in would make it real? Or was it because he was too emotionally overcome to call in the tag? That question was never answered.

Dispatch tried to contact 'Hollywood' again for the information but to no avail. The park ranger was approaching the campgrounds in the golf cart and approximately seventy-five yards from the deputy and the gray truck. Simultaneously he saw the deputy come to the car resulting in an unimaginable painfilled scream. 'Hollywood' Baxter fell to the ground on his hands and knees. Not knowing what had occurred, the ranger immediately called the Lakeland County Communications Center to report a deputy down. After his phone call to the communication center, the ranger did not approach the deputy but continued to hear him sob uncontrollably.

After receiving the information from the park ranger and still not hearing from 215, dispatch made a broadcast, "Signal 43 (Officer Needs Help) for 215 at Birch Canyon Park." Sierra 12 believed the call might be bogus and designed to ambush and kill a responding deputy. Hence, Sierra 12 came upon the air and requested the south end unit 214 to "Set a perimeter around the park!" He added, "213 respond to Sector One (North Lakeland Substation) to establish and run Staging."

Sierra 12 added, "Lakeland, units in the sector respond to the scene, units outside Sector One respond to staging!"

Dispatch acknowledged and put the information out on all radio channels.

When 'Hollywood' Baxter approached the truck, he saw the spray and droplets of blood running outside the driver's side door. The window was also rolled down. Baxter noticed the long auburn hair. Cindy, his beloved wife, wore the same white patterned sundress when she made him breakfast that morning.

Sergeant Owens was the second unit on the scene. When he arrived, he found Deputy Baxter sitting in the front seat of his wife's truck, holding her hand and sobbing. As Owens approached the vehicle, he found a note on the dashboard that said, "I'm sorry." The message appeared to have been written by a woman, Cindy Baxter, as was confirmed later. A Smith and Wesson stainless two-inch revolver was found in the lap of Cindy Baxter, with one round of .357 ammunition fired into her right temple. Owens recognized Cindy from the many squad parties and BBQs at his home. Owens' wife and Cindy had become friends.

Sergeant Owens canceled Signal 43 and requested Homicide Detectives, Victim Advocates, and a Sheriff's Chaplain. The Sheriff was also notified. The reason Cindy took her own life was never determined. She had no history of depression, and the two did not have any marital or financial problems. 'Hollywood' was off work for six months, and after counseling and treatment, he could not return to work after being dispatched as the initial officer to his wife's suicide. Bill Baxter resigned from the Lakeland County Sheriff's Office. He left the State of Jefferson, returning to his roots in Southern California.

"Howie the Good!"

Alistair Carter was born and raised in Newport Beach, Orange County, California. Alistair was the quintessential tough guy, strong, silent, and self-contained. The son of a liquor salesman, Alistair looked like he could have been one of the founding members of the Beach Boys. However, after working twenty years as a cop in the methamphetamine capital of Greenwood County, Alistair looked just as weathered as the original Beach Boys. Tom Stevens had been friends with Alistair Carter for those twenty years. Alistair was a Sergeant with the Meadow Woods Police Department. At the same time, Tom was a sergeant with the Hudson Falls Police Department. Both worked as team leaders on the Greenwood County Formalized Intervention Street Thugs (F.I.S.T.) task force.

Tom and Alistair were teamed up working the hood in El Camino during one operation doing knock and talks. As Tom approached the next house of a known banger, Alistair started to fall behind. Tom called out, "Come on, slowpoke!"

Alistair said, "Don't worry about me."

Tom asked, "And why is that?"

Alistair proclaimed, "Because I carry a Big Gun!"

This was said and heard by the probationer they were about to visit as the piece of shit opened and was coming out his front door. From that moment on, Alistair Carter was nicknamed. He was called 'Slow Poke' after Speedy Gonzales' cousin Slow Poke Rodriguez because he also carried a "big gun and has the evil eye!"

Alistair 'Slow Poke' Carter had been married to his wife Karen for two years longer than Tom and Marcie Stevens. Besides, Karen and Marcie had been friends for many years. Karen was a program manager for the Hudson Falls Police Athletic League and worked for Tom. After twenty years in Greenwood County, Alistair and Karen retired and moved to Washington Park, Jefferson, where he eventually joined the Lakeland County Sheriff's Office at the behest of Tom. Alistair 'Slow Poke' Carter currently works on the midnight shift in Sector Five, the casino and resort corridor known as Jefferson Promenade.

Howard Goodman, also known as 'Howie the Good,' was a forty-five-year-old businessman in Alameda County, California. He owned a lumber yard with his partner Bruno Lamb. He had been staying with Bruno for the previous weeks. His wife of ten years, Annie, threw him out of their house so she could move in her younger female tennis coach as her new lover and life partner. 'Howie the Good' had additional threats looming over him. The Internal Revenue Service looked for him for income tax evasion. He was out on bail, being considered for indictment by the grand jury for a 'shady deal' with a local hospital foundation. 'Howie the Good' had also been renting foreclosed houses that were not his to do as a form of quick cash to unsuspecting out-of-state vacationers.

Howie realized his life was a mess, so he decided it was time for a road trip to Santiago Springs, where he could stay in a nice suite, have some fun, play golf, and find some broads. Howie's business partner, Bruno, had a five-gallon glass water bottle in his bedroom closet hidden behind a rack of suits. Bruno had spent ten years filling it with quarters for a rainy day. Howie knew it could rain any moment since it was summer in Jefferson, so the opportunity was knocking! Bruno found the empty five-gallon water bottle on his kitchen floor with a note at the bottom. "You should have known better!" Signed, 'Howie the Good.'

It was a beautiful Tuesday morning at Santiago Springs Marriott Resort and Casino. The CEO and board of directors for Anheuser Busch were in town for a shareholder meeting at the new SeaWorld Santiago. They always stayed at the Marriott and hired a small army of off-duty deputies. The deputies would see to their security at the hotel and the traveling to and from the new SeaWorld. Deputy Alistair 'Slow Poke' Carter was in uniform. He parked his marked patrol car south of the main porte-cochere near the convention center. 'Howie the Good' came back from the golf course's pro shop when he first saw Deputy Carter.

Alistair was standing outside his patrol car enjoying the morning breeze when the two men spoke. One thing Alistair Carter had was the ability to talk to people. That skill was gathered from years of working with juveniles and the occult and providing security measures for houses of worship. That, coupled with the natural con man known as 'Howie the Good,' was quite a combination. The two men spoke for several minutes and covered topics ranging from politics to sports to movies to action on the South JFK Trail of Santiago Springs. Howie asked Alistair how long he would work this off-duty job and if that position was his for the whole day.

When Alistair acknowledged it, Howie said, "Try not to be bored to death!"

Alistair replied, "I always have movies."

'Howie the Good' disappeared into the hotel's main entrance. Approximately thirty minutes later, a room service attendant was seen pushing a cart across the front lobby and into the porte-cochere towards the convention center. Alistair Carter was sitting in his car watching *The Shootist* with John Wayne. He was surprised when a waiter stopped at his open driver's side window and confirmed he was Alistair Carter.

The deputy replied, "Yes, I am."

The waiter said, "Very well, sir. I'm here to deliver your lunch compliments of Mr. Goodman."

When Alistair signed the check, it said, "Thanks for your service!" It was signed 'Howie the Good.' The waiter delivered a steak sandwich with French fries and a strawberry milkshake. Howie liked Alistair Carter. He seemed like a stand-up cop. A cop, Howie would like to investigate a significant event in his life.

After his time in Santiago Springs, 'Howie the Good' decided to end his life that afternoon rather than face the music back home. He figured Alistair would be the first on the scene since he was sitting in a patrol car near the front entrance. Howie believed Carter would not say anything disparaging about him. Carter would not stand for some young cop or another first responder to shoot off their pie hole after responding to the call.

About an hour later, Deputy Alistair 'Slow Poke' Carter stopped by the hotel's front desk to ask what room Howard Goodman was in.

The clerk told the deputy, "In room 465 facing the golf course."

The deputy replied, "Thank you."

Alistair wanted to stop by the room and thank him for the lovely lunch. As Alistair Carter was about to knock on the door of room 465, he heard a single gunshot. Instinctively he drew his weapon and kicked in the door. Howie was dressed in a brightly colored golf outfit, lying on the king-size bed with a gunshot wound to his chest above his heart. A Glock Model 30 .45 caliber handgun was still in his right hand. Nothing could be done. He was dead.

An extensive suicide note addressed to Deputy Alistair Carter was found on the desk in the room. The message outlined all the issues facing Howie at home and his admission to all of them. After an apology to all his family members, thanking the first responders for what they do, the note ended with "P.S. Alistair, you should have known better…There is no such thing as a free lunch!"

Signed, 'Howie the Good.'

Deputy Alistair Carter thought, "You mean Howie the Dead!"

J.J. Hightower's Night Club

Jack Cleaver liked the kid Yehuda Goldberg and took him under his wing as his protégé in the Lakeland County Sheriff's Office Training Division. During one of his 'lessons of life' training sessions, Jack spoke of when the NBA All-Star Week and Jam Session arrived in town. It was during the week of February 22-26, 1995, when Sergeant Jack Cleaver was the midnight sergeant in Sector 5, the Jefferson Promenade Corridor. The evening shift sergeant was Dennis Adams, a well-respected former SWAT operator, and Gang Unit supervisor. He should have been promoted to lieutenant years prior. Jack Cleaver had worked for Dennis Adams as his corporal for a couple of years in Sector 5, and the two got along very well. One problem with Dennis is he never drank the Cool-Aid.

Most good cops realize that you have to think like a criminal if you want to catch a criminal. The same holds for a terrorist or anybody with an ax to grind. Some sporting events had gotten out of hand in Lakeland County, resulting in hotels, not on Jefferson Promenade, being overrun and property destroyed. Jack Cleaver considered the temperature of the country and the fact that these games were broadcast worldwide. Jack Cleaver did not want a wingnut or another group with some cause to throw a burning couch out the window of one of Saul Cohen's hotels. Or get 'whiskeyed' up and start shooting the ducks in the lobby of the Roosevelt Hotel. Cleaver vowed that the Lakeland County Sheriff's Office of 1995 at the NBA All-Star Jam Session would not be the Chicago Police Department of 1968 at the Democratic National Convention, how an agency should not respond to an event.

Jack met with Dennis, and once the two talked, Dennis shared his concerns. If an incident went down, Dennis would assume the position of Operations Section Chief and supervise the law enforcement response at the scene. Jack would take the role of Incident Commander. Jack had learned that a well-known and controversial rap singer was scheduled to sing at J.J. Hightower's Night Club. This event was scheduled at the Premiere Hotel and Casino Santiago Springs, on Friday night, February 24, 1995, at 8:00 PM. Trouble seemed to travel with this rap singer, and it was reported that the nightclub and the hotel were sold out for the performance. The lounge had contracted six deputies to work the concert in the club. The Premiere Hotel, the entertainment complex where the club was located, hired ten deputies to operate the hotel lobby and casino floor. Based on years of experience, Jack believed this was where the trouble for Sector 5 would begin.

Sergeant Cleaver had contacted the High-Risk Incident Commander for the NBA All-Star Jam Session and requested additional deputies to assist in Sector 5. His request was denied without further proof that there would be a problem. Cleaver's and Adams' squad were well-trained and versed in the Seven Critical Tasks and the Incident Command System. The basics were reviewed in a briefing with both teams, and everyone was told of the plan. Jack had selected one of his best and most trusted deputies to fill the role of the Staging Manager, Paul Sabo.

Sabo was a hard charger who initially resisted ICS but soon realized how valuable it was to control and manage an incident or event successfully.

When one of the newer deputies asked the sergeants how they would know when it started, Sergeant Jack Cleaver replied, "You will hear what sounds like a twelve-year-old little girl coming up on the radio screaming for help! That means it's game time!"

After that, everyone received their instructions, and it was just a matter of waiting.

Friday's evening shift briefing reminded everyone of the plan for that night's festivities, and everybody was prepared and ready. Considering the number of people they had on the promenade and at the convention center, it was an uneventful shift. The rap singer was scheduled to start his set at 8:00 PM. However, his flight was late from New York.

At 8:30 PM, an unidentified unit came up screaming on the Sector 5 primary channel, "… we're taking rocks and bottles at J.J. Hightower's Night Club at the Premiere Hotel!! Need help!!"

The little girl screaming for help as Jack Cleaver had briefed his deputies.

Lakeland County Dispatch broadcast after an alert tone, "Signal 43 (Officer Needs Help) for units at J.J. Hightower's Night Club Premiere Hotel and Casino, Units respond Code 3."

Sergeant Jack Cleaver came up on the air and stated, "All units stay off the air and respond. Lakeland, have responding units 10-96 (Change radio channels) to Sector 5 Tactical North. Lakeland, have units currently in Sector 5 respond to the scene, and other units outside of Sector 5 respond to Staging."

Dispatch acknowledged the instructions and broadcasted them to all responding units. Paul Sabo, Unit 150, had switched to the Sector 5 Tactical North Channel and made the following broadcast, "Lakeland, 150 is changing designator to Staging."

Lakeland acknowledged, and 'Staging' added, "Lakeland, the staging area is the north side of the north-south convention center parking lot. East of the north concourse."

Lakeland acknowledged, and Sergeant Adams came on the air and advised, "Lakeland Sierra 53, change my designator to 'Operations,' and I am en route to the call." Lakeland acknowledged the information and made the change. From this point, Sergeant Adams supervised the response to the riot on the Tactical Channel.

At the same time, Deputy Sabo gave dispatch information on Sector 5 Tactical North. Sergeant Cleaver was providing information to communications on the Sector 5 Primary channel. "Lakeland Sierra 55, change my designator to Premiere Hotel Command. Sierra 53 will become 'Operations,' and Unit 150 will become 'Staging'."

Sergeant Cleaver added, "The Command Post is located at the Lakeland County Convention Center Parking Garage. At the open lot to the rear of Tyler Loop Parking west of Fillmore Drive." Lakeland Dispatch acknowledged the information, made the changes, and updated responding units.

Sector 5 Primary was used to handle calls for service unrelated to the Premiere Hotel and Casino Incident. Sergeant Cleaver had arranged with Sergeant Andy Hughes in Sector 6 to cover supervision in Sector 5 while taking care of business at Premiere Hotel and Casino.

Unbeknownst to Sergeant Cleaver, Lt. Eddie Ames, Commander of the Tactical Unit, had a thirty-person field response team working in Sector 5 for reasons similar to the Premiere Hotel calls. His units were both in patrol vehicles and bicycles. Lt. Ames and Sergeant Adams had been SWAT teammates long ago, and the effect at this call was seamless. Sergeant Cleaver canceled Signal 43 once he had twenty units in staging.

The crowd was eventually dispersed. Only a handful of arrests were made. Other than trash, there was no damage to J.J. Hightower's Night Club or the Premiere Hotel and Casino. Most importantly, no deputies were injured. This call lasted approximately one hour from dispatch to conclusion. After the call, Jack called all the responding units to the Command Post for a debriefing.

When Jack started to talk, the new Watch Commander, Lieutenant Roy Nguyen, began to ask a minor question. Lieutenant Eddie Ames, the senior lieutenant, interrupted Lt. Nguyen and said, "Stand down, lieutenant. This sergeant and the others who helped run this incident know precisely what they are doing. Unless you have something positive to add…."

Lt Nguyen remained quiet, and Sergeant Cleaver responded to Lt. Nguyen that his concern was addressed in the planning stage of the response to this incident. Both good and bad points were discussed during the debriefing. Once it was over, two corporals, one from Sector 3 and the other from Sector 4, came up to Sergeant Cleaver and told him they had been listening to the operation. It was the smoothest one they had ever heard. They asked the sergeant if he could teach them how to do that.

Sergeant Cleaver replied, "Absolutely." He laughed a little and said, "Apparently, it's my life's calling!"

At the end of the story, Sergeant Cleaver spoke to Yehuda Goldberg. He said, "We will have succeeded in emergency management training if all first responding supervisors and managers handle a call (like the Premiere Hotel and Casino riot) just as quickly and smoothly as they call a vehicle stop." That night, Sergeant Cleaver became known as Jack 'CP' Cleaver. The 'CP' stands for Command Post.

"You Always Wanted My Heart..."

Stagecoach Country Club and Estates was the oldest and most respected country club in Lakeland County. The course's design almost forty years ago was done with help from the PGA, and many a PGA Tournament was held at the site. Besides that, it was one of the best off-duty jobs in the county. The reason is it paid on time. Additionally, the country club contracted for a four-hour shift each day. The deputy who was working was allowed to work whatever hours they wanted to. They could split the hours in any combination needed so long as the four hours each day were covered. This off-duty job had been around for so long that it had its designated radio call sign for deputies working in the estates. Tom Stevens was given one of the off-duty slots because the person who had it needed to spend more time at their church preparing for Sunday service.

It was a beautiful Sunday morning in early February. The sky was crystal clear with no wind and a temperature of sixty-five degrees Fahrenheit. Tom was down the street finishing his first cup of coffee at the 7-Eleven store and talking with two Sector Three deputies about some in-progress calls handled by the midnight shift.

Ambrose Scott spent the night on the couch in his office. He wore his clothes from the previous day, minus his Hush Puppies. On the coffee table in front of him was an empty bottle of Chivas Regal and a highball glass next to it. Ambrose finished the bottle off last night after a fight with his wife of thirty-five years, Sophia. She stormed off to bed in another one of her dramatic 'exit stage left' routines from his office.

This morning, the wooden blinds of the office had been closed. Still, the position of the couch in comparison to the window allowed the sun to sneak in and shine its light on the lower half of the sofa as Ambrose slept. As the sun continued to rise, the small beam of light grew inch by inch until, like a child holding a magnifying glass on a leaf, the light settled on Ambrose's partially closed eyes and unmercifully woke him. Still feeling the effects of the scotch, Ambrose woke up and, attempting to shut off the sunbeam, knocked the empty bottle of Chivas on the floor. Ambrose sat up for several minutes, rubbing his head and deciding if he wanted to start the day or not.

Ambrose had recently retired as CEO and President of the Pacific and Atlantic Outdoor Advertising Agency in Santiago Springs. At sixty-five years of age, Ambrose still had a full head of grey hair. Ambrose stood six foot three inches tall with a great tan and weighed a slim one-hundred-and-eighty-five pounds. Ambrose was an avid golfer who spent most days on the links and in the county club.

Sophia Scott, Ambrose's wife, was a striking woman. At fifty-seven, she still looked like a retired runway model from Paris. She had recently let her hair go grey, but she was still a beautiful woman at five foot ten inches tall and one-hundred-thirty-five pounds. Mrs. Scott spent most of her time playing bridge and working as a socialite with the country club. She was never seen without makeup and had piercing blue eyes that could look right through you. She was not a woman to be casually dealt with or ignored.

The couple's net worth was approximately 47 million. Sophia believed Ambrose was having an affair with one of the waitresses at the country club, and she would have no part in it. Ambrose thought his wife needed psychiatric help and should stop using prescription pain pills and wine. Last night's argument was just another in a long line of theatrics initiated by Mrs. Scott! The disagreements between the two were always verbal and never physical.

The Scotts had two children. The eldest, their son Gideon, was a thirty-year-old Lieutenant Commander in the Navy. He instructed military history at the Naval Academy in Annapolis, Maryland. Gideon Scott was single and devoted his life to his military career. The Scott's second child is twenty-seven-year-old Audrey, who had married a dentist in Manhattan. Audrey and her husband, Trevor Santoro, had twin girls, Bella and Sadie. Gideon and Audrey had not spoken to their mother or father in over a month.

Ruby Mendez had been their housekeeper for twenty-five years when the Scotts purchased the two-story white with black trim Colonial-style mansion. The mansion has five bedrooms and seven bathrooms, approximately five thousand square feet. The house has a large front yard with professionally maintained lush green grass separated by a circular driveway in the middle large enough to park fifteen vehicles easily. The mansion at 30527 Palomino Parkway in the estates backs up to the sixteenth hole of the Stagecoach Golf Course.

Ruby stopped this morning at Vaughn's Market to pick up some fresh fruit for Mrs. Scott, so she ran a little late for her shift. Ambrose had made his way from his office to the kitchen, where he made an entire pot of coffee. Once he poured himself a large mug of coffee, he returned to the sanctity of his office. Ambrose was not looking forward to continuing his conversation with Sophia last night. When Ruby arrived at the Scott home, she immediately went to the kitchen, where she found the new pot of coffee. Ruby prepared a tray for Mrs. Scott consisting of a blueberry muffin, sliced peaches, hot coffee, and a small glass of freshly squeezed orange juice.

The main bedroom was on the second floor in the mansion's east wing. As Ruby entered the bedroom, she saw that the bed had been turned down, but it did not appear as if anyone had slept in it the previous night. Ruby called, "Mrs. Scott, Mrs. Scott, are you here?" Ruby approached the main bathroom. The next thing Ambrose heard in his office was a blood-curdling scream from Ruby and the sound of broken glass. The breakfast tray was dropped on the white marble floor of the bathroom, breaking all the China dishes and glassware on the tray.

Ambrose was reading the Santiago Springs Sentinel newspaper in his office. As he started to rise after hearing the commotion upstairs, he uttered, "Jesus Christ, what now!"

When Ambrose reached the top of the stairs and walked towards the Main bedroom, he called out to Ruby. "In here, Mr. Scott, hurry!" she replied.

So, Ambrose entered his and his wife's bedroom. Ruby was sitting on their bed, crying hysterically. When Ambrose got to the bathroom, he looked in and said, "Oh my God! What have you done?"

After which, overcome by emotion and sight, he threw up his morning coffee and the remains of dinner and scotch from last night. Ambrose said to Ruby, "Call the Sheriff!"

Tom Stevens was about to walk into the 7-Eleven when the alert tone on the Sector Three radio went off. "Attention! Available Sector Three units and Stagecoach One, a report of a possible homicide or suicide occurred at 30527 Palomino Parkway. The reporter is the housekeeper with broken English. Stagecoach One, your call is Code Three."

Tom came up on the air and said, "Lakeland Stagecoach One en route from Polk Way and Manchester Square!"

The zone car said, "Lakeland 231 to back." Dispatch replied to both deputies, who arrived at the scene within minutes.

When the patrol cars arrived, they parked in the circular driveway, steps away from the mansion's front door. Ruby Mendez met the deputies as they approached the front door.

Deputy Edwin 'Eddie' Hernandez was riding unit 231 this morning and was Tom Stevens' backup. When the two deputies arrived, Ruby Mendez provided both deputies with a synopsis of what had occurred. Ambrose was now in the foyer near the front door. Deputy Hernandez went over to interview Ambrose. Tom asked Ruby to take him upstairs to the body. Ruby stood outside of the primary bedroom and pointed toward the bath. When Tom entered the doorway of the main bath, he realized that he was looking at the bloodiest crime scene he had ever experienced in his career.

The bathroom alone was more extensive than most people's living and dining rooms combined. The entire room had white marble floors, high gloss white wooden cabinets, and white marble countertops. All the walls were covered in mirrors, making the room look three times its actual size. In the corner of the room was a large walk-in shower, large enough for three people, with ten shower heads to cover all parts of the three bodies. In the center of the room was an eight-foot porcelain claw foot bathtub. Next to this bathtub was a large white roman pillar with a tabletop.

An open bottle of Beaulieu Vineyard Georges de Latour Private Reserve Cabernet Sauvignon was on the table. Sitting next to the bottle was a large wine glass containing a partially consumed glass of this fine red wine.

Tom looked around the room and saw blood splattered all over the counter and on both sinks. Smeared blood covered the floor along with the morning continental breakfast, broken dishes, and Chivas-enriched vomit. The room smelled like every bit of it! On the counter, Tom found an opened and spilled bottle of prescription sleeping medication for

Mrs. Scott. The prescription date was last week, but most pills were already gone. Tom also found an open tube of lipstick from the Francesca Valentino Cosmetic Company. The color of the lipstick was Del Monaco Red. Mrs. Scott used this lipstick to write her parting thoughts across the large mirrors over the two sinks. First, she drew a broken heart picture, then wrote: You always wanted my heart, well here it is!

Investigation revealed that, after arguing with her husband Ambrose the previous night, Sophia retired to the main bedroom, where she turned down her side of the bed. Then she went to Ambrose's side of the bed, where she retrieved a large hunting or tactical knife similar to one Rambo might use. This knife had a ten-inch blade and was razor-sharp. Ambrose kept the knife for protection from an intruder in the drawer of his nightstand. Sophia entered the bathroom, drew herself a hot bath, poured herself a glass of wine, and grabbed and consumed a handful of sleeping pills.

Sophia used her husband's tactical knife to slice a four-inch vertical cut on the inner side of both arms. She began to bleed profusely when she started to draw and write her farewell message to her husband. Blood was splattered all over the bathroom mirrors, the floor, and the side of the white porcelain bathtub. Sophia, who was starting to get cold from the blood loss, still with the knife in hand, sat in the tub filled with approximately a foot of water. Sophia thrust the knife into her naked body and through her heart in her last moments on earth. She was submerged underwater when Tom found her with the knife handle still standing erect in her body. Three white carpets on the bathroom floor were soaked in her blood.

Homicide Detectives responded to take over the investigation. Sophia's death was ruled a suicide by overdose and self-inflicted knife wounds. At the time of his investigation, Tom thought what a pretty color of lipstick Mrs. Scott used to write her farewell message.

Six months after the death of Sophia, Ambrose found himself sitting on a beach in Acapulco, Mexico. He was wearing a ruby red European cut Speedo with his body covered in suntan lotion. Sitting next to him is his new twenty-three-year-old wife, Pixie Walker. She wanted to keep her name to show her independence.

Pixie no longer worked at the Stagecoach Country Club as a cocktail waitress but was a club member since she married Ambrose. Pixie was learning how to play bridge. Ruby Mendez retired after finding Mrs. Scott. Pixie thought it was time for a change, so she hired a twenty-six-year-old English gentleman who had just finished butler training overseas. Audrey and Gideon had yet to meet their new twenty-three-year-old stepmother despite being offered an all-expense-paid trip to spend the week in Acapulco. Ambrose still had regular intercourse with Chivas Regal but couldn't seem to scare away all those demons.

Tom bought his wife Marcie a tube of the Francesca Valentino Del Monaco Red lipstick. Marcie was both surprised and excited that Tom even thought of her. Marcie scolded Tom about spending that much money on a tube of lipstick. After Marcie reprimanded Tom, she gave him a big hug and a kiss. When he bought the lipstick, Tom thought about how elegant Mrs. Scott had been before her death. He felt that by purchasing that lipstick, he would send Mrs. Scott a message that this lipstick belonged on beautiful lips. Not on a mirror in some bathroom, sending a final note of desperation. Tom just smiled and enjoyed the view.

Atticus

At 5:45 A.M. Sheriff Atticus Lee walked into the back door of Sector One, past the briefing room that was starting to fill with dayshift deputies, and proclaimed, "Morning troops!"

The Sheriff was dressed in a grey wife-beater shirt, navy-blue shorts, and white athletic shoes. He was headed toward the gym facility in Sector One and did not wait for a reply from the deputies. Sheriff Lee lived in north Rockwell, and he and his family regularly used the gym in Sector One. When Tom Stevens was in training, Asa Williams first took Tom to the Sheriff's neighborhood. He instructed Tom to respond as soon as possible and do an excellent job if he ever got a call in this neighborhood.

Tom messing with Asa, asked, "Shouldn't we do that on every call?"

Asa turned his head, raised an eyebrow, and replied, "You know what I mean!"

"Lakeland 213 Alpha 10-8 (in-service), Stevens, Unit 1101." Tom Stevens returned the radio microphone to the holder on the center console of his patrol car.

Dispatch replied, "213 Alpha 10-8 at 0630 hours."

Tom turned southbound onto Birch Canyon Road, heading to downtown Rockwell. Asa Williams told Tom as they finished briefing that he would meet him at the BP station on north JFK Trail. The gas station was less than a year old, had a full car wash, and was kind enough to give the cops free car washes for their patrol cars. Additionally, the morning crew at the store consisted of young, good-looking, and very energetic ladies who always greeted the customers with smiles and a positive attitude! Many dayshift cops would stop at the BP station on the way to their zones because the coffee was always fresh, and they had a wide variety of delicious pastries.

When Tom pulled into the BP lot, several cars were at the pumps, and the store had the usual morning rush. Tom parked on the north side of the store, away from where most customers would park. When Tom entered the store, he found one of his favorite gals behind the counter.

Tom said, "Morning, Britany!"

Britany nodded with a big toothy smile. Asa Williams was just moments behind Tom Stevens. He, too, parked on the North side of the building, away from the crowd.

When Asa entered the store, he proclaimed, "Good morning, ladies! Isn't it a lovely morning?"

The three clerks replied, "Morning, Asa!"

Tom and Asa both got a cup of coffee. They walked to their usual table in the Northwest corner of the building near the large plate glass windows where the table could comfortably seat four persons.

Asa began to tell Tom of his plans to buy a used motor home for him and his family to use on vacations when Sergeant Travis Nelson pulled into the lot. He, too, parked on the north side of the business, where he, like the others, backed into the parking stall. Sergeant Travis Nelson entered the store. The senior clerk named Barbara, a tall 36-year-old redhead still with her teenage shape, called out in a sultry voice, "Good morning, Sergeant Nelson."

Travis replied, "Morning Barbara!" with no effect from her efforts.

Sergeant Nelson has been happily married for almost twenty years. Travis grabbed a cup of coffee and joined his troops.

As the three men finished their first cup of coffee, a dispatcher called, "211 Alpha Lakeland."

Asa Williams was working that zone. He reached over the microphone in the center of his chest for his handheld radio. He pushed the transmit button saying, "Lakeland 211 Alpha, Go ahead."

"211 Alpha, we have a report of a residential burglary at the Babcock residence located at 2483 Branford Ave. The crime occurred sometime overnight; your call is Code 2."

Asa told dispatch, "Lakeland 211 Alpha is en route from JFK and Monroe Ave." With that, Asa swallowed his last bit of coffee and bid farewell, saying, "Duty calls."

As Asa was heading to his call, Sheriff Atticus Lee pulled right in front of the business. He exited his dark gray unmarked Ford Expedition decked out with the newest and best lights and sirens available for testing. These same lights and sirens were also installed in the new patrol cars to see how beneficial they would be.

When the Sheriff entered, before he could say anything, all three of the clerks said, "Good Morning, Sheriff Lee!" He replied, "Good Morning, Girls!"

Sheriff Lee walked over to the pastry counter and ordered two 'bear claws.' Afterward, he walked over to Sergeant Nelson and said, "Morning, Travis," and the Sheriff shook Travis' hand.

Tom Stevens was greeted with a very enthusiastic "Good Morning, BIG!" Tom Stevens thought the Sheriff must have remembered him because he called him 'BIG' at his hiring interview. Sheriff Lee shook Tom's hand. Sheriff Lee told both deputies that, unfortunately, he had to get going; he was late for a meeting at Central Operations. With that, Sheriff Lee grabbed a large cup of coffee and his bag of bear claws, walked over to the counter, and asked for a car wash coupon, which the clerk happily gave him. The Sheriff waived again as he drove south on JFK Trail toward Central Operations.

As the Sheriff drove away, Tom told Sergeant Nelson, "I can't believe he still remembers me! He called me BIG as he did in my hiring interview!"

Without trying to sound like too much of an asshole, Travis told Tom, "He calls everybody he doesn't know 'BIG.' It is his go-to name for people!"

Tom didn't feel bad because he also had difficulty remembering most people's names.

Travis added as a consolation, "He only knows my name because we were on specialty teams together when we worked patrol. And we were both on the SWAT team."

Finally, Tom asked the sergeant, "Is he as nice and good as he seems?"

Travis told Tom to go and top up his coffee. Tom returned. Travis started speaking with the same demeanor and admiration in his voice that Asa Williams demonstrated when he talked about Travis Nelson. "Law enforcement is the family business for the Lee family. Most family members have or are still involved in the family business. Atticus Lee comes from a large family of law enforcement professionals. His father, Malachi Lee, was the Chief of Police for the City of Santiago Springs for twenty-six years. He was the chief during the expansion years and dealt with out-of-state riffraff that thought they would come to Jefferson and take advantage of the 'country folk'! Old-timers still talk about Malachi Lee's exploits as the head lawman in Santiago Springs."

Sergeant Nelson continued, "Atticus's younger brother, Moses, is currently the Chief of Police for the City of Greenville. He is well respected as an innovator and a chief who gets things done. The sheriff has a 'smoking hot' sister who works for the Lakeland County Sheriff's Office as a Master Deputy in Community Relations. Besides her looks, being raised in a family of all boys, she is one of the toughest cops Travis said he knew. He would have Chloe Lee back him any time and on any call. Unfortunately for Chloe, her career was dead in the water because her brother was Sheriff. She could never be promoted due to the hard feelings and hostile work environment caused by nepotism."

Tom interjected, "When I went to Sheriff Lee's office for my hiring interview, I was there for approximately forty-five minutes. I wasn't a bit nervous and felt like I was speaking with an old friend. I noticed that he had received the Sheriff of the Year for both the Jefferson Sheriff's Association and the National Sheriff's Association."

Travis said, "This agency is one of the best-equipped agencies in the state, if not the nation. No deputy is short of any equipment to do their job. We may not be at the top of the pay charts, but we more than make up the difference with our assigned equipment; that is directly the result of Atticus Lee."

Sergeant Nelson felt like talking this morning. Since the radio was still quiet, he sat back in his chair and asked Tom if he had heard the story about how Atticus Lee was elected Sheriff. Tom said he had not. Travis Nelson started with, "The former Sheriff, Scott Price, was a piece of shit lawyer. He received his law enforcement certification as he had been a Reserve Officer for the Town of Riverside in Lakeland County for two years. His regular job was corporate law. He ran under the premise that he would clean up the 'good old boy' sheriff's office and bring them into the twentieth century. He barely beat the incumbent, Duncan Mac

Williams. At eighty years, Duncan had been Sheriff of Lakeland County for thirty-five years. Mac Williams was also a founding member of the Ku Klux Klan in Springfield forty years ago."

Sergeant Nelson continued, "Once elected, Sheriff Price decided to move the Sheriff's Administrative offices from Central Operations to an upper-level floor of the Bank of Lakeland building in downtown Santiago Springs. He effectively separated the Sheriff from all his employees. Price, only five foot five inches tall, had a four-foot oil painting of himself in dress uniform. It was commissioned and placed in the new Sheriff's Administration lobby to be seen by all who had business there. Sheriff Price often told people he did not need the support of the deputies or his employees because the public would re-elect him based on his performance. Sheriff Price was despised by the rank and file of the Lakeland County Sheriff's Office. While Price was completing his first term as Sheriff, Sergeant Atticus Lee worked with his family and supporters for his first run at Sheriff, come the next term."

Nelson added, "Atticus' father called his long-time friend for advice and help. Malachi called Asher Roth, known as the 'Prince of the Esplanade.' Asher was one of the wealthiest and most respected men in Santiago Springs. A self-made man from New York owns seven hotels with casinos on the Jefferson Esplanade and two other golf and tennis resorts near the attractions. Each of Asher Roth's properties was paid for before construction.

Jefferson state law required Atticus to resign from the Sheriff's office to run for Sheriff. When the time came, Atticus submitted his letter of resignation to a "frosty" Sheriff Price. Asher Roth hired Atticus Lee as the Security Director for the Asher Center Hotel next to the convention center while he ran for Sheriff."

Moreover, "Another thing Malachi Lee did for his son was hire a former detective named Silas 'No Chance' Brown. 'No Chance' got his name because once he determined that you were the suspect in the case he was working on, there was 'No chance' you would get away with it! Silas stood six feet seven inches tall and weighed approximately three hundred and seventy-five pounds. Silas' job was to do nothing but attend all of Sheriff Price's public events and stand as close as he could to the candidate to help illustrate how small of a man the Sheriff was.

As the campaign continued, Atticus started to gain weight because everybody wanted to feed their new friend or have a piece of pie and coffee. Atticus never disappointed his voters but let us say his former SWAT body was gone. Atticus also had unbelievable support from most members of the Sheriff's office, who would go door to door on their days off and campaign for their candidate. On election day, the race was called early in the evening. The polls were closed because it was obvious that Atticus Lee was going to be the next Sheriff of Lakeland County by a landslide."

Tom reminisced about how welcome Sheriff Lee made him feel when he was at the hiring interview. He made you feel as if you were a member of the family. As if you were one of the deputies he selected for his team. Those same thoughts were confirmed time and time again throughout Tom's career with Lakeland County. One night when Tom was working in the rural part of the north county, he was dispatched to a commercial burglar alarm at a produce packing facility. No units were available to back Deputy Stevens.

Suddenly Tom heard on the radio, "Lakeland Unit 1 will back 310 on that call."

Tom could not believe that. When he worked for Greenwood County, he only heard the Sheriff come up on the radio maybe four times, and he never responded to calls for service. As Sheriff Lee was pulling up, Tom was finishing checking on the perimeter of the building.

Sheriff Lee rolled down his window and asked, "How does it look, Tom?"

Tom replied, "All good, boss!"

Atticus told Tom, "I have to get going. My wife has dinner on the table, and I'm already a half-hour late! Take care, Tom."

Sheriff Atticus Lee was in office for four terms. In the end, the media took every opportunity to destroy his legacy and the image of the Lakeland County Sheriff's Office. Sheriff Lee was highly trusting. He cared too much about his employees and surrounded himself with some of the wrong people. Nevertheless, Sheriff Lee had many fine qualities that made him a great sheriff. The agency has never had the same atmosphere or the same feeling as home since he retired.

Protective Shield and Response Section

The day after April 20, 1999, the Columbine High School Massacre in Littleton, Colorado, the Lakeland County Sheriff's Office created the Protective Shield and Response Section under the command of Captain Warren 'Hair on Fire' Smith. Smith got the nickname from his troops based on his failure to plan for incidents or events and then taking that planning process on at the last minute with a ridiculous due date. His troops always made him look good! Smith was also known for routinely calling a staff meeting on Friday afternoons at 4:30 PM. He knew full well that most of the staff routinely went home at 4:00 P.M. Sheriff Atticus Lee promoted Smith to help create his dream section. Captain Smith and his management staff hand-picked each of the members of that section.

Second in command of the Protective Shield and Response Section was a shameless self-promoter named Albert Garcia. The unit nicknamed him 'Harley' due to his recent passing of his beloved Motor Officer School. Garcia commanded the Emergency Management Unit and the Crime Prevention Unit. Accordingly, Garcia's sole mission was to get promoted to Captain, and nothing would stop him from reaching that goal. Lt. Garcia's counterpart was Lt. Victor Clark, a Yankee from New England. He managed Research and Development for PSRS and the Vital Systems and Facilities Protection Unit.

By all means, the Lakeland County Sheriff's Office policy was to increase the security of the citizens and visitors of Lakeland County from domestic and foreign terrorism or manufactured and natural disasters. Specifically, these efforts were accomplished through the Units within the Section and the programs and grants the Section administered.

To illustrate, the Protective Shield and Response Section was responsible for acting as the agency's terrorism and Weapon of Mass Destruction coordination point with private, municipal, county, state, and federal agencies. Additionally, they support the rapid response and containment of acts of terrorism and natural and manufactured disasters utilizing the Critical Incident Management Team. PSRS regularly advises the Sheriff on disaster-related issues. Besides, they will also disseminate National Security information from the federal, state, and local governments[9].

---

[9] Orange County Sheriff's Office General Order 17.1.5 Homeland Security May 7, 2010, Sheriff Jerry L. Demings

Furthermore, PSRS coordinates the activities of the Regional Domestic Security Task Force, the Jefferson Sheriff's Statewide Task Force, and other related multi-disciplined partnerships. Similarly, PSRS coordinates comprehensive and related grant projects and liaisons with the Lakeland County Office of Emergency Management. Upon activation, the section also diligently and professionally staffs the Emergency Operation Center (EOC).

The Protective Shield and Response Section is easily the coordination point for activities involving the Jefferson State Police Regional Domestic Security Task Force (RDSTF). Besides, PSRS remains the point of contact for disaster-related mutual aid requests. This section also dutifully and exceptionally coordinates updating the Jefferson Mutual-Aid Resource System (MARS).

Moreover, the Protective Shield and Response Section regularly and routinely directs information, activities, media releases, and recommendations to the Intelligence Section. In addition, PSRS utilizes the Intelligence Squad for all investigative issues and as a point of contact with the Federal Joint Terrorism Task Force, the U.S. Attorney's Terrorism Task Force, and the Intelligence Committee of the Regional Domestic Security Task Force. Finally, the Protective Shield and Response Section will facilitate the release of general non-specific information to the public received through the Federal Alert System.

To illustrate, the Protective Shield and Response Section include the **Emergency Management Unit**, The **Vital Systems and Facilities Protection Unit,** and the **Crime Prevention Unit.**

The Emergency Management Unit is tasked with aggressively and frequently developing, exercising, and facilitating emergency management plans. Emergency Management is also the Sheriff's coordination point for the various anti-terrorism and emergency management task forces, the Incident Command System (ICS), and the National Incident Management Systems (NIMS)[10].

The Vital Systems and Facilities Protection Unit boldly and carefully identifies the Vital Systems and Facilities in Lakeland County and

---

[10] Orange County Sheriff's Office General Order 17.1.5 Homeland Security May 7, 2010, Sheriff Jerry L. Demings

conducts vulnerability assessments. These missions are designed to prevent, prepare against, and mitigate terrorist attacks.

Crime Prevention Unit is proactive in reducing crime and the fear of crime by participating in various prevention programs. To clarify, Neighborhood Watch and Business Watch are two of the most notable. In addition, other programs provided by the Crime Prevention Unit include Personal Safety, Robbery Awareness, Workplace Violence, Counterfeit Currency/Fraud, and Identity Theft. The Crime Prevention Unit maintains and continuously communicates with various organizations, including the Lakeland County government, South Jefferson Crime Prevention Association, South Jefferson Report-a-Crime, and different community outreach groups, including community organizations, religious organizations, and various trade and alliance organizations. In addition, Crime Prevention Deputies provide free safety and security checks for homeowners and businesses to ensure their homes and commercial companies are safe and secure without cost.

The Emergency Management Unit is supervised by Sergeant Jack 'CP' Cleaver, a seasoned former training supervisor and SWAT member. Sergeant Cleaver, however, never brags or speaks of his involvement with the SWAT team. Jack received his nickname 'Command Post' from Patrol Commanders for the professional way he managed High-Risk Incidents when he worked in Uniformed Patrol. Jack Cleaver would gladly have stayed a corporal his entire career if not for Sergeant Ethan 'Gunny' Thomas. The latter encouraged Jack to take the promotional test when Jack was his corporal. Eventually, 'Gunny' took Jack's hesitation to Sheriff Lee, who ordered Jack to take the Sergeant's test! As a result, a sergeant was born!

Undoubtedly, the Emergency Management Unit develops and facilitates the implementation of the Protective Shield and Response Section Traffic Evacuation Plan. EMU also develops, maintains, and promotes the agency Incident Command System manual and Critical Incident Management Guide. The unit also supports the mobile command post and related equipment.

The Emergency Management Unit develops, implements, and facilitates emergency management-related training by designing agency-initiated exercises and coordinating with public and private entities involving our agency in their exercise process.

Lastly, the Emergency Management Unit coordinates the Mutual Aid Response Unit and the Jefferson Sheriff's Statewide Task Force.

Sergeant Ethan 'Gunny' Thomas supervised the **Vital Systems and Facilities Protection Unit.** He was a thirty-year Marine reservist who was a subject matter expert on the Incident Command System (ICS). Tom Stevens learned that the hard way one day when he and the 'Gunny' were at a meeting with some local government employees and business owners. One of these people opened their mouths, and it was apparent they had no idea about ICS, the subject on which they were speaking. The 'Gunny' took great pleasure in packing and eating this poor man's lunch. Tom Stevens realized that you either know ICS or you don't. Most professionals with ICS knowledge will take no prisoners from those who don't know ICS! Never bluff your way through it. You never want to be that guy!

Additionally, 'Gunny' is honest to a fault. If you ask his opinion, he will tell you. The problem is that most people do not want to know the truth! They find his honesty disturbing!

Vital Systems and Facilities Protection Unit's roles and responsibilities include coordinating communications between the federal, state, and local governments, private industry, media, and citizens of Lakeland County about terrorist threats and preparedness. Moreover, they coordinate detailed efforts to protect the citizens of Lakeland County against biological, nuclear, incendiary, chemical, and explosive weapons of mass destruction.

VSFP Unit guides the development and implementation of innovative and informative training programs for first responders regarding Protective Shield and Response Section efforts. They also suggest and direct the procurement of equipment for first responders in response to a terrorist or a Weapon of Mass Destruction (WMD) incident.

The Vital Systems and Facilities Protection Unit identifies vital systems and facilities within Lakeland County. Additionally, VSFP Unit participates with the Lakeland County Office of Emergency Management to maintain the Threat and Risk Assessments for unincorporated

Lakeland County. Finally, they assist public and private vital systems and facilities in completing comprehensive vulnerability assessments.

The Crime Prevention Unit is supervised by Carl 'Two Guns' Evans, a former sniper on the agency's SWAT team. Carl got his nickname as a patrol deputy working in Dayton. One night Carl engaged an auto theft suspect in a shoot-out, with the suspect being shot and the deputy going home. After that night, Carl never went to work without a backup gun, hence 'Two Guns.' Carl Evans is a consummate professional who takes great pride in the Crime Prevention Unit. He is also the Deputy Unit Commander for the Critical Incident Management Team. Sergeant Evans is often the voice of reason, going head-to-head with Lt. Garcia on operational issues.

Crime Prevention roles and responsibilities include sharing or clarifying information regarding agency policies, regulations, rules, requirements, and applicable state and federal laws, policies, or procedures. The Crime Prevention Unit faithfully and frequently researches these. They consider audience characteristics, the time allotted for the address, and the environment where the speech is given. After that, they present a well-prepared speech or lesson plan that meets the needs of the topic and the audience's interests.

The CPU actively participates in various community outreach and public awareness activities, functions, and events to promote community involvement in law enforcement and law enforcement involvement in the community. Additionally, the Crime Prevention Unit methodically maintains the strategic criminal information flow between entities within the agency to maximize agency effectiveness.

The Crime Prevention Unit will regularly liaise with community leaders. Its purpose is to identify community policing needs and develop, coordinate, implement, and support effective crime prevention activities, programs, intervention strategies, and problem-solving activities. To illustrate, the Crime Prevention Unit distributes crime prevention, community policing, and public safety information and literature to the public. They also answer questions and direct inquiries to the appropriate agency personnel according to agency policies.

The CPU provides appropriate, accurate, and detailed crime prevention and reporting information and literature to the public per agency policy.

For instance, the Crime Prevention Unit will develop and produce factual and informative crime prevention materials.

The final member of the Protective Shield and Response Section Team is Trenton "Ham Samich" Amato. The latter worked as the political analyst and liaison for Sheriff Lee. Director Amato, who had a history and was well-connected in the medical community, was a civilian employee with the well-earned equivalent rank of Captain in the agency. Late afternoon, Trenton would stop by most of his colleague's offices in the Protective Shield and Response Section. He would ask if anyone had a spare 'Ham Samich' in their office. Now and then, he would find one!

During the glory days of the Protective Shield and Response Section, the Section consisted of a Captain, a Director, two Lieutenants, four Sergeants, and four Corporals. Emergency Management had one Corporal and one Deputy, radio designator 'BBQ 1' as that was his job with the Critical Incident Management Team. Vital Systems and Facilities Protection had one Corporal and an Emergency Management Coordinator named Donald "MacGyver" Leone. Don got his nickname because he could make chicken salad out of chicken shit and did so whenever PSRS needed him to.

Research and Development for Protective Shield and Response Section had two deputies. Crime Prevention had two Corporals and an additional six deputies, each assigned to the six sectors. If you were to ask anyone in the PSRS, most would agree that it was a high point in their career; however, nothing lasts forever.

Emergency Management created the Traffic Plan for the mass evacuation of south Jefferson in case of a pending catastrophic event. They also worked splendidly with the Lakeland County Fire Rescue Division and Lakeland County Public Schools to create the needed disaster training. The Vital Systems and Facilities Protection Unit created the Continuity of Operations Plan (COOP) for the Lakeland County Sheriff's Office. The second in the state at the time. Finally, Crime Prevention continues to introduce innovative crime prevention programs throughout the county to improve the quality of life for Lakeland County residents.

The Briefcase Squad

Sixty minutes into his new job, Reuben Johnson found himself flat on his back and sweating profusely onto the well-manicured green grass of the parade ground at the Los Angeles Police Academy in Elysian Park in the City of Angels. It was only 7:30 AM, yet on this warm August morning, the temperature was already eighty-five degrees with no breeze. As a result, the brown L.A. haze was sitting heavy. Reuben could feel the beginning of the burning pain in his lungs that most Angelenos have come to expect in early mornings during the summer.

The never-ending past hour consisted of several hundred pushups, sit-ups, and burpees. A staff of four drill instructors continued calling all the recruits everything but children of God. During the first grueling twenty minutes of the day, the recruits were told they were not fit to wash police cars, much less be police officers. The trainees were berated and said their training would only get more challenging and they should leave now while they still had dignity. Suddenly, three recruits picked themselves off the parade ground and walked to the student parking lot, where they got into their cars. The three former recruits were last seen driving southbound on Academy Drive towards Academy Road. Reuben Johnson would later wonder if these same 'recruits' were just plants that would start on the first day of each academy and leave at the appropriately scripted time. Reuben Johnson would eventually become an outstanding detective.

Reuben was a white male who stood five foot eight inches tall and weighed approximately one hundred and eighty pounds. Reuben had sandy brown hair and blue eyes. He kept in shape by playing racquetball and softball in the San Fernando Valley. If you dressed Reuben in a pair of khaki pants, a shirt and tie, and a button-up sweater, he could be a stand-in for Mr. Rogers. However, Rueben's colleagues soon realized that being quiet and non-assuming did not mean he was not aggressive. He could throw a punch, apply a pair of handcuffs, or pull a gun and stick it in a suspect's ear before most people realized what had happened.

Reuben momentarily thought to himself, this smoggy morning about thirty minutes into the training, "Have I made the right decision? I wonder if I could get my job back at Pacoima Junior High School?"

Reuben was a history teacher who thought, "I wouldn't give those little bastards the satisfaction in thinking I was not tough enough to be an L.A.P.D. officer." In the distance, while Reuben was considering his career choice, a current police academy class platoon dressed in Class A uniforms marched toward the parade grounds. They were singing police cadence as well as any U.S. Marine boot camp platoon. This well-polished and professional-looking class were scheduled to graduate from the academy within a week.

The lead Drill Instructor shouted at Reuben and his fellow recruits that they should not look at this group of soon-to-be L.A.P.D. officers. "You derelicts are not good enough to wash their laundry, much less good enough to watch them marching." Another Drill Instructor told Reuben's class to keep their heads down as they passed by. Reuben thought to himself they could march a little slower or at least make another pass by his class. The break from the exercises was terrific!

Suddenly the Lead Drill Instructor declared, "All right, maggots, get up. We are going for a run with your new friend, Mister Hose!" Rueben's academy class had started with sixty recruits, minus the three students who took the threat of the drill instructors and fled this morning. As they began their five-mile run, the now fifty-seven recruits grabbed ahold of Mister Hose, a used 150-foot fire hose courtesy of the L.A. Fire Department. The objective was to hold onto Mister Hose during the entire time of the run. If you let go during the run and fell behind, you owed the drill instructors twenty-five pushups for every occurrence. At the end of the five miles, only a hand full of recruits still had Mister Hose in their grasps. Reuben Johnson was one, and Amos Abrams was another. Unfortunately, there was not much time for celebration. Most of Reuben's classmates were on the ground paying for their weakness with pushups. The handful that stayed with Mister Hose were sent off to the showers and told to get dressed for class. The last comment heard by the recruits headed to the showers was, "Class will start in thirty minutes and if you thought this morning was tough, show up late for class!"

The students spent most of the day learning criminal law, report writing, and police ethics. Finally, at 3:30 PM, the class was dismissed. The recruits had at least three hours of homework. As the future officers walked out to the student parking area, the north forty of the academy,

Amos Abrams came up to Reuben and introduced himself. "Hi, I'm Amos Abrams. My friends call me "Highball.""

Reuben replied, "My name is Reuben Johnson. Where did 'Highball' come from?"

Before Amos could answer, Rueben said, "Here I am." Reuben had parked his gold 1972 Ford Pinto Hatchback in the first spot in the row closest to the academy structures and near the main entrance. 'Highball' parked his red 1973 Chevrolet Corvette Stingray about three spots west of Reuben, who told 'Highball,' "Nice car!"

'Highball' asked, "Are you hungry? I know a little place near Dodger Stadium that makes a killer Buffalo Chicken Sandwich served with the coldest beer in town!"

Reuben replied, "Sounds good! I'm starving. Let's go!"

When the two arrived at The Dugout Bar and Grill, 'Highball' was greeted by the bartender Bobby Perez, a former minor league pitcher for the San Diego Padres. Both men ordered the Buffalo Chicken sandwich and two draft beers. Reuben learned that 'Highball' was a C.P.A. at one of the big firms downtown. He, his colleagues, and customers often would go out to have a three-highball lunch. So 'Highball' was the bar glass that Amos' favorite drink came in. To be sure, Amos had an affinity for Johnny Walker on the rocks and a weakness for the ladies who served him. So, his friends at the firm laid the nickname 'Highball' on him.

'Highball' was raised in the Fairfax District of Los Angeles. The son of an upscale Jewish tailor and custom shirt maker, 'Highball' attended the University of Southern California, where he obtained his master's degree in economics. He was six feet two inches tall and weighed two hundred pounds. He had dark brown curly hair and dark eyes and, at twenty-eight years of age, looked like a younger brother of Mac Davis. He was a member of the Los Angeles Athletic Club downtown, not for the sporting equipment but for business lunches, dinners, and the infamous Blue Room. 'Highball' has also been an L.A.P.D. Reserve Officer for six years. The law enforcement 'bug' finally bit him hard one day when he sat at a conference table in his office building. While looking out the windows, watching downtown activity, he wondered how much more of this accounting bullshit he could take! 'Highball' was also into Tae Kwon Do, the Korean martial art, and he had just finished receiving his brown belt certification. 'Highball' told Rueben that he would help him through the academy because he knew what it was all about and what they expected. After the early dinner, the two recruits said goodbye, and each drove to their respective apartment to start their homework. Neither of the two men recognized the beginning of a lifelong friendship on which legends would be built.

Reuben and 'Highball' became fast close friends because they were the stellar opposite of each other in looks and personality. However, 'Highball' was right about knowing how the academy operated. Reuben would later find out that the Commercial Crimes Division, Complex Financial Crimes Unit had their eye on "Highball." After a year on patrol, he would be transferred to Parker Center, also known as the P.A.B. (Police Administration Building).

During a classroom discussion on the history of the Los Angeles Police Department, the Zoot Suit War of 1943 was dissected and batted around the room. A relatively slow recruit from Oklahoma named Hank Baker was in the back of the class discussing the history of race relations in Southern California. Hank, who had a size six hat and a forty-eight shirt, also shared his vast knowledge of the tensions between the military and the Hispanic community. Another young Anglo from the small town of Eustis, Florida, named Jack Ross, spoke up about the Sleepy Hollow Murder of August 3, 1942. Reuben could stand no more. Reuben, a history teacher in the San Fernando Valley, was very familiar with the Zoot Suit War in Los Angeles. Many of Reuben's students had family members involved in the riots. Some of his students even asked Reuben if he would be like the cops of those days! The students were worried and afraid that Reuben would change and become an asshole like most cops they knew.

Reuben told his colleague that it was not the Sleepy Hollow murder. The young recruit took offense and challenged Reuben on how he knew what he was talking about. Reuben told Jack Ross that *The Legend of Sleepy Hollow* was a fictional story written by Washington Irving set in the year 1799. It was not a story about a Chicano riding a horse packing his head in one hand and a taco in the other. Instead, the Sleepy Lagoon Murder of Jose Diaz and an immigrant crime wave in Los Angeles fueled the Zoot Suit War from June 3–8, 1943. Jack Ross continued pushing back by saying, "How do you know these things?" Reuben replied, "Because I am a history teacher who likes to read, study, and learn things. I like history because it always repeats itself, you know, Jack like stupid inaccurate information shared by morons who call themselves want-to-be scholars."

The academy class burst out in laughter. Jack, who was caught off guard by Reuben's comments, merely responded by saying, "All right, Professor, whatever you say." From that moment forward, Reuben Johnson became known as 'Professor Johnson.' Reuben wore the nickname like a badge of honor throughout his L.A.P.D. career!

The 'Professor' and 'Highball' took the defensive tactics class at the academy very seriously. Officer survival was strongly stressed daily, and it was drilled into the recruit's head that you would always go home at the end of your watch. Each of the drill instructors enforced this message at every available opportunity. 'Highball' had gotten the 'Professor' interested in Tae Kwon Do. Likewise, 'Highball' was now learning to play racquetball with the 'Professor.'

'Highball' became the Inspector Clouseau of this L.A.P.D. academy class, and the 'Professor' became Cato as in the *Pink Panther* film series. 'Highball' even started to call the 'Professor' 'My little yellow friend,' as Peter Sellers did in the movies. Once a day, either the 'Professor' or 'Highball' would attack the other, like a wildcat on the hunt, to keep alert and train their minds to be ready. This continued throughout the academy and long after they both graduated.

After four long months, graduation day finally arrived. The 'Professor' was assigned to the midnight watch in the Foothill Division, and 'Highball' was assigned to the evening shift of the Rampart Division. Both Officers decided to rent a four-bedroom two bath house in Van Nuys to save and invest their money. After a year in Rampart, 'Highball' Abrams was transferred to the Commercial Crimes Division. 'Professor' Johnson remained in Foothill Division for almost two years, after which he was transferred to Robbery Homicide, Parker Center. Working criminal investigations allowed both the 'Professor' and 'Highball' to work traditional schedules, which allowed them to continue their education. 'Highball' started law school at Southwestern University on Wilshire Boulevard in Los Angeles. The Professor returned to the University of California Los Angeles, where he continued working toward his Ph.D. in Education.

Two years quickly went by when Reuben first met Beth Simpson. Beth was an English teacher at San Fernando High School. She came from the Midwest and was raised by her Christian church-going parents, who worked and owned a farm in Kansas. She had three brothers and two sisters and all the kids worked on the farm. Ms. Simpson had witnessed a drive-by shooting involving a group of emotional and not-too-bright students from her school. Detective Johnson met Ms. Simpson as the lead Detective of the homicide investigation. The Detective's investigation was a slam dunk case with the shooter eyeballed by several witnesses and requiring minimal investigative effort. The suspect was arrested within two days. During the next six months pending trial, Detective Johnson became very close to and very fond of Ms. Simpson. After the suspect took a plea deal and was sentenced to an extended term with the California Youth Authority, Reuben and Beth started dating. Within six months, Reuben Johnson married Ms. Beth Simpson at a small wedding in Santa Barbara. Amos Abrams was naturally the best man.

This brisk Autumn evening, around 8:00 PM, the 'Professor' returned home after an early dinner with Beth. Once they entered the house, Beth went towards the bedroom when suddenly Rueben was attacked from behind. He removed his two-inch Colt Detective Special .38 caliber revolver from the holster. When the attack occurred, he was about to place the revolver on the counter of the breakfast bar in the kitchen. The 'Professor' was worried about Beth, who was now out of sight in the back bedroom. As the 'Professor' struggled with his assailant, the suspect moved, and the revolver discharged, striking its target, the suspect's left buttock. As the 'Professor' stepped back, 'Highball' screamed, "You shot me in the ass!" The 'Professor' replied, "You dumb bastard, what are you doing?" 'Highball' replied, "What we always do, officer safety training!" By now, Beth was on the phone in the bedroom, calling in a home invasion at the residence of two L.A.P.D. detectives with shots fired. Every unit in the division was going to this call.

'Highball's' injury was nothing more than a flesh wound. Patrol responded to the scene, and when the sergeant was told what had occurred, he found it hard to believe. Like most of the patrol officers that knew the two detectives, the sergeant thought that the 'Professor' was covering for one of 'Highball's' cocktail waitress girlfriends who had shot him. Everyone believed that if the 'Professor' were going to shoot 'Highball,' it would be right between the running lights, not in the ass! Internal Affairs and the Officer Involved Shoot Team responded. Patrol units knew they would be tied up for months because every cocktail waitress in the city and county could be suspect. Every Vice and Narcotic Unit Supervisor knew if you needed intelligence on a cocktail waitress, contact Detective Abrams in the Complex Financial Crimes Unit. The shooting was eventually determined to be accidental. Throughout the investigation, the two detectives remained as close as ever. Even Beth forgave her two 'fools'!

Everyone decided it was a good idea to cut back on self-directed training. The Officer Survival Training should be left to the folks who provide such service in the Training Division of the L.A.P.D. Once Reuben and Beth married, they moved out of the house with Amos. They started their life together in the valley, closer to her work.

Beth Johnson was the love of Reuben's life. He considered her to be the most glorious creature on earth. She was also one of only a handful of women whom Amos Abrams admired and trusted. Amos listened to Beth's counseling and guidance on decisions he needed to make. Amos considered Beth to be a true friend. Six years into the marriage of Beth and Reuben, she was diagnosed with pancreatic cancer, which was very fast-moving. Within a month and a half of being diagnosed, Beth was admitted to the U.C.L.A. Medical Center for treatment. She would remain in the hospital for a fortnight before passing. Toward the end of her life, in her hospital bed, Reuben was by her side. Amos, too, visited her as much as Reuben.

Beth asked Reuben to go to the hospital gift shop and pick her up the latest edition of Cosmopolitan and a package of peanut M&M's. When Reuben left the room, Beth called Amos over to her bedside.

When he sat beside her, Beth said to Amos, "Promise me you will take care of Reuben. He needs you, and he won't be the same without you. Amos, you are the big brother Reuben never had!"

Reuben returned, and as he came back into the room and approached Beth, Amos said, "I promise!"

Two days later, Beth started the dying process. Her husband, Reuben, and Amos were at her side when she drew her last breath. Reuben pulled Beth close and embraced her. Both men openly wept and sobbed.

Eight months after Beth died, Amos told Reuben that he was planning to B.B.Q. a couple of porterhouse steaks that Saturday and some corn. He was even going to toss a Caesar salad. Amos said that if Reuben was good, he might open up a new bottle of Johnny Walker Black.

After dinner, the two friends sat around the backyard fire pit.

Amos started by saying, "Ok, let's recap our lives. The L.A.P.D. has employed us for twelve years. We have been detectives for ten of those years. I went back to school and obtained a Juris Doctorate Degree. I have recently received my Second-Degree Black Belt in Tae Kwon Do. You have recently achieved your First-Degree Black Belt in Tae Kwon Do. We have recently won the Division C San Fernando Valley Championship in Doubles Racquetball. I have tested for and passed the bar examination in California, Jefferson, and Nevada. I still hold my C.P.A. certification in California. I also recently lost one of my best friends. You have completed your education at the University of California Los Angeles with a Ph.D. in Education. You have recently lost the love of your life.

From one erudite to another, we need a change! I think it is time to close this chapter of our life and start a new chapter in the Life and Times of 'Professor' Johnson and 'Highball' Abrams!"

Reuben sat in his chair. He was not used to keeping up with 'Highball,' especially with Johnny Walker Black on the rocks. Reuben, starting to slur his words, told Amos, "I'll have to get back to you on that! How about another drink?"

The two friends submitted their letters of resignation to the L.A.P.D. They left Los Angeles for the State of Jefferson and the City of Santiago Springs. Amos had convinced Reuben that Santiago Springs was an up-and-coming community with plenty of career opportunities. With their retirement money, years of financial investments, and life insurance money from Beth's death, the two were set to take on this new life challenge. Amos and Reuben purchased a large home in the Stagecoach Country Club Estates of Santiago Springs. The house was located near the clubhouse. 'Highball' was not interested in golf; he just liked the idea that the 19th hole was within staggering distance from his new home! The two former detectives had enough money to live comfortably for several years without financial hardship.

After a couple of months of wasting time, hanging out at the casinos, and enjoying the restaurants and nightlife of Santiago Springs, Amos convinced Reuben to apply to the Lakeland County Sheriff's Office as a deputy sheriff. Amos told Reuben, "It will be fun. We can work in adjoining zones and only have to worry about ourselves! So, what could go wrong?"

Flora Newsom, Sheriff Atticus Lee's Executive Assistant, entered the Sheriff's office and said, "You have two more new hire interviews this afternoon, boss! Amos Abrams at 1500 hours and Reuben Johnson at 1600 hours. Both are from L.A.P.D., and both are well qualified." Sheriff Lee replied, "Thanks, Flora. You can leave their files on my desk. I'll get to them in a moment." After reading the files on the two potential deputies, Sheriff Lee was quite impressed and interested. The interview with Amos went better than expected. After the interview, Sheriff Lee asked Amos to hang out in his private waiting area until he was done interviewing Reuben. The interview with Reuben went equally as well. When they were finished, Sheriff Lee called Amos back into the office and told both men, "Congratulations, I am offering you a position as Deputy Sheriff with the Lakeland County Sheriff's Office. I have great plans for you two! The next sergeant's exam is about a year and a half away. When you both take and pass the test, you will be promoted to sergeant and assigned to me as part of the Sheriff's Administration. In the meantime, you two will have to do your time on the road." Amos and Reuben accepted the Sheriff's offer, and the three men shook hands. Sheriff Lee asked both of his new deputies to keep his plans to themselves.

Reuben was assigned to uniform patrol in Sector One evening shift in Rockwell. Amos was assigned to uniform patrol in Sector Three evening shift in Springfield. Lakeland County Sheriff participated in the Indianapolis Plan and assigned take-home cars to each deputy. This was new to Reuben and Amos because L.A.P.D. did not have take-home cars. Reuben and Amos loved parking the two green and white patrol cars in the driveway of their new home in the Stagecoach Country

Club Estates. The local highbrows would always walk or drive by very slowly, and you could feel the concern about what their new neighbors, obviously 'low life,' had done to have the cops called on them. It was a while before the neighborhood realized that the new 'low lifes' were deputies.

Nineteen months had passed since the hiring interview with Sheriff Lee. Amos and Reuben took and passed the sergeants exam, with Amos placing fifth and Reuben placing seventh on the list. Amos naturally took every moment available to rub it into Reuben. Sheriff Lee promoted the two deputies and administratively assigned them to Sheriff's Administration, where they, along with Assistant Sheriff Langston Hall, worked directly for Sheriff Lee. The two new sergeants would investigate cases of interest to the Sheriff or other political heavyweights in local government and agency civil liability. It did not take long for all patrol supervisors to realize that if Reuben and Amos showed up on one of your calls, somebody with some juice was interested.

Another program Reuben and Amos took care of was something Sheriff Lee learned when he was the National Sheriff's Association Sheriff of the Year. He learned about a new way of doing business from his fellow sheriffs in California. Whenever one of the deputies in Sheriff Lee's department did something stupid, and the department was facing civil liability, Sergeants Abrams and Johnson would go and visit the victim. It would be in the hospital room or at their house, and the sergeants would pass on Sheriff Lee's condolences and sorrow for the action of his deputies.

Looking at it purely statistically, most victims of police brutality are lower income. Amos Abrams, a seasoned detective, and lawyer could sell ice to an Eskimo. Amos would smooth things over with his melt-in-your-mouth butter voice, explaining that Sheriff Lee assured them that he would personally correct this problem. Sergeant Johnson would open his briefcase and remove a stack of one-hundred-dollar bills freshly wrapped by the bank. A one-inch stack of wrapped one-hundred-dollar bills is $10,000.00. Sergeant Abrams would take the pile of money and tell the victim, "This $10,000.00 is for your pain and anguish." He would place the money into the hands of the victim, knowing that a person of low income will not quickly return the stack. Sergeant Johnson would say, "All we need is a signature from you saying you have received this money and all is good!" Most of the time, while holding onto the stack of money, people would gladly sign the release of liability for the quick cash. The Lakeland County Sheriff's Office, which is self-insured, would save thousands, if not millions, of dollars if the case had gone to a civil trial.

Most people did not know that Amos Abrams became Sheriff Lee's personal attorney, and C.P.A. Amos met Asher Roth, the hospitality mogul of the Jefferson Promenade, through one of his cocktail waitresses and eventually through Amos representing Sheriff Lee's interest in the community. Asher Roth tried to steal Amos away from Atticus Lee many times. He told Amos that he would give him anything he wanted as long as he, Asher, was his only client.

Amos told Asher that he would only come to work for him if his partner, Reuben Johnson, were offered a professor position in History or Criminal Justice at Santiago Springs University.

The only persons at the Lakeland County Sheriff's Office who called Amos and Reuben 'Highball' and 'Professor' were Sheriff Atticus Lee and Assistant Sheriff Langston Hall. The rest of the department called them 'The Briefcase Squad.'

Sergeant Abrams and Sergeant Johnson remained with Sheriff Lee till the end of his career with the Lakeland County Sheriff's Office. After that, Amos Abrams went to work for Asher Roth as his attorney. He also married a red-headed cocktail waitress, Bambi, from one of his casinos. Reuben Johnson now teaches history at Santiago Springs University, where everybody calls him 'Professor.'

April Fools

Seth Roberts and Daniel Deluca thought they were quite the 'Cock of the Walk' as they strutted through the Administration Section of the Santiago Springs Police Department. The two young detectives were part of a program Chief Roland Greenberg had taken and adapted from the Hudson Falls Police Department. Hudson Falls called their program the Special Enforcement Team. Santiago Springs called their new and improved program Special Projects. Seth and Danny were part of the four-person squad hand-picked and assigned directly to Chief Greenberg. They were here to get their assignments for the day from the Chief.

Chief Greenberg made his career when Sheriff Atticus Lee's father was Chief of Police. He was sitting behind his desk, talking on the phone, when the two detectives entered the office. Chief Greenberg motioned for the two to enter and sit in front of his desk. The Chief offered the two a cup of coffee, but only Danny accepted. After pouring Danny a cup from his personal Mr. Coffee, the Chief sat down. He told the two that he wanted them to attend a community meeting at the Southside Community Center from 1630-1800 hours that night.

Special Projects often worked as the enforcement arm for Community Relations. Captain Angelique Colombo from the Community Relations Section would present the evening's program. The Chief wanted Seth and Danny available to answer any enforcement questions from the gallery. The two units had been working together recently, cleaning up a rental property and related crimes in the southeastern portion of the city. While wiping his brow with a white handkerchief, Chief Greenberg reminded Seth and Danny that Captain Colombo was the 'warm and fuzzy eye candy' and they were the 'long arm of the law.'

Chief Greenberg concluded the meeting by telling his two detectives that he wanted them to shut off their cell phones from 1630-1800 hours. They had to give complete attention to the meeting and Captain Colombo.

"I don't want you two clowns checking your stocks and bonds! Capeesh?"

Both detectives replied, "Yes, Sir," as they left the Chief's office and headed towards their assigned car in the parking lot.

Seth told Danny, "I usually check my stocks while driving to work."

As the two left the Police Administration, many 'coppers' who saw them thought Seth and Danny would be promoted to Sergeant during the next round of promotions.

Seth Roberts, the sweeter of the two detectives, is a ten-year Santiago Springs Police Department veteran. He lateraled from the Greenwood County Sheriff's Office and has a degree in Political Science from Cal State Berkeley. The conservative Republican stands five foot ten inches tall and weighs approximately one-hundred-and-eighty-five pounds. His mother tells him she thinks he looks like John Denver. Mrs. Roberts would often bloviate about her son to her friends. Seth, who thinks he looks like Elton John, is married to his wife, Abigail, of ten years. Abigail is an emergency room nurse at the Santiago Springs Medical Center. Seth and Abby have two girls, Violet and Madison, nine and eleven years of age. The family lives in the Washington Heights subdivision in western Lakeland County. The family has lived in an upper-middle-class home that has been cared for by their Guatemalan housekeeper and nanny, Ellie Martinez, for ten years. Ellie's husband, Francisco, is the family's gardener.

Danny DeLuca is of Sicilian ancestry. Danny Deluca was born in Brooklyn, New York. At thirty-five years of age, he was also a ten-year Santiago Springs Police Department veteran. He was a handsome man who was tall and lean with chiseled features, and jet-black hair combed straight back. He spent four years at San Diego State University, where he graduated with a degree in business, a mountain of debt, and a desire to do anything but business! Upon first inspection, one might expect to be introduced to the latest lieutenant of the Gambino crime family. Instead, Danny lateraled from the San Diego Police Department, where he walked a beat in "Old Town."

Danny's wife, Skylar, a tall blond who looks like the actress Veronica Lake, is the Human Resources Director for the huge Hilton Hotel and Convention Center downtown. Skylar and Danny have been married for twelve years and live in southwest Santiago Springs. They have two sons, Curtis and Edward, who are nine and seven years old.

Despite the husbands being close and trusted partners for four years, Abby Roberts and Skylar Deluca were not that close due to conflicting and opposite intense careers. But that would change that night when the world of Special Projects would collide head-on with the 'Old Man' of Sector Three.

Sergeant Sylas Brown has been with the Lakeland County Sheriff's Office for thirty-six years, mostly in uniform patrol in Sector Three. A handful of remaining old-timers call him 'Hogleg.' Sheriff Lee, Sylas' zone partner, gave him that nickname back in the day. Because of the six-inch Colt Python .357 Magnum, he carried in a swivel holster when the two worked the road together. The rest of the sector refers to Sylas as the 'Old Man.' Sergeant Brown was still as proud to wear the uniform today as the first day he put it on. He had a ten-member squad with an average experience of seven years. Brown was very good at running his team and expected specific tasks to be completed on every 'Hot Shot' call over the radio. Sergeant Brown's corporal, Harold Miller, was one of the best supervisors in patrol, mastering command and control thanks to Sergeant Brown.

Trent Jones was the ambitious and high-strung Sector Three Watch Commander. When Trent graduated from the academy, he was anxiously assigned to Sector Three evening shift on Sergeant Sylas Brown's Squad. That was fifteen years ago, and Sergeant Brown still intimidated the good lieutenant. Lt. Jones also learned quite a bit from Sergeant Brown and, as a result, did an excellent job as Incident Commander.

Seth Roberts had been waiting for that day since the previous year. Seth and his wife, Abby, are intelligent and well-educated individuals. They love playing practical jokes and pranking each other on April Fool's Day! During the last ten years, practical jokes have become even more intense. Abby set up a false residential burglary scenario the previous year at their home. Seth's beloved baseball card collection had been stolen from his ransacked office within the house. Abby had even arranged for a mutual friend, Deputy Emanuel Sanchez, to be at the house when Seth got home, pretending to take the burglary report. Seth Roberts naturally called his partner to come by the house to drown their sorrows. Seth complained, pouted, and moaned for almost three hours before Abby, who was beside herself, broke down and shouted, "April Fools!!"

Seth was determined to beat Abby this year. The prank had been planned for weeks. Seth had told the housekeeper, Ellie, that he would prank Mrs. Roberts. Ellie, who was very aware of the competition between Mr. and Mrs. Roberts but did not understand it, continued to listen to her boss.

She thought they were both locos! Abby got home around 4:30 PM most evenings. Ellie was given money to take Violet and Madison to one of the theme parks and for dinner. She was told not to bring them back until 8:00 PM and not to mention the prank to the girls. Ellie was instructed to answer phone calls only from Mr. Roberts during this time. Ellie had to ignore phone calls from Mrs. Roberts, no matter how many times she may have tried to call. Finally, Ellie was told to gather the two girls' cell phones and leave them in the car while they entered the theme park. Ellie reluctantly agreed.

Ellie and the two girls left around 3:00 PM. Seth jumped into action! He had bought a quart of Stage Blood for use in his plan. First, Seth knocked over a potted plant in the living room, spilling some soil onto the carpet. Seth knocked over a couple of the dining room chairs and spread the mail and other papers on the table onto the floor around the room. Next, he opened the bottle of Stage Blood and poured some on the white porcelain kitchen tiles, where he smeared some about the floor and the white tile countertops. Seth grabbed a butcher knife from the kitchen drawer. He strategically placed the blade onto the kitchen countertop with some blood on the handle. Seth exited the kitchen and into the garage, where Abby would park her car. As he left home, the scheming detective left a smeared bloody handprint on the back kitchen door that he planned to leave ajar, awaiting Abby's return home.

As the two detectives pulled into the Southside Community Center parking lot, Danny asked Seth, "Are you sure you want to go ahead with this?" Seth replied, "Oh hell yes! Come on, let's get to our meeting, partner!" Both Detectives turned off their respective cell phones as instructed by the Chief and left them in the center console of the unit. Captain Colombo arrived moments later. After parking her car, Danny stayed back and waited for her. Seth had already made it to the meeting room and scoped things out. Danny thought to himself, "What a beautiful woman!" The Captain had long dark hair and dark eyes. Her skin was olive, and she always had a lovely smile.

The always graceful Captain graduated with a Master's degree in Education from Jefferson State University in Santiago Springs. Her husband, Dominic, is a thriving personal injury attorney downtown. The couple, married for fifteen years, have no children. The community meeting started on schedule, and the Captain did an excellent job representing the Santiago Springs Police Department. The two Special Project Detectives only took a few questions each.

At 4:38 PM, a call came into the Lakeland County Sheriff's Office Communication Center. The woman at the end of the line was hysterical, but the communication center professionals could decipher.

A broadcast was made to Westend Sheriff's units. "Special Attention Sector Three Units and 331, respond to a Signal 8 (Missing Persons) times two with Signal 13 (Suspicious Circumstances) at 424 John Street. Signal 8's are the daughters of a 10-37 (Law Enforcement Officer)."

Deputy Laurel Campbell grabbed the mic and advised, "Lakeland 331 is en route."

Deputy Marvin Rossi, her zone partner, also advised, "Lakeland 331 Alpha to back."

Communication advised, "Additional information on the two missing girls along with the housekeeper is in the call narrative." (On the MDS computer in the car).

Sergeant Brown directed dispatch, "Lakeland, Sierra 31, send me the call!"

Sergeant Brown took a moment to read the narrative of the call and said to himself, "Oh hell no, not on my watch!"

Two minutes after the call went out over the radio, telephones in the Public Information Office of the Lakeland County Sheriff's Office began ringing off the hook. The reason for the avalanche in the PIO was simple. All three major news agencies in the county had been issued non-transmittable radios from the sheriff's office to monitor activity in patrol. Missing Person reports are never put out Code 3. Likewise, Suspicious Circumstances are rarely put out with Missing Persons. So, when they tied in a law enforcement officer, every news outlet in town was rolling requesting additional information or at least a location for the Media Staging Area.

Charlie 31, Corporal Harold Miller, advised units 334 and 333 Bravo to switch to the tactical channel. When the two units responded on the tactical channel, Corporal Miller instructed Deputy Leroy Harris, car 334, to set the outer perimeter. Next, Corporal Miller ordered Deputy

Olivia Wright's car, 333 Bravo, to set the inner perimeter. The corporal told both deputies to return to him within fifteen minutes when this task was completed.

Deputy Olivia Wright advised dispatch, "Lakeland 331 and 331Alpha are both on the scene."

Dispatch replied, "331 and 331 Alpha 10-97 at 1642 hours.

Captain Hector Caruso of the Lakeland County Sheriff's Public Information Office was on the phone with the responding Sergeant Brown. Caruso had called Brown to advise of the mass media response. Sergeant Brown replied, "Thanks for the update. You coming out to take care of that part of this?" Captain Caruso responded in the affirmative and asked the Sergeant, "Do you have a Media Staging Area in mind?" Brown, expecting that question replied, "Let's make it Roosevelt Avenue south of Timothy Lane." Caruso said, "Got it. Thanks, Sylas!"

Sergeant Brown advised dispatch, "Lakeland Sierra 31 on the scene."

Communications replied, "Sierra 31 10-97 at 1645 hours." The Watch Commander, Lt. Trent Jones, arrived seconds later.

Deputy Leroy Harris called, "Charlie 31, 334 The outer perimeter has been set"

Deputy Olivia Wright chimed in, "The inner perimeter has also been set."

Corporal Miller acknowledged the information from the two deputies. He knew that when both set their perimeters, they obtained the deputy's name, their radio designator, and the exact location where they were assigned. The outer perimeter took five units with the help of Sector 3 detectives and a pair of SROs (School Resource Officers). The inner perimeter required four marked patrol units. Once they arrived for resource tracking, the assigned deputy information would later be given to the Critical Incident Management Team (CIMT).

Deputy Marvin Rossi, Unit 331 Alpha, gave a detailed in-person briefing to Lieutenant Jones and Sergeant Brown, including observations in the kitchen and dining room. There was no sign of the three missing persons. After receiving information from Deputy Rossi, Sergeant Brown and Lieutenant Jones left the residence. They drove to the intersection of

Roosevelt Avenue and Timothy Lane, establishing the Command Post for this incident. Once they arrived, Lieutenant Jones came up on the air and advised, "Lakeland, Patrol 31, change my radio designator to 'Command' of the Washington Heights Incident. Lakeland also change Sierra 31's radio designator to 'Operations.'"

The Communications Center responded, "Copy 'Command' at 1655 hours."

Charlie 31 said, "Lakeland, change my radio designator to 'Staging.' Lakeland, please advise all responding units outside Sector 3 that the staging area is the Ronald Reagan Elementary School on the Van Buren Highway north of Madison Canyon Trail. Specifically, on the east side near the bus loop."

Dispatch replied, "10-26 (message received), 'Staging' at 1656 hours."

Lieutenant Jones called the High-Risk Incident Commander, Major Marshall Allen, and briefed him on what was occurring in Sector 3. Both specialty teams would be responding to this incident. HRIC included Critical Incident Management Team (CIMT) and the HRIC Intelligence Unit. Major Allen also told Lieutenant Jones that he would place the 100-member Emergency Response Team (ERT) on standby in case a ground search was warranted.

"Lakeland, 'Operations,' please notify the on-call chaplain and victim advocate to respond to the scene." "Operations" continued, "Lakeland, can you also notify CID that we have an area set aside for their Major Case Response Team to set up their trailer." Lakeland responded, 'Operations' 10-26 at 1705 hours."

Dispatch notified 'Operations' once all of the specialty teams requested to respond had been notified, and the time each acknowledged their response.

'Operations' told communications that the CID Operations area was on Roosevelt Avenue north of 'Thisa' Way. (The subdivision developer at the time talked the county into allowing him to name the street Thisa Way).

"Lakeland, 'Command,' I need two deputies to respond to the Command Post. One for the scribe and the other to staff the Command Board."

Before dispatch could respond, two CIMT deputies working off-duty in Sector 3 advised that they would handle it and were en route.

At 1815 hours, Detectives Danny Deluca and Seth Roberts were walking toward their unit in the Southside Community Center parking lot. The two had stopped and talked to some citizens who were too embarrassed to ask questions in the meeting. Just as Danny was about to unlock the driver's door, he heard Captain Colombo's calling their names.

Captain Colombo asked Seth, "Have you spoken to your wife lately?"

He replied, "No, not since this morning."

"You may want to give her a call. She's looking for you."

And with that, Captain Colombo showed Seth the text message she received from the police department communication center. When Danny and Seth returned to their vehicle, they turned on their cell phones. Danny had the usual news and weather reports, but Seth's phone indicated that his wife had tried to call him at least twenty-two times since 1640 hours.

Once inside the unmarked unit, Seth made the call to his wife. A strange women's voice answered Abby's phone.

"Hello, this is Mrs. Gianna Lewis. May I help you?"

"Mrs. Lewis, this is Detective Roberts with the Santiago Springs Police Department. Why are you answering this cell phone?"

"Oh, Detective Roberts, I am with the Victim Advocate Unit of the Lakeland County Sheriff's Office. I am here with your wife, Abby, who is distraught and unable to answer the phone. Detective, your two daughters, and the housekeeper are missing. Do you have any knowledge of their whereabouts?"

Detective Roberts paused for a moment and thought, "Man, she's good! She realized it was an April Fool joke. To win, she had one of her friends play the role of a Victim Advocate! Perfect, Abby, but you will not win this year!"

Detective Roberts told the strange voice on the phone, "I'll be right home. It will be about thirty minutes. I'm stuck in the evening rush and at the opposite end of the county." Seth hung up.

Seth told Danny about the phone call. Danny looked at him and said, "Seth, I don't have a good feeling about this one."

Seth replied, "Are you kidding me? This is going to be great!"

At about 1845 hours, Seth and Danny were eastbound on Harrison Street approaching Roosevelt Avenue when they arrived at the Washington Heights subdivision. The two detectives could see the numerous media trucks and vans parked along the roadway with flashing lights and north of the intersection in the media staging area.

Seth kept repeating out loud, "Oh God, Oh God, Oh God!"

Finally, Danny turned left onto Roosevelt Avenue and talked to the deputy blocking the street, "We need to get to the Command Post. We have additional information they need to know."

The deputy pointed north on Roosevelt Avenue and told the two detectives the Command Post was located just south of Timothy Lane.

Once the deputy let them in, Danny told Seth, "We must get you home now!"

But, when Danny pulled up Seth's driveway, they saw a Lakeland County Sheriff's Office Forensics van on the scene with yellow crime scene tape around the house. Danny told Seth he would take care of notifying the Incident Commander. But, first, he just needed to take care of his wife.

When Seth entered the house, and his wife saw him, she started to cry again and came running toward him with high emotion. Abby said, "They are gone, and nobody has seen or heard from them!" Seth replied with a large lump in his throat, "The kids and Ellie are fine. This was just an April Fool's joke."

Abby stepped back and took a moment to look at her husband. She doubled up her fist, hit him in the chest above his heart, and said, "You son of a bitch! I can't believe you did this to me!"

Abby, an Emergency Room nurse, knew that she needed to keep her emotions in check. Seth quickly called Ellie on his cell phone, and she immediately answered. Ellie and the kids were finishing up their dinner at Denny's. She told Seth that the girls had a great time at the theme park.

Seth requested that Ellie put the kids on the phone, and he handed the phone to Abby, who put the call on speakerphone. When Abby heard the girl's voices and knew they were all right, members of the Forensics Team let out a cheer!

In the meantime, Danny had the unenviable job of telling the Incident Commander that this call was unfounded and just an April Fool's Joke. As Detective Deluca approached the Command Post Vehicle, he was stopped by a member of CIMT who was acting security for the Command Post Vehicle. Not everyone can get inside the vehicle without official business. The member of CIMT told Command who was outside, and they granted permission to enter. As Danny started climbing the truck's stairs, the door swung open, and a supervisor with the Forensics Team was coming out. This supervisor had just told Incident Command that his team found that the blood found at the scene was, in fact, not blood but a product called Stage Blood. Therefore, forensics believed that this scene was staged and not actual.

Detective Deluca entered the Command Post Vehicle and found the Incident Command sitting at a table. It consisted of the Operations Section Chief, an Investigative Section Chief, a CIMT Scribe, and the Major of High-Risk Incident Command, who was merely observing. A Planning Section Chief was also present. Additionally, the truck had additional members of CIMT. They work under the Incident Command System and provide personnel as leaders representing the Situation Unit, the Documentation Unit, Resource Unit, and Technical Specialist. CIMT also sent two team members to assist with the staging area. Additionally, the Ground Support Unit Leader and the Supply Unit Leader were outside the Command Post Vehicle and available as needed.

Det. Deluca explained to Incident Command what had happened and said it was meant as an April Fool's joke between a husband and wife.

Sgt. Brown chuckled under his breath and said, "Son, I've spent my whole career dealing with law enforcement officers who make stupid mistakes and poor choices. You and your partner are right up there near the top of the list."

Sgt. Brown looked at Lieutenant Jones and said, "Command, this one is all yours!"

Danny told the group that his partner was present with his wife at their home, explaining what he had done and why. When Detective Deluca finished his explanation, he was asked to standby at the Command Post Vehicle outside the doors.

Major Allen called Sheriff Lee to appraise him of the outcome. Within ten minutes, Major Allen received a call from Chief Roland Greenberg of the Santiago Springs Police Department. Chief Greenberg apologized for the actions of his two detectives. The Chief asked Major Allen to tell the two detectives to report to police headquarters as soon as possible and report to the Watch Commander, who would take it from there. Chief Greenberg apologized again and assured the Major that something like this would not happen again. The message was passed along to Detective Deluca, who patiently waited outside the Command Post Vehicle's back door. Danny went by and picked his partner up. Abby was no longer speaking to Seth and Ellie. The two kids made it home before their dad had to leave and go back downtown to deal with the police administration over the matter.

Lakeland Communications broadcasted to all units that the Signal 8's had been located and were in good health. The Incident Commander instructed all units to stand down and return to normal operations. All squad leaders, team leaders, and supervisors were asked to come to the Command Post for debriefing. After the hour-long debriefing, supervisors were told to ensure the safety and account for all of their personnel. When the incident was secured, there were over one hundred and twenty personnel and assets assigned to the incident. Twenty units were in Staging and available as needed.

Sheriff Lee is friends with Chief Greenberg. He first met Roland when his dad promoted him to lieutenant, and he would come by Chief Lee's home to brief the Chief on information or to say hello. Sheriff Lee prepared an accounting of the cost of responding to the Missing Person call involving suspicious circumstances and a law enforcement officer's family. Each expense was broken down, and the price was just over $200,000.00. Sheriff Lee presented the cost breakdown or bill to Chief Greenberg, not for payment. But for reference for the next time, Seth Roberts and Danny Deluca wanted to play a practical or April Fool's joke again.

The Forensics Team would later receive a Commendation from the Santiago Springs Police Department for performance above and beyond the call of duty. They helped Abby clean up the house and the scene before leaving. The girls were exhausted, went to bed, and passed out. They never really acknowledged what was happening in their place since their dad had always been a cop, and his friends would always come over to the house.

Seth was in such a hurry, or he didn't care, that he did not read the fine print on the Stage Blood bottle, which warned the consumer that this product might stain areas where it comes in contact. Despite the best attempt from the Forensics Team and Stanley Steamer, the Stage Blood left its mark. The good news is that Abby got new countertops in the kitchen along with new tile and new carpet in the living room and dining room.

Seth Roberts was banned from his residence for three days before Abby caved into her, missing Seth and the girls begging their mom to let dad come home.

When Skylar Deluca heard about what had happened, she called Abby. She apologized for her husband's stupidity and conveyed her sorrow for the pain and anxiety the two 'morons' and 'assholes' put her through. As a result, Abby and Skylar have since become best friends, and the two families now spend time and do things together.

Two promotional cycles came and went with no promotions. However, the two Detectives remained partners and continued to work in the Special Projects Squad. After the third promotional cycle, Detective Seth Roberts and Detective Danny Deluca were promoted to Sergeant and assigned to Midnight Patrol at opposite stations in the city.

Abby told Skylar that she reacted so strongly at what Seth had done because, on the morning of April 1, there was a rollover traffic collision on the Interstate. One little girl, an eight-year-old, was killed instantly when the vehicle rolled and crushed her skull. The other one, a little older, was airlifted to the trauma center where Abby works. Despite the best efforts of the doctors and nurses, she died at only eleven years of age.

When Abby told this story to Skylar, she concluded by saying, "It was a bad day at the office!" She started to sob.

The Interview

It was Wednesday, August 1. It was hot and humid in Santiago Springs. It felt like the dog days of summer have arrived. Despite the weather, Tom Stevens had been waiting for this day for eternity. Today was Tom Stevens' Transfer Review Board for the position in the Training Section of the Lakeland County Sheriff's Office. This would be Tom's opportunity to accomplish his career goal of teaching law enforcement officers how to manage the response to critical incidents properly. Tom got up early and prepared his Class 'A' uniform for the interview. Marcie also got up to rally Tom and make his breakfast. She didn't want his stomach growling in the middle of the interview. LCSO allowed its sworn personnel to wear awards from other agencies on the dress uniform and hash marks for every four years of law enforcement service. With his prior service, Tom had six gold hash marks on the left sleeve of his uniform shirt. He also had three rows of ribbons under his gold Lakeland County badge.

Tom thought he looked like a Mexican General. Marcie thought he looked handsome. She reminded him to check his tie before he went into the interview and to keep his hands out of his pants pockets. Tom was buzzing with anticipation and excitement. He had kept his nose clean at the Sheriff's office for the two years he had been here. Tom had experience working patrol in two sectors. He had been a Field Training Officer for six months. He had taken the Corporal's promotional examination, which he successfully passed. He was currently on the Corporal's list to be promoted. Tom felt well-informed about the training position and knew he would be victorious at the end of the day.

Transfer Review Boards were a big deal at the Lakeland County Sheriff's Office. Every manager in the agency had to chair or participate in a TRB once a year. Each member, from the chair to the evaluators, had to wear a Class 'A' uniform with all ribbons earned. Tom Stevens learned this while participating as an evaluator on a new hire board. Tom signed up for that job in preparation for today. He wanted as much inside information on the process as he could get. The TRBs were always held in a conference room in Human Resources. All the candidates waited in the waiting room at the entrance of Human Resources. Tom learned that five candidates had submitted for the position, and one had already pulled out of contention, thus leaving four. When Tom arrived at the Human Resource Division, he would learn he was the second interview of the day. The first candidate had already finished and left the building. Tom sat alone in the waiting room. In less than five minutes, Tom was called into the conference room, where he was used to being on the other side of the table with other evaluators. Tom boldly entered the room and smoothly moved around the chair and table to shake hands and say "Good morning" to the TRB Chair and each evaluator. Tom casually knew each person in the room from seeing them around Operations. The Chairperson of the Transfer Review Board was Captain Francesca Gomez, who commanded the Training Division. She was self-confident, ambitious, and determined. Captain Gomez wore no lipstick or nail polish, and she appeared to be about ten days late for an appointment with her hair colorist. Captain Gomez came to the Sheriff's office simultaneously with Captain Colombo, and they became friends and colleagues. Gomez had her sights on being the next Major, and she wouldn't allow anything or anyone to stand in her way. Many of her associates considered her, a black woman married to a Hispanic female, to be abrupt.

Sitting to the right of Captain Gomez was Sergeant Jack 'CP' Cleaver, who was the supervisor of the Emergency Management Unit. Sergeant Cleaver wore more ribbons than anybody else in the room and was the only deputy, other than Tom Stevens, who wore the uniform and looked like a street cop. The rest looked like office dwellers. Sergeant Cleaver pioneered law enforcement emergency management and was straightforward and inventive. Some in the agency found him cynical. Sergeant Cleaver, like many others, suffered from male-pattern baldness. A former SWAT Operator (which he never talked about), Jack Cleaver was still physically fit. More important, he was intensely loyal to his friend and boss, Captain Warren Smith.

Sitting in the middle of the evaluators was Captain Warren Smith of the Protective Shield Section. Captain Smith was a man in his middle fifties with a full head of salt and pepper hair and a pot belly. Smith was well-connected with counterparts throughout the state and federal governments. Despite thirty years of service, he was still hard-working and well-liked by Sheriff Lee. One of the founders of Law Enforcement Emergency Management, along with Sergeant Cleaver, Captain Smith, was intelligent and forceful in ensuring work from his section was top shelf. Smith worked with the Command Staff, primarily former SWAT Operators, and most disliked him, believing he was arrogant. He was just arrogant in a different way, not the SWAT way. The Sheriff's office recently hired Captain Smith's son, and many were watching to see if and how far the acorn fell from the oak tree.

The last evaluator was Captain Angelique Colombo of the Community Relations Section of the agency. Captain Colombo was a tall and thin raven-haired olive-skinned beauty. Her uniform was tailored, and she wore a French manicure. Captain Gomez asked her at the last minute to sit on this board. Since they were friends, the end of the year was fast approaching, and she had not completed her TRB mandates, Captain Colombo agreed.

Captain Colombo looked like she had just come off Vogue magazine's cover. She was friendly, charismatic, and intelligent. Captain Colombo had a natural attractiveness despite being married to a successful husband for several years. Tom Stevens thought she was the most feminine deputy in the agency. Like her friend, Captain Gomez, Captain Colombo also has aspirations of becoming the next Major. She, too, was not inclined to sit by and watch her friend or anyone else get promoted to Major without a fight. Many deputies who work in Community Relations have found Captain Colombo to be inflexible. People who work for her say, "It's her way or the highway!"

After Tom Stevens shook each board member's hands, he sat in the chair and made himself comfortable. Next, Captain Gomez began to read a welcome greeting from a script. She read a script from Human Resources about how the interview would proceed and the scoring process. Captain Gomez said, "Good luck and are you ready?" Tom Stevens replied. "I sure am!"

The evaluators rarely ask questions. Instead, they document what the candidate says in response to each question. Tom had prepared in his mind to respond to questions as if he was teaching the board members the topic at hand.

Ten minutes into answering the first question, Captain Smith interrupted Tom and said, "You know, Tom, each of these interviews is scheduled for forty-five minutes, and we have several more candidates to go!" Captain Smith was not trying to be rude since he knew Tom from when Tom served on a new hire board the Captain chaired. He reminded Tom that time was limited, and they wanted to get through all the questions. Besides, Captain Smith was just cranky because he had a meeting scheduled after lunch with Assistant Sheriff Hall about some 'Bullshit' project he came up with. Captain Smith thought for a moment, then realized, "Why am I upset? I'll give it to Sergeant Cleaver like he always did!"

Tom got through the interview in time with all questions answered. When he left, he was very confident that he had done well. Tom called his wife, Marcie, and broke the news to her. After Captain Smith finished meeting with the all-mighty Assistant Sheriff Langston Hall, Smith returned to his office, where he gave the project to Sergeant Cleaver.

Cleaver told Smith, "We need Tom Stevens in this office working in Emergency Management. He gets it!"

Captain Smith replied, "You are right, Jack, but I don't have a deputy position open!"

Sergeant Cleaver countered, "Then have the Sheriff promote him to Corporal and assign him to Emergency Management as my Corporal."

In a coy voice, Captain Smith said, "I'll think about it."

Cleaver insisted, "Damn it, Warren, if you want to accomplish what the Sheriff wants, you need to talk to the Sheriff. Ensure he promotes Tom and assigns him to our unit. Do you remember what the Sheriff told us, 'Corporal positions are a dime a dozen!' Besides, you know as well as I do, that Emergency Management is an appointed position, not a tested one!"

Captain Smith abandoned his thinking and said, "Ok 'CP' I'll talk to the Sheriff."

Sheriff Lee and the Command Staff respected Sergeant Jack 'CP' Cleaver. Sheriff Lee had given Cleaver "Open Door Access" to his office since he did so many projects for Administration. Later that afternoon, Sergeant Cleaver met Sheriff Lee as he was walking out to his vehicle in preparation to go home. Sergeant Cleaver shared his opinion with the Sheriff and selfishly recommended that Tom Stevens be promoted to Corporal and assigned to Emergency Management. Sheriff Lee's only comment was, "Oh yes, I know Tom. He is a good man. Have a good night, Jack." And with that, the Sheriff drove away, giving the sergeant a thumbs up.

Sheriff Lee has told many people that the best part of his job is when he can promote someone. So, two days after talking to Sergeant Cleaver, Sheriff Lee called Tom Stevens, who was at home with his wife and family.

The Sheriff's voice dropped an octave and became very serious and professional. "Good evening, Tom. I hope you are doing well. The reason I am calling is regarding the Training Division position. You came out number one on the list, but as you know, the Sheriff has the final say. Tom, you have been an excellent employee for the past two years. I wanted to be the one you heard it from. I will not approve your assignment to Training."

Tom, who had just taken a punch to the gut and whose heart was beating out of his chest, suddenly allowing a considerable lump to form in his throat, could only speak, "Yes, sir."

The Sheriff continued, "Tom, I am promoting you to Corporal and assigning you to Emergency Management. I think you and that team will accomplish great things!"

Tom said, "Thank you, sir. We will." Tom realized that his prayers had been answered, and he thanked the Lord under his breath.

The Sheriff concluded the phone call by saying, "Tom, I want you to report to Captain Warren Smith on Monday, August 27, at 0800 hours."

Tom said, "I will, and thank you again, Sheriff. I won't let you down!"

It was a typical Tuesday morning in the Stevens household. Tom and the kids were sitting around the breakfast table off the kitchen, finishing breakfast. Marcie was putting the finishing touches on Simone's hair when she asked Tom, "What do you think about Venus Williams defending her U.S. Open Women's Tennis Championship by beating her sister Serena?"

After reading the morning sports page, Tom said, "I don't think it makes for good conversation or great ambiance at William's household during the family Sunday dinner."

Gunner chimed in and said, "Mom, I have to go to work tonight at 5:00 P.M."

Gunner has a part-time job at Vaughn's Supermarket in north Santiago Springs. He is a bagger and works until midnight three days a week.

Marcie acknowledged both Tom and Gunner. After that, Colt reminded his parents that he had baseball practice after school. He would not be home until around 7:00 P.M. Simone mentioned to her mother that she had cheerleading practice after school. She would not be home until the same time as her brother. The three kids excused themselves, said their goodbyes, and headed out the front door to school. Tom stayed for ten minutes longer and swallowed his third cup of morning coffee. Marcie was at the kitchen sink rinsing off dishes before she put them into the dishwasher. Tom walked by his wife, paused to give her a big kiss on the cheek, and told her, "I love you, sweetie, have a good day!" Tom put his coffee mug in the dishwasher.

Marcie said, "I love you too! Say hi to Jack for me."

"I will," and with that, Tom entered his Grey 2000 Ram 2500 Pickup, recently provided to him as a result of his new assignment in Emergency Management, and headed toward Central Operations. When Tom started the engine, Brooks and Dunn sang, *Ain't Nothing 'Bout You*. Tom said out loud, "Oh man! I love this song!"

Tom arrived at the office at about 7: 55 A.M., and Jack Cleaver was already at his desk reviewing emails. Tom entered his office and turned on the lights and computer. He also turned on the large television mounted on the wall and watched a few moments of Fox News. The Emergency Management Unit monitored National News, Local News, and the Weather Channel. But, of course, it was always Fox News. Nobody would ever have the nerve to turn on, much less watch CNN.

Tom was sitting across from Jack's desk when at approximately 8:50 A.M. Fox News advised of a Fox News Alert. The announcer stated the day and date which would stick in the minds of this generation as

December 7, 1941, did in previous generations. The two new associates were diligently working on updating the Critical Incident Management Guide. Something unthinkable occurred that morning that would change the way the nation's emergency services would respond to significant incidents or events forever:

Tuesday, September 11, 2001

Islamic Terrorism, Aircraft High-Jacking, Suicide Attacks, and Mass Murder

Sergeant Jack 'CP' Cleaver and Corporal Tom Stevens watched the events of this horrific day unfold, along with the rest of the nation. Neither could realize this day's effect on them professionally and personally. The adventure was about to begin!

Footnotes and References

The Laguna Fire

1. History of ICS-EMSI Retrieved August 23, 2021
   https://www.emsics.com/history-of-ics/
2. Laguna Fire – Wikipedia Retrieved August 23, 2021
   https://en.wikipedia.org/wiki/Laguna_Fire

The Sicilian

3. Encyclopedia of Detroit – Uprising of 1967 Retrieved July 7, 2021
   https://detroithistorical.org/learn/encyclopedia-of-detroit/uprising-1967

Pacific Northwest Savings and Loan Robbery

4. Norco Bank Robbery Documentary Part 1 of 3 – Youtube
   Retrieved June 15, 2021
   https://www.youtube.com/watch?v=OQXXcFmMVNE
5. Norco Bank Robbery Documentary Part 2 of 3 – Youtube
   Retrieved June 15, 2021
   https://www.youtube.com/watch?v=cdbdfAc2E2g
6. Norco Bank Robbery Documentary Part 3 of 3 – Youtube
   Retrieved June 15, 2021
   https://www.youtube.com/watch?v=HDQrvW5-Pdc

Her Voice

7. Shaaron Claridge – Wikipedia Retrieved April 3, 2021
   https://en.wikipedia.org/wiki/Shaaron_Claridge

The Menagerie

8. WMD RESPONSE: 7 CRITICAL TASKS – American Public
   University System. Retrieved May 2, 2021
   http://start.amu.apus.edu/common/dl/visor-cards/visor_wmd.pdf

Protective Shield and Response Section

9. Orange County Sheriff's Office General Order 17.1.5 **Homeland Security** May 7, 2010, Sheriff Jerry L. Demings. Retrieved September 5, 2021
10. Ibid.

About the Author

Steven D. Thomas

Steve Thomas started his emergency management career in Southern California in 1976. Working with and learning from the traditional "four seasons" of California, which include: flooding, fires, mudslides, and earthquakes, he could hone his skills in the newly created Incident Command System. Steve has worked in municipal and county law enforcement arenas and subsequently held various positions, including Operations Section Chief, Planning Section Chief, Logistics Section Chief, and Assistant Commander of a Critical Incident Management Team.

Steve recently retired after working in Central Florida for the Orange County Sheriff's Office. He had been assigned to High-Risk Incident Command, Homeland Security, and Emergency Management. His emergency management duties included preparation, mitigation, response, recovery, and Continuity of Operations Planning and Development.

Steve was on the design team, the lead instructor, and eventually the Director of the Orange County Sheriff's Office Command School. Command School brings together law enforcement, fire department personnel, and school administrators for hands-on training in managing the "first critical hour" of any significant incident or event.

Steve has instructed various criminal justice and emergency management agencies on topics such as Terrorism, Vulnerability Assessments, the Incident Command System, and Homeland Security.